THE MASTER

Gordon Houghton

Also by Gordon Houghton

The Dinner Party (1998)
The Apprentice (1999)
The Journeyman (2001)
Game Boy (2005)
Max (2011)
Another World (2012)
Mute (2016)
The Invisible (2018)

Anthologies

Dystopian Dreams (2019)
Undead Nightmares (2020)

THE MASTER

by Gordon Houghton

Amazon Edition

ISBN: 9798656097284

for the three who did

Taking back control

After three thousand years of stabbing, strangling, starving, poisoning, asphyxiating, dismembering and generally cutting short the lives of men, women and children in all manner of cruel and imaginative ways, the Four Horsemen of the Apocalypse had been disbanded.

No one was quite sure what happened to them in the decades that followed. War, it was rumoured, became a roving mercenary-for-hire. Pestilence, it was alleged, continued to inflict terrible diseases on any passer-by whose general good health irritated him. And Famine, it was claimed, had retired to a cave in the Himalayas, where he devoted his meagre energies to a rigorous routine of silence, abstinence and contemplation. Death's fate was equally uncertain, but some reports placed him on a small Caribbean island, where he spent his days lying on the beach, attempting to mitigate the severe pallor of his complexion.

No trace remained of the Agency, their former workplace: it had been razed to the ground shortly after their departure, leaving no sign of their existence and destroying all evidence of their activity. At the same time, four ramshackle old cars were found burned-out in a second-hand lot on the far side of town, an incident which yielded no more than a brief column in the local tabloids and provoked a cursory response from the police. Everyone soon lost interest; the news cycle moved on.

The business of death had to continue, however: there were just too many people. Though it had become a burden for the Four Horsemen, there were others more than eager to replace them—creatures with keen minds and restless hands; a foul and subtle horde that took pleasure in suffering and inflicted it with pitiless efficiency. A plan was devised, contracts were drawn up, infrastructure was put in place.

5

Mankind would be downsized by the only workforce with the requisite power and ruthlessness for the task.

It wasn't a smooth transition. Records went missing, mistakes were made, new systems and rules took time to work out, and some regrettable excesses were committed in the name of productivity. Nonetheless, in a few short years the new recruits had infiltrated every village, town and city in the world and had created a formidable network of liars, cut-throats, propagandists and saboteurs.

Among the most eminent was Abaddon—an ancient creature riddled with malice and mischief. He regarded the demise of the Four Horsemen with enormous satisfaction, and relished his part in their downfall. It was a matter of pride: he remembered when his kind had been treated with fear and respect by the living and was determined to reawaken those feelings as quickly as possible. For him, authority had not been transferred, it had been *restored*.

He was simply taking back control.

A knock on the window of his private chamber interrupted his reveries. It was irritating, but he knew that none would dare encroach without good cause. Naturally, he could ignore the incursion, but something about the knock—its rhythm, its insistence, perhaps nothing more than his own intuition—caused him to reply.

'What is it?'

'Very sorry to bother you, sir, but I have news that you might find interesting.'

They couldn't see each other and spoke only through the grille, but the intruder's voice had given him away immediately: Abaddon was pleased to note that it was his most loyal servant, one who could always be relied on for some juicy titbit to assuage the boredom.

'Well?'

'It seems we've found another diversion.'

'I hope it will prove more amusing than the last.'

'I hesitate to say so, but I trust you will be more than satisfied.'

He wanted to believe, but blind faith always ended in disappointment. All the same, he couldn't deny that the prospect excited him. Diversions of this sort were rare; the promise of another ought to be cherished.

'That remains to be seen.'

'Of course, sir. I mean no offence.'

'Very well—you may go.'

'Just one more thing, if I may.'

'Do you intend to try my patience, worm?'

'Not at all, sir. However, according to our records, it may please you to know that you've met this particular diversion once before. There is a certain *history* between the two of you.'

'Really? Well, I suppose that *is* interesting.'

'Thank you, sir... I'll make the arrangements, as usual.'

The servant's footsteps faded. Abaddon relaxed in his chair, savouring the news. An old prey newly encountered. A pinch of spice for the routine. A trick or two, a few words in the right place; a subtle promise, a just reward.

He was *really* looking forward to this one.

PART ONE

Malache the Liar

The master

I keep my soul in a box. It's safe there. No one can touch it.

The box is small, without hinge or seam, and is made of polished wood inlaid with ivory and precious stones—though the ivory has yellowed over the years, many of the stones have been lost, and the once bright veneer has peeled and cracked. But this outer shell is insignificant compared to what it protects: that weak and quivering essence that once gave me life.

However, there remains a doubt. I glimpsed my soul only fleetingly, many years ago, and sometimes I question what I saw with my own eyes. Was it an illusion? A false memory? Some demonic trick?

To put my mind at ease I need to open the box again. But the lid is sealed by some intricate mechanism, and my hands are practically useless: the bones are fused together in a club, the skin is melted over them like a child's mitten. The dexterity required to unpick that hidden lock is beyond my power.

Perhaps I should be content with what I have. Though the greater part of me is curious to look inside—to check once and for all that my soul is there—a small part of me would rather leave it in peace. That small part remembers what it was like to be a corpse, locked in total darkness. It remembers the security of the coffin.

But the coffin is gone, and I am no longer a corpse. I am a zombie, and I keep my soul in a box.

In the shadow of an old building, huddled against myself, I sheltered from a winter storm. Occasionally, a gust of wind blew needles of rain against my skin; but I didn't mind. I was content to let the world happen.

After a while I uncurled from my damp huddle and paid attention to the city around me. I wasn't worried about making contact with its inhabitants: my clothes shielded me from scrutiny. My black trackpants, black sweatshirt, black trainers, black woollen hat and long black overcoat could easily have passed for a pile of rags. So I watched this dark, rainy city with impunity, smelled the mould of rain-soaked rotting leaves, heard cars hiss by on rain-swept roads, tasted raindrops on my lips—

'Why should I give *you* money? I have to look at people like you every day. You should pay *me*.'

A man was standing on the pavement before me. His eyes lay buried in his face like little black stones, but his mouth was wide and red.

'I don't want your money,' I said quietly.

'So why the hell are you sitting here?'

'I just want to be left alone.'

He grunted. 'I work nine hours a day, five days a week, and every night I see tramps like you sitting here looking for hand-outs. This used to be a good neighbourhood full of decent, hard-working people; now it's riddled with filth. So I'm giving you some friendly advice: why don't you fuck off to your soup kitchen and get out of my fucking sight?'

He continued to speak, but I stopped listening. It wasn't the first time I had been confronted by a Lifer, and most were kinder than him; however, I had little in common with any of them. I didn't need much in the way of food or water, I could survive on very little money, and I was prone to melancholy and sentimentality.

At last he fell silent; I was aware of him once more. I saw the rain bouncing off his umbrella, the neat lines of his grey pinstripe suit, the wet shine of his expensive leather shoes. The easiest way out of this situation was for me to move, so I stood up, expecting him to let me pass. But he remained where he was.

Something had changed in him. His face was ashen, the black eyes were fuller, his mouth was pale and tight. He was swaying slightly, breathing heavily; his chest heaved in spasms. Suddenly, his legs buckled and he vomited on the pavement in front of me.

I wondered if I should help him up, but before I could do anything I caught an odour of woodsmoke and became aware of another figure standing beside me—someone who seemed to be both present and absent at the same time.

'I hate rudeness, don't you?' this new stranger said.

As I turned toward him his appearance solidified. I saw a perfectly ordinary man of average height, dressed in a fitted black suit with a white shirt and black tie. His blond hair was wild, with a slight curl and no defined crown, but he had a friendly face with warm blue eyes, and an expression that was almost angelic in its innocence.

I started to walk away.

'Wait, friend,' he said. 'I would like to speak with you.'

Below me, the ailing man continued to retch, but his spasms were fruitless and painful, and he moaned loudly as the rain beat against his back. Then, through the rain and the vomit, I smelled something else, faint but familiar, repulsive, nauseating...

'What do you want?' I said.

'First, allow me to introduce myself.' The stranger extended his hand, which I accepted reluctantly. His flesh was dry and smooth, like snakeskin. 'My name is Malache. If you would come to my office, I have a proposition which you may find attractive—'

'I'm not interested.'

'Naturally. You are reluctant to trust an outsider. This is perfectly understandable; indeed, it would be foolish for one such as you to do otherwise. All I ask is that you listen to what I have to say, and if at the end of it you reject my offer, I give my word that I shall not trouble you again.'

Whether it was the manner of his speech, his sympathetic demeanour or some other inexplicable force,

I felt my resistance crumbling. In any case, by not leaving immediately I had already lost.

'Okay, I said.

'Excellent.' He grinned, revealing a wide mouth and two rows of small, pointed teeth. 'However, if I may, I would first like to clarify one or two administrative details.' He looked me up and down. 'To begin with, you fit the description, more or less.' He leaned toward me and inhaled diffidently. 'A faint odour of the sacred river, too—very good... Would you mind if I examined your neck?' I loosened the collar of my overcoat obediently as he read the number seared into my flesh. '7218911121349—as it should be. Thank you.' He straightened my collar vigorously and patted me firmly, high on the back; then he pulled a phone from his jacket pocket and studied it. 'Everything checks out. You're a little thinner than I was expecting, but I don't need to confirm your various mutilations and disfigurements. Keep your clothes on.'

I was grateful for his discretion, but at the same time I felt an overwhelming sense of déjà vu, as if my life was about to repeat a familiar and inevitable pattern.

'I won't tell you how long I've been looking for you,' he continued. 'Suffice to say, it's a pleasure to find you alive and in one piece. And I can assure you that our association will be of great mutual benefit.'

As he was speaking, I clumsily manipulated the box from my overcoat pocket, clasped it roughly between my stumps and offered it to him.

'Help me open this. Then I'll gladly come with you.'

'Absolutely not!' he said firmly. 'That box was intended for you alone, and only you may unlock it. Even if I wanted to, I couldn't. I'm sorry.'

My hope wilted. I sank to the ground in despair. Malache bent down beside me and rested his fingers lightly on my shoulder—a gesture accompanied once more by that revolting stench. I knew then that he wasn't a Lifer, or even a creature of this world; but it didn't matter. Nothing

14

mattered anymore. The rain would always fall, and I would always be a zombie.

With infinite tenderness, Malache put his arms around me and held me as my mother had once held me, without judgement; and I wept now as I had wept then, without shame. When my tears had dried, I turned toward him and saw that he was looking at me with compassion, and I felt blessed, and loved.

'How would you like a new pair of hands?' he said.

Babylon Bookbinders

Malache revealed nothing more of his proposal; but I suspected any offer he made would depend upon accepting his terms. I didn't ask. The longer I remained in the dark, the more I could dream of replacing these withered stumps with ten fingers that would unlock the box containing my soul— and when the box was open I would absorb that bright, quivering essence and draw it deep inside me.

And I would finally live again.

'Let's go,' he said. 'A crowd is gathering.'

In my fantasies about phantom limbs, I hadn't noticed the people helping the bilious stranger in front of us— some of whom were now casting accusatory glances in our direction. Malache stood up and offered me his hand; I took it willingly. We walked quickly away without looking back.

'Will he be okay?' I asked.

'In a couple of days. If he manages to forget the smell.'

Even as he spoke I inhaled another wave of that unpleasant stench emanating from my companion; but it seemed less potent than before, and the further we travelled the more tolerable it became. It was still present—as the unguarded disgust on the faces of passers-by confirmed—but it no longer made me want to throw up.

We soon reached the main shopping area. Bargain stores, restaurants, phone outlets and fashion retailers jostled for attention; but Malache turned down a narrow side street, away from the crowds. Again, I was grateful for his sensitivity: the dead have little to fear from the living, but a zombie is constantly threatened by the anxiety of exposure.

He stopped outside a noodle bar and put a comforting hand on my arm. 'I know you want to hear the details of my proposal, but first I have to prepare you for what lies ahead. I'm an administrator in the Bureau of Infernal Affairs. My office is one of many throughout this city, and there are many more across the country and beyond. However, we like to keep a low profile, so whether or not you agree to my offer, I must stress the need for confidentiality and discretion with regard to anything you might witness over the next few days.'

He looked at me expectantly; I nodded my assent.

We stopped outside a narrow stone building at the end of the street. I saw a stained glass door and two plate glass windows displaying a range of antiquarian books. Above the entrance, in plain white lettering on a black background, I read the words:

BABYLON BOOKBINDERS
Prop. Nergal, Ereshkigal & Dumuzid

Four Vespa scooters of varying colours—black, red, green and purple—were parked at an angle to the kerb. I tried to examine them in more detail but Malache urged me toward the door. He opened it to the tinkling of a bell.

I walked inside.

I saw a workshop, much longer than it was wide, stretching to a windowed office at the rear. I saw shelves filled with books and binding materials, craft supplies and tools, scissors, knives, presses of all kinds, folders, boxes and filing trays, sheaves of paper and jars crammed with brushes. I smelled paper, leather, wood, glue, polish and a dozen other subtle odours I couldn't name. I heard the faint sounds of a machine, whirring and grinding in the distance. I tasted hot, musty, metallic air.

Three wooden workbenches were spaced equidistantly along the room, burdened with many of the same tools and materials I had seen on the walls. At each workbench stood a carved wooden chair.

The chairs were occupied.

At first glance the occupants looked like people—and to a Lifer visiting the shop, that first impression of humanity would have overcome any latent doubts—but I sensed there was something not quite *right* about them. They were all dressed in jeans, cotton shirts and jerkins, and their physical appearance was unremarkable: a stocky youth with ginger hair and matching beard, a slim, muscular woman with a keen gaze and narrow lips, and a drowsy old man whose green baseball cap offset his rheumy eyes and sallow complexion. However, alongside these superficial characteristics, their bodies exuded a faint *shimmer* and an almost imperceptible iridescence.

'Who's the startled rabbit?' the woman asked Malache.

'Isn't it obvious?' said the youth, closing the laptop on his desk. 'He's the overseer's latest thing.'

'Fresh meat for the grinder,' said the old man, morosely.

'What's your name?' asked the woman.

'I don't remember.'

'Well that won't do, will it? We have to call you something. We can't just say *you there*, or address you as *that thing in the corner*, can we? You need a title.'

'How about He Won't Get Through This In One Piece?' said the youth.

'Don't be facetious, Nerg.'

'Do you have a preference?' Malache asked me.

I shrugged.

'Fine,' the woman said. 'My first instincts are always reliable. If no one has a better suggestion, I'm going to call you Rabbit.' She looked defiantly around the room but no one challenged her. 'That's settled, then... Come and sit beside me, Rabbit. Tell me all about yourself.'

'You'll have to wait, Resh,' said Malache. 'We have one or two clerical matters to discuss first.'

'Don't be rude, Mal. Introduce us at least.'

Malache sighed and indicated each speaker in turn. The woman: 'That's Ereshkigal.' The youth: 'Nergal.' The old man: 'Dumuzid.'

'Former gods turned petty devils,' the old man grumbled.

'Speak for yourself, Dum,' said the youth.

Malache ushered me into the office at the far end of the room. He closed the door behind us and drew down a set of metallic blinds.

I looked around. It was a small, minimally decorated space containing a polished wooden desk, a large executive leather chair, a smaller mesh chair and a two-seater sofa. The walls were adorned with several framed Employee of the Month certificates, all of which bore Malache's name, as well as two posters promoting a company called Green Devil Recycling. The sound of the grinding, whirring machinery was louder here; it seemed to be coming from a second door opposite the entrance. It drowned out the noise of the ceiling fan.

Malache settled into the executive chair and indicated its mesh cousin in front of the desk. 'Take a seat,' he said.

I sat down and folded my arms.

'Would you like a drink?'

I nodded. My mouth was as dry as a mummified corpse.

He opened the bottom drawer of the desk and produced a litre bottle of Southern Comfort and two tumblers. I hadn't drunk alcohol since my death, and right now—when I needed to make an important decision—probably wasn't the best time to dive back in. For all I knew, one shot would pickle my undead brain and turn me into a mindless, unfeeling vegetable incapable of planning ahead, acting responsibly or talking to people in coherent sentences.

'Pour me a large one,' I said.

'It would be my pleasure.'

He half filled the tumbler and pushed it toward me.

I hesitated, then took a tiny sip. Immediately, I felt the smooth mix of whiskey, orange and spice linger on my lips and tongue. I rolled it around my mouth awhile, then swallowed; it seared and scratched the lining of my throat as it flowed, burning, into my stomach. I wanted more, so I took a longer drink and held the tumbler at eye level as Malache spoke. His face was transformed by the glass into a grotesque mask.

'So here's my proposal... Essentially, you will perform a series of minor tasks for the Bureau. You will come to the office every morning at the specified time. I will provide you with information relevant to the day's task. You will go away and absorb that information. In the evening you will come back and I will take you to someone who needs help. You will help them. When you have finished helping them, you will report to the overseer.'

'What about my hands?'

'If you do everything asked of you in a timely and dependable fashion, the overseer has assured me that he will personally furnish you with a complete set of fingers.'

'Like my old ones?'

'Exactly so.'

I sighed, and took a third sip; then took a swig for good luck. I felt seasick and happy and weightless. I wanted to dive into the bottle and drown. But a thought rose from the bottom of my mind and sprang from my mouth as if it didn't belong to me. 'No contracts, though. There's always some clause I don't understand or a commitment I can't keep.'

'We have what we like to call a Verbal Zero Hours Contract. It's like a normal zero hours contract but without the paperwork—that's good for you and good for us. In truth, it's not really a contract at all: there's nothing to sign and you can walk away at any time.'

'I don't understand.'

'It's simple. This discussion is our deal. These words are our bond. I have stated my requirements, you have stated yours. I agree to your terms. All you have to do is agree to mine.'

The alcohol rampaged through my brain, diluting reason and nudging my mind off vertical. My existence had reverted to its habitual form: bafflement, a sense of dread, the desire to acquiesce. How could I trust him? What exactly did the work involve? And what was he not telling me? I didn't care. My head was floating in a liquid bath of Southern Comfort, and it felt good: a burning, drowning, demon's trap of goodness.

'I accept your terms,' I said.

Malache smiled. 'I would offer to seal the deal with a handshake, but given your condition I have no wish to offend you... Nonetheless, we have an agreement and I trust that you will honour it.' He rose from his chair, took the glass from my hand and placed it on the desk; then he opened the door to the workshop. 'Dum!' he called. 'I have a job for you.'

I turned around as the sallow old man appeared in the doorway. I found it hard to focus on his precise shape, either because of the brain vinegar I'd drunk or that inherent quality of shimmer I'd noticed on arrival.

'What can I do for you, Mal?'

'I have a meeting with the overseer, so I'd like you to take our friend to lunch and tell him about our work here at the Bureau.'

'Can't you ask Resh? I'm on a hot streak.'

'What are you doing?'

'Dead Sea Scroll 973: The Ten Commandments Moses Didn't Tell You. *Thou shalt not misuse a gourd, however lonely thou art. Beware a burning bush, lest thy ass be singed—*'

'It can wait. I've left the note for tonight's assignment on your desk. Pick it up on your way out.'

Malache turned around and looked at me with a gaze of glimmering crystal blue. I felt as if he were enfolding me with kindness. 'Good man,' he said, patting me on the shoulder. 'Everything will work out fine. You'll see.'

Noodles

I followed Dumuzid to his workbench and waited as he searched for the note. He rummaged through stacks of paper and piles of leather, but found nothing; with increasing irritation, he scoured the floor and walls, combed through the pages of a dozen books, and examined the shelves, tool drawers and message boards.

'Is this what you're looking for?'

We both turned toward Nergal, who was brandishing a wax-sealed white envelope.

'Where did you find it?'

'On your desk.'

'Why did you take it?'

Nergal shrugged. 'I needed a bookmark.'

Dumuzid sighed and snatched the envelope from his colleague's hand; then he put on a heavy overcoat and led me outside.

The rain had turned to a faint drizzle, a cool and prickling counterpoint to my alcoholic haze. I stood by the Vespas, expecting to ride pillion on a journey to some distant restaurant. The old man regarded me with puzzlement.

'Do you like noodles?' he asked.

'I don't remember.'

'Well, let's go and find out.'

21

We walked the short distance to the café Malache and I had passed earlier: a small, cheerful and brightly-lit place decorated with an array of lush green plants. It was called, unimaginatively, The Noodle Bar. Immediately to the right was a haberdasher which, riffing off its neighbour, was titled The Needle Bar. To the left was a nail bar; but the owner, evidently a maverick, had named it The Oxford Manicure.

We entered and sat on a bench at a polished wooden table. A couple of Lifers glanced in my direction; I averted my gaze and kept my back to the wall. Almost immediately, a chubby man with thick glasses approached and addressed my companion.

'Hello, Mr D,' he said. 'Good to see you again. How are you?'

'I'm fine, Ignazio. I brought a friend today.'

To my horror, the chubby man turned to look at me— but if he felt any disgust at my shabby appearance he masked it with a gracious nod. 'Any friend of Dumuzid is a friend of mine. He's my best customer. He makes the plants shine!' He gestured at the greenery around us which, in fact, appeared supernaturally lustrous. 'His mere presence draws people to my café, and if I had my way I would pay him to eat here... But I do not wish to embarrass him. What can I get for you? I recommend the chicken udon, the tempura king prawns, the vegetarian seaweed soup—'

'Plain noodles,' I said.

'Plain noodles?' he repeated incredulously. His expression implied that I had just stabbed his prize coy carp.

'Yes.'

'No sauce?'

'No.'

'I have yakisoba, black bean, green curry, oyster sauce. I have pickled ginger, peanuts and shallots. I can add meat or fish—'

'Just plain.'

He took my order with a look of profound distress, but brightened again when Dumuzid requested sizzling calamari and sesame prawn toast followed by Singaporean egg noodles with beef and vegetables. He nodded once more, then returned to the kitchen and relayed our order to the chef. The chef responded by smashing a plate and unleashing a stream of abuse, which our host quickly neutralised with a smile and a friendly arm around the shoulder.

Dumuzid removed the envelope from the pocket of his jerkin, turned it over in his hands, then put it away again. 'I expect you're feeling somewhat agitated,' he said.

'Yes. But I'm trying to stay calm.'

'The alcohol should help. We offer it to all the interns. Some refuse it; others, like you, use it to medicate their anxiety. There is no right or wrong. Only choices.'

I considered debating the point. When I was alive I had often made the wrong choices: emotionally, I had wrecked all of my intimate relationships and had made no lasting friends; practically, I had taken on a job for an old flame that I should have left alone—and which, coincidentally, had led to my death. Nor did I make any better decisions as a zombie: I had worked for people who disliked me in jobs for which I was totally unsuited; and I had, regardless of the danger, almost entered into a meaningful association with a Lifer.

As a corpse, of course, I had felt nothing, said nothing and done nothing, so had never had cause to make any significant choices at all.

I didn't argue; instead I said with the ponderous emphasis of a drunk: 'Why me? I have no particular skills, I've never excelled at anything, and if I hadn't been promised my hands I wouldn't even be here.'

'I wouldn't be so sure,' he said. 'The overseer usually gets what he wants.'

I didn't understand what he meant, and the arrival of our lunch cut short any attempt to question it. I was presented with a beautiful bowl of plain, steaming noodles with the same ceremony and civility Dumuzid received for his array of dishes. I gripped a fork between two stumps and set about the meal with relish; the delicate tang of the soft, salted noodles made me feel much better. I couldn't remember the last time I had eaten hot food.

I settled into contented silence as—between mouthfuls of squid, beef and prawns—Dumuzid told me about his work.

'So. The Bureau is an organisation created to rationalise the task of population control; however, there are many disciplines subordinated to that goal, and every aspect of our work must reflect the Boss's guiding ethos. I confess that I don't always know precisely what that ethos is—I'm only a minor devil, and our branch is small compared to those you find in the larger cities and capitals—but I am assured that we all make a valuable contribution to the cause.' He paused to remove a rubbery calamari from his teeth, then continued. 'Our particular team is just one of thousands worldwide responsible for redefining the truth. For example, my specialty is the forging of antique manuscripts, which are chemically aged and relocated to various archaeological sites throughout the world. These fakes are then discovered and analysed by historians—many of whom also work for us—and the moral narrative is subtly shifted in our favour.'

I blissfully rolled a thick udon over my tongue.

'Fundamentally, our main aim as devils is to propagate the lie. It doesn't matter what the lie is, how credible, how ridiculous, how important or otherwise; the point is that it multiplies and continues to grow until it is believed, despite all evidence to the contrary. However, one must be careful not to be blatant, so all of our cadres use legitimate businesses to provide cover for the activities we undertake.'

'And Malache?'

'Well, he's in charge of the grinder, of course; but he's also our link to the overseer—he reports on our progress and provides us with feedback. You might say he's a go-between, but his work is more eclectic than that. Half of what he does is a mystery, even to us.'

'I still don't understand why he needs me.'

'The answer is simple. There are two classes of citizen in the Underworld. The majority are *devils*, like Nerg, Resh and I: intelligent creatures with the wit and skill to deceive the living. Through various means we encourage Lifers to kill themselves or each other; and if I might be permitted a small boast, we have achieved remarkable success in this regard... The second group—a less numerous and somewhat atavistic strain—are *demons*: reckless beasts with a primitive hatred of the living. These creatures are more hands-on: they enjoy the visceral thrill of killing—and if we didn't keep them occupied the resulting chaos would threaten our mission here.' He removed the envelope from his pocket, placed it on the table and pushed it toward me. 'However, demons have one major flaw: they need guidance to find the right prey. Many of them work among Lifers and can recognise familiar individuals by sight; but strangers baffle them. Put simply: they can hardly tell one human from another... Now, the basic task of identification is too menial for a devil, the living are too compassionate to be of any use, and the dead don't care. So who does that leave?'

'Zombies,' I said.

I left the café with the envelope in my coat pocket. If I had interpreted Dumuzid's words correctly, it contained the details of someone who would be killed; and though I believed that life and death were not so different, and both had their advantages, I didn't relish the prospect of watching someone die again.

But what choice did I have? I wanted my soul.

I thought Dumuzid might accompany me further, or at least stay until I had opened the envelope, but he clasped my right stump, gave it a weak squeeze and said, 'I must get back to work. Good luck.'

I headed for the place where I had first met Malache. The rain had stopped and no one paid me any mind, but I felt suffocated, trapped. The grey sky pressed down on me, the pavement felt thick and heavy. This was a world I had to drag myself through, a world that had set itself against me. Would it feel any different with a soul inside me? I had been a zombie for so long I couldn't remember what it was like to be anything else.

All I knew was:

There were days when I longed for the coffin. There were days when I longed to be alive. There were days when I felt nothing at all, and I sat in the darkness and didn't think. And there were days when I thought and felt too much and I wondered at the thinking and feeling, and it was too much to bear, and I wanted to push it outside of me and leave it all behind.

I pressed my broken hands against the box in my coat pocket. Of late this world has lost it lustre, and I have forgotten how to love.

I arrived at the steps in the shadow of the old building. The stranger I had spoken to had disappeared and all trace of him had been washed away by the rain. Even so, I settled down warily in case someone connected me to that shameful incident.

Then I huddled inside my coat and took the envelope from my pocket.

I have forgotten how to love. When I was alive I found it easy: I loved my parents, I loved my work as an investigator, I fell in love with people utterly and without fear of the consequences. As a corpse I had no strong feelings either way: love had no more significance than the muffled echoes of life penetrating my coffin from six feet above my head. But since my resurrection I have been afraid of love, terrified of the danger it holds: the exposure of my self, the peril of commitment, the fear of being hurt by another without recourse or remedy. So I have forgotten.

Or rather, I have tried to forget.

I still remember Zoë, the only Lifer who came close to unwinding these chains from my undead heart; and she sat beside me now, as I broke the wax seal on the envelope with my teeth.

I found a handwritten note and a colour photograph inside. The photo showed a man in his early forties with a thick neck, a wide toothy smile and faint streaks of grey in his hair. The note was singed at the edges. It said:

1224364860728. Normal, average face, medium height (by their standards). Wish they all didn't look so alike. I'll bring Xael along for the ride. 9pm—Master of Fire.

A small price to pay

I should have drunk more when I had the chance. The tang of alcohol still lingered on my tongue, but the numbing warmth had faded and the melancholy unease of existence had returned.

The photograph was self-evident, but the note was far from clear. The number was an identifier with thirteen digits, like my own, and would presumably ensure we found the right Lifer; but I'd never seen identifiers on the living before. The time confused me, too: was it an appointment with the demon, an instruction to meet Malache at nine, or simply the time of death? I had no idea. After several minutes of internal debate I decided to pursue the safest option: I would return to the workshop at eight.

The sun was low in the sky; I estimated it was mid afternoon. I was tired from this morning's events and wary of how long tonight's task would take. I decided to find somewhere to sleep.

There are many corners and hollows where the barely visible can find shelter. At night I have curled up in gardens and garages, inside bins and skips, beside lamp posts and tree trunks; I have slept in doorways, alleyways, parks and private squares. During the day there are fewer places to hide unguarded; but they exist, if you're prepared to take the risk.

On the main road south out of Oxford, before the park, there are rows of terraces: a mixture of student digs, residential dwellings and sheltered housing. Many of these have basement flats with unused coal stores outside: the coal has gone but the space remains—an empty room with a door; a dry place to rest when no one is home.

And that was what I found.

I curled into a ball beneath my coat and fell asleep thinking about my hands. They were the keys to a new life: a life with a soul, like the life I had once lived; a life with friends and the love I had tried so hard to forget. I would find a job, I would eat hot food every day; and I would find a place to live, a place of my own with a door I could close against the world.

If I had to make a deal with a devil for all that, it was a small price to pay.

When I woke it was dark. At first I panicked, thinking I had missed my appointment; then I heard the throb of rush hour traffic and realised I had plenty of time. I rose stiffly, rolling over and pressing my stumps to the tiled floor, then raising myself to a crouch. With great care I crept forward and looked through a crack in the door. The curtains in the front window were closed; the owner had returned. I eased the door open. The porch was dark but there was light in the hallway beyond. I crawled out of the coal store—

The front door opened and a young man stood over me. He was around twenty years old, slightly built, with short blond hair. The smile on his face quickly turned to disgust; he recoiled instinctively, retreating to the threshold.

'Who are you?' he said.

He noticed my stumps and drew back further, into the light of the hall. A young woman appeared behind him, but showed no inclination to move closer.

'Who is it?' she said.

I didn't want to alarm them. In life I had hurt people, both privately and professionally—sometimes unavoidably, occasionally out of spite—but I was different now. I didn't want to harm anyone. So I stood up, bowed politely and said: 'I'm no one. I just needed a place to sleep.'

I turned around, climbed the steps to street level and left without looking back. The hair on my neck told me I was being pursued by a vengeful, axe-wielding mob; but undead neck hair is an unreliable guide to the truth. I arrived at St Aldates unmolested.

At the top of the slope I reached Carfax Tower. I had once seen a woman throw herself from its high parapet: I remembered her body lying at the base, broken in a spreading pool of blood. I had written a suicide note on her behalf, though I hadn't cared enough to find out what happened to her afterward. I didn't even know where she was buried.

The clock on the tower told me it was seven-thirty. I still had half an hour before my appointment. I passed the time gazing at the shining displays of consumer goods on Cornmarket. The stores were closed and I had no money, but the brightly glittering Christmas baubles mesmerised me for a while.

'You're early,' said Malache. 'I wasn't expecting you until nine. Didn't you read the note?'

'I misunderstood what it said.'

'Never mind. You're here now. Would you like a drink?'

I knew I shouldn't, I had a job to do, first impressions were important and it had taken me a long time to recover from the previous glass.

'Yes,' I said.

We sat in his office again. The air was cooler, the lights of the workshop were dim and there was no sign of his three colleagues. He took the bottle of Southern Comfort from the drawer, half-filled a glass and pushed it toward me. I thanked him and took a burning sip—which slid into a drink, which stumbled into a full-throated glug. I felt better, which is how alcohol works, right until the moment it kills you.

We sat without speaking for a while, listening to the low machine hum from the other side of the wall. The door to that area appeared to be locked: I saw a brass key in a brass keyhole. I sensed Malache observing me as I looked at it, but he looked away when I looked back at him. He was still dressed in his black suit, black shoes, white shirt and black tie. Emboldened by the drink, I said:

'You look like a funeral director.'

'And you look like a zombie,' he replied.

That shut me up for a while. It was a warm, spicy, golden shutting up with a hint of orange: a peaceful, floating, this-won't-be-so-bad silence. Malache watched me with a faint smile on his lips. I emptied the glass quickly; I hoped it would get me through the next few hours. *Master of Fire*. I remembered the demon who had taken my hands—was it the same one?

'It is time, friend,' said Malache.

'Can I take the bottle with me?'

'I'm afraid not.'

I stood up and shuffled around unsteadily, until I realised I had two feet, then I followed Malache through the workshop to the stained glass exit. He opened it, led me outside, then closed and locked the door behind him. I looked up at the sign again; something about it struck me as odd.

'Why isn't your name there?'

'I prefer to work in the shadows,' he said, climbing onto the black Vespa. 'Anyway, let's go. Sit on the back and hold on tight.'

I did as he asked: for a moment it felt as though I was mounting a wild horse, then I wrapped my arms around his waist and the world stabilised. But only briefly: Malache immediately took off at high speed, the engine beneath him growling like a giant, enraged wasp. I closed my eyes, pressed my cheek against his jacket and absorbed the noise until it became a part of me. I felt the wind, the cold winter's night, the relentless beating energy of the machine. I felt alive!

It was over too soon. I had been vaguely aware of a long, steep hill, the curve of a roundabout, an undertone of traffic surrendering to the quiet of country roads. I had dreamt an alien dream and woken in moonlight.

I found myself on a gravel driveway leading to a clump of redbrick buildings. The largest of these appeared to be a chapel, with a square chimney where the spire might have been; the rest seemed to have no obvious purpose. There were benches along the path, formal gardens all around, trees in the distance. Long swathes of grey fields linked everything together, and every field was dotted with rows of gravestones like tiny silver teeth.

'We're still early,' said Malache, checking his watch, 'but Haborym should be along in a minute or two.'

'Who's Haborym?' I slurred.

'Your demon... Do as he says and try not to provoke him. He becomes reckless when he's excited.' I rolled off the Vespa onto the gravel, but Malache remained seated. He turned the scooter around. 'I have to go, but I'll be back when it's over. You'll be fine, trust me.'

He waved goodbye and vanished into the night.

I sat on one of the benches and settled into my overcoat, a cord of dread ravelling inside me. *Haborym, Master of Fire.* I didn't know what those words meant. All zombies are afraid of the unknown; but the half-known, the threatened, the implied—these are much, much worse.

A moment later, I heard tyres rolling across gravel and the whine of a car in low gear. Someone was coming.

31

Ring of Fire

As soon as I saw the headlights, I panicked, leapt from the bench and concealed myself in the nearest bush. I observed the vehicle's slow, cautious approach with mounting terror.

The car came to a halt. The door opened and a man got out. I saw his face in the moonlight—and felt an overwhelming sense of relief. It was the same face I had seen in the photograph this afternoon. The note described him perfectly: normal, average, medium. The kind of man you might miss in a crowd, even if the crowd consisted of three people.

He closed the door and looked around unhurriedly. He didn't see the zombie in the bush. He didn't hear the zombie's troubled breathing. He didn't care that the zombie was paralysed by the conflict between empathy and self-interest. He didn't know that the zombie felt ashamed because he wanted to warn the man that he would soon be murdered, but was too afraid to do so.

He opened the boot and took out a spade, a lump hammer and a stone chisel. Then he began to whistle a tune from a film I had watched with my father when I was a teenager: *Twisted Nerve*. I liked the tune because it was sinister and melancholy, but somehow upbeat and cheerful too—words which also described the stranger as he trampled across an ornamental garden toward the nearest row of gravestones.

I followed at a safe distance, keeping to the shadows of the trees. My limbs stumbled forward, my head was drunk and stupid, but the detective within was focused and alert. My senses responded to every detail: the blinding fullness of the moon, the pale glimmer of frost on grass, the stranger's heavy footprints leading me onward. I wanted to know who he was, where he had come from, what his intentions were.

He paused at the first headstone, read the inscription, then passed quickly on to the next; but this pleased him no better than the first. He moved slowly along the row in this way, carefully checking every grave, until at last he found one that satisfied him. He stopped whistling, took the hammer and chisel in hand, knelt on the raised earth and began to strike the headstone. I thought he intended to vandalise it, but his blows were restrained and precise: he was carving a message. And each stroke was punctuated by a few words.

'Where are the goods, Frank?—You said you'd look after them—Fifty-fifty, remember?—Your wife doesn't have them—Don't worry, I asked her nicely—At first, anyway—Then she told me where you were buried—But she wouldn't say anything else—She was loyal right to the end—Your daughter, on the other hand—She wasn't so loyal—She said she owed you nothing—And she told me right away—Everything, Frank—So I'm leaving this message for you—People should know what kind of man you are—And after that, I'm taking what's mine—And maybe I'll take what's yours, too.'

When he was finished, he threw his tools onto the grass, traced his fingers along the fresh carving and stood up to admire his handiwork. Then he picked up the spade and began to dig, and the only sound I heard was the slice of a blade and the thump of discarded earth.

How long does it take a man to dig a hole two and half feet wide by eight feet long by six feet deep? I started to calculate the answer—one hundred and twenty cubic feet of soil at a rate of five cubic feet every ten minutes, on average, without resting—when I was distracted by a presence alongside me in the shadows. At first it was merely a pleasant warmth, then a prickling sensation across my back, and finally a firm prod to my right kidney.

I turned and saw a figure in a pinstripe suit and bowler hat, carrying a folded black umbrella. But beneath this human form I caught flickering glimpses of another: a hairy, foul-smelling creature with three grotesque heads; and something black and glistening that slithered and writhed at its feet.

'Are you the undead, or are you my prey?' he said.

'The undead,' I replied, suddenly quite sober.

'And that featureless thing over there...?'

'Your prey.'

'You're absolutely sure?'

'Yes.'

'That's settled, then.' He set off at a brisk pace toward the grave digger, leaving a patch of scorched grass where he had stood. I followed him, but after a couple of steps he turned around and pointedly sniffed my torso. 'Your odour is rather distracting. Perhaps you should wait here.'

The man caught sight of the demon. He stepped back and raised his spade menacingly.

'Who the fuck are you?'

'I am Haborym, from the Bureau of Infernal Affairs.'

'The what?'

'It doesn't matter. Please accept my apologies for what I am about to do—'

'Get away from me, you fucking freak.'

The man swung his spade to within a couple of inches of Haborym's face. The demon didn't flinch; but on the second swing he seized the weapon, tore it from his opponent's hands and turned it against him, delivering several heavy blows to the head and chest. They were executed swiftly and without fuss, and after the ninth or tenth strike the man lay motionless on the ground.

Haborym summoned me with a wave. When I arrived, I saw a bruised and battered body lying face-up on the freshly-dug mound of earth. Wielding a jagged blade, the demon was quietly cutting a number into the unconscious man's neck.

I turned away and looked at the headstone. I saw the forename *Frank*, engraved in florid italics. But the surname had been obliterated by a single word carved with clumsy strokes: LIAR.

'What do you want me to do?' I said.

'Wait until I've finished the ID. Then you can help me carry this thing to the crematorium.'

Haborym's shape was alternating rapidly now between the pinstriped gentleman and a three-headed beast standing beside a giant black viper. One of the heads—a crude parody of the human form—was focused on the cutting; the other two—a sardonic cat and a black-eyed serpent—watched me closely. The viper shifted restlessly as he worked, coiling and uncoiling its tail, its scaly skin iridescent in the moonlight.

I tried to move away, but the serpent and cat heads hissed an ominous warning.

'All finished,' he said. 'We normally imprint the tag much later, but needs must... Wait—is that *my* handiwork?' He prodded the melted flesh of my hands with his fingers. 'Intense heat. Powerful grip. Subtle use of the palms. Fine craftsmanship—but *not* mine, sadly.' He sighed. 'Anyway, you'd better take the head end.'

I bent down, hooked my stumps under the man's armpits and lifted him, synchronising my movements with Haborym, who picked up the legs as if they were straws. My companion was more demon than human now. His rosy, elongated face boasted a thin nose, two pendulous ears and a wide mouth filled with thick yellow teeth. His eyes were black with patches of red, like embers. Sparks and tiny flames leapt from his flesh. Faint wisps of smoke rose from his torso.

I felt nothing.

We reached the crematorium—the functional redbrick structure I had identified as a chapel earlier. Haborym skirted the building to the rear and kicked open a wooden door. We found a small, sterile room inside. I saw an extractor fan set into the wall, three cupboards and a steel sink. A metal preparation table in the centre completed the picture. We placed the man's body onto it.

'Did you read the Life File?' I said.

'What are you talking about, undead?'

'The client: what do you know about him?'

'My prey, you mean? Nothing at all.'

'Aren't you interested?'

'Why would I be? One sack of meat is much like another. Walking on the earth or rotting below, it's all the same.' He shrugged. 'This is what I do. I enjoy it and I'm good at it. What else is there to say? Now, guard this thing while I check the equipment.'

He strode into an adjoining room; the viper trailed sluggishly behind him.

The man on the table lay very still. His breaths were slow and shallow.

I lowered my head and whispered in his ear: 'Get up. There's still time. All you need to do is wake up. The door is open; this creature will never find you. You can live out the rest of your life in peace.'

But it was hopeless. I was talking to myself, trying to assuage my guilt, pretending that I wasn't just a pawn in someone else's game. But I have always been a pawn, and it has always been a game.

I rested my head on his shoulder and stroked his greying hair softly, hoping it would bring him comfort.

Haborym returned with a metal trolley covered in a black cloth. He didn't seem to notice that I was offering consolation to his victim. Perhaps it made no sense to him.

'Not the biggest furnace I've ever seen,' he said, 'but it will allow you to witness my performance in all its glory... Let's get him onto the catafalque.'

He indicated the trolley. I helped him transfer the unconscious man onto the cloth; then he wheeled him feet-first into the adjoining room. Another functional

36

space: grey walls, a second extractor, two great silver furnaces with glass doors, and a pair of wooden cabinets containing a variety of urns. He steered the catafalque to the door of the left furnace.

'Once I'm inside I want you to push the body toward me. I'll do the rest.'

My mind was so thick with shame, I didn't understand what he was saying. Why would he climb into the furnace?

I was about to ask, but at that moment the viper reared its massive head above the trolley, sank its fangs into the man's flesh and—with a couple of vigorous shakes—tore off his right ear. I recoiled in horror as the victim moaned and shuddered; Haborym smiled, and caressed the snake as if it were a beloved pet.

'Xael takes a trophy from every kill,' he said fondly. 'She has quite the collection back home. Normally I remove something for her'—he addressed the snake directly—'but I forgot this time, didn't I? Don't worry, I'll make it up to you later.'

I closed my eyes and waited for the madness to go away, but when I opened them again it was still here. The snake had slithered beneath the table and the demon had squeezed himself into the furnace. All I could see were his three heads.

'Give it a shove!' he said.

I didn't move.

I thought: you live, you die, you live again, and nothing changes, because everything is part of the same endlessly repeating pattern—words, feelings, actions, choices, innate behaviours, learned behaviours, the people you like, the people you don't, the jobs you choose, the things you buy, the mistakes you make, over and over again—and you take yourself with you everywhere you go, and there's no escape, even after death.

'Hurry up, undead! I can't contain myself much longer.'

I wedged my stumps behind the man's shoulders and pushed him forward. Our faces were so close we were

37

almost kissing. I felt the bristling life within him, the warmth of his breath against my cold cheek; but a greater warmth came from the furnace. Looking up, I saw the demon's form changing again: his heads and torso were surrounded by a glowing orange halo which crackled and roiled, sending sparks and jets of fire in all directions. I gave the body a final shove; Haborym seized the man's legs and pulled him rapidly into the growing flames.

'Seal me in. Unless you want me to melt your face off.'

I pressed a button to lower the glass door into place. As it clicked shut I saw a violent burst of light through the window. I wanted to look away but I couldn't. I believed I owed this man something, though I wasn't sure what. Respect? A moment of mourning? Perhaps it was simply the acknowledgement of the unspoken connection between two human beings. The impulse to value someone who was like you, but wasn't you.

Time passed. The man became less like me. He turned into a corpse surrounded by a blazing orange plasma, a mass of seared and scorched flesh flickering inside a churning ring of fire. The ring incinerated his clothes and set his hair alight. It melted his eyes until they ran down his face in thick steaming tears. It liquefied, then vaporised, his skin. It charred his muscles and calcified his bones; then the muscles were consumed by the flames and the bones disintegrated into ash. And still the fire turned.

I felt it in my shrivelled hands. I remembered black claws tightening around my fingers, softening the flesh, crushing the bone. I remembered a pain that cut through my body like a flaming sword. But there was no pain left now. Only the memory of pain.

I heard a light tapping on the furnace door. I looked up and saw Haborym's face pressed against the glass. He was sweating and his lips were moving, but I couldn't hear what he was saying.

I opened the door. A thin cloud of fine grey ash drifted outward on a wave of hot air. A pinstriped gentleman crawled free and brushed himself off. I smelled, or imagined I did, the sweet odour of burning flesh.

'I thought you weren't going to let me out.'

'I didn't hear you.'

'Never mind. Do you have a toothpick?'

I looked blankly at him.

'Or a skewer—anything small and sharp will do.'

I shook my head.

'Fine. I'll do it myself.'

He leaned back into the furnace and began to dig for some unseen object in the remains. I tried not to breathe, because every breath was laced with the ash of a dead man. Haborym didn't seem to care: he licked his lips greedily and raised puffs of powdered bone as he searched.

'Eureka!' he announced at last. 'Here, take this.'

He turned around and opened his fist, revealing a dark granular sphere about the size of a marble. It looked insignificant, but when he pressed it into my clawed stumps it felt gelid and heavy, and it possessed a strange energy that discomfited me. I quickly transferred it to my coat pocket.

Haborym smiled and slapped me on the back. 'Right, I'm off!' he said breezily. 'I have to be at the bank by seven-thirty; I've got a full day of meetings ahead. It's tedious, but someone has to keep the economy going. Thanks for your help.'

He left the room via a second doorway—through which I glimpsed a small chapel and several rows of wooden benches. The door closed noiselessly behind him, leaving me alone with a few pounds of ash.

I didn't know what to do, so I waited in silence.

This gave me time to think. As a zombie I had never felt the urge to harm anyone, but I had often stood by as others were harmed—a fact demonstrated both by my apprenticeship at the Agency and the events of the last few hours. But this aspect of my personality troubled me: it was a flaw. After my resurrection I had experienced feelings for others, but they had never been strong enough to spur me to action: I had allowed deaths to occur without a word of protest or a hand raised in anger.

Perhaps opening that box in my pocket was only one step on the road back to humanity. I needed to nurture the feeble shoots of kindness within me first, so they might nourish my wakening soul. But I had no idea how to go about it.

My thoughts were interrupted by footsteps coming from the chapel. I looked around frantically for somewhere to hide, my gaze focusing on every shadow, my arms flapping in panic.

But the door was already opening.

The Chimera

It was Malache: a man with cherubic blond hair, dressed in a funereal suit. He scanned the room, examined the open furnace, traced a finger through the ash on the polished floor.

'Has he gone?'

'Yes,' I said. I took the cold, heavy lump of darkness from my coat and showed it to him. 'He gave me this.'

He glanced at it briefly, but didn't touch it. 'I'm sure the overseer will be pleased. Put it away for now.'

I returned the object to my pocket. Its weight felt even more oppressive than before. I had no idea what it was or why Malache's superior took an interest in it; I just wanted to dispose of it as soon as possible.

'We should go,' he said. 'The fire has already taken hold.'

I didn't know what he meant, but as we reached the doorway I heard the crackle of flames and smelled the acrid odour of burning wood. The chapel was on fire: the chairs were alight, the drapery was ablaze, the altar was a torch. Several of the roof beams were burning furiously.

We departed quickly through a set of double doors and walked out into the cold, moonlit night. Malache crossed to his black Vespa and straddled the leather seat. As I put my arms around his waist once more, I heard a rafter from the chapel roof crash to the ground.

We returned the way we had come: through country lanes to a broad roundabout, then along populated roads to the centre of town. The rhythmic glow and fade of street lights punctuated our only exchange, as we descended the long hill toward the city centre.

'When you meet the overseer, be on your guard,' he said. 'You can't hide your wounds from him.'

My torso was criss-crossed with stitches, and several minor body parts were missing as a result of my death; but I was puzzled by his caution. 'My deformities are nothing special. I'm not ashamed of them.'

'I'm referring to the wounds inside you. The lesions and abrasions of your character; the cuts and sores that never heal... He will probe them. He will prey on your weaknesses.'

'Thanks for the warning. But I'm not sure anything could be worse than death and resurrection.'

'I hope you're right,' he said.

We rode on, past fields and houses, people and places drifting by in a dreamlike haze. I drifted too, carried on unknown currents toward a shadowy goal. I knew Malache was taking me to his superior, which would conclude the first of the tasks required of me. A few more tasks would give me my hands, my hands would open the box, the box would yield my soul—and I would be a Lifer once more.

But at what cost? As a private investigator, I had formed intimate bonds with my clients. Even at the Agency, I had known something of the lives that we had ended; I had experienced a connection. But now I was merely an instrument. Knowledge of the victims was immaterial.

What would happen to me if I continued on this path? During my lifetime, I had seen ordinary people become brutal automata, their souls withered by malice and corruption. Would this be the fate of my soul, too? Or did that small wooden box in my pocket provide some protection from my actions? It seemed unlikely; but I couldn't know for sure until this ordeal was over.

'We're here,' said Malache.

We had stopped outside a pub. Its grubby white façade was decorated with hanging baskets and window boxes, in which a few wilted cyclamen battled for survival alongside frost-bitten pansies and clumps of heather. The name above the door was The Chimera; the accompanying sign featured a lurid depiction of the mythical three-headed beast. It had been called something else when I was alive, but I couldn't remember the old name now.

Malache and I dismounted. He lowered the centre stand on the scooter, approached the entrance and produced a ring of keys of various sizes and designs. He selected a Yale key with a curiously flat blade and jiggled it in the lock.

The door sprang open.

It was dark inside and the room smelled of stale beer; but there was enough reflected light to make out the broad outlines of furniture, the glint of bottles behind the bar, a narrow fireplace. Malache strode through the shadows like he knew his way around; I trailed him clumsily, stumbling over a bar stool and banging my shins on a low table. We passed through a doorway at the far end, which led to an enclosed courtyard with several alcoves at the rear. Malache stopped in the centre of the yard and addressed me directly.

'This is the final and most important part of our agreement. The object in your pocket is more precious than you can imagine; you must treat it with care and surrender it when required. Answer the overseer's questions honestly. Do not interrupt him.'

'Aren't you staying?'

He shook his head. 'I have other business to attend to; but I'll see you tomorrow morning at nine... Now, go and sit in the alcove by the grille. He's expecting you.'

He turned and left.

I sat in the place he had indicated, on a seat that faced the courtyard, so I might see what was coming. I waited anxiously, watching the shadows and doorways. At last, I became aware of a warm, foul breath wafting through the latticed grille behind me. I retched instinctively, not from the stench itself but because I immediately recognised it. It belonged to a creature I had met before, a monster I had every reason to fear.

It was the demon who had taken my hands.

The deal

He didn't speak for a few minutes, but his presence was tangible: heavy, laboured breaths and that repellent faecal odour. A long-buried memory surfaced in my mind: the mottled fire of his reptilian torso, the cruelly clawed feet, the muscular arms and enormous wings—and the black claws that had wrapped around my hands. I didn't need eyes to see him, because he was already inside my head.

'We meet again, Half-life,' he said at last. 'And though many years have passed, I must apologise for the nature of our previous encounter. I had been hunting you for a very long time; there had been several missteps along the way. I was overcome by the stress of the search and the pleasure of discovery. I behaved in a manner that was both unorthodox and unjust.' I heard something flitter behind the grille, a delicate sound, like the quivering of insect wings. 'But the past is the past. You are here now because of the deal you made with my subordinate; though in truth, you made that deal with me... Did you complete your first task successfully?'

'Yes.'

'So you have a gift for me?'

'Yes.'

'Very well. Place it in front of the grille.'

I did as he asked, fumbling the black, heavy ball of matter from my pocket onto a ledge beneath the wooden lattice.

'That perfume...' he said. 'Quickly—turn around.'

I faced the courtyard once more; a moment later the lattice creaked open behind me. I felt the demon's heat, smelled his squalor and rot, tasted his abject foulness on my tongue. He seemed to hesitate a moment—the hair on my neck bristled as I imagined him reaching forward with those terrible claws—then he closed the grille gently.

'The dark meat is the best,' he said, noisily licking his lips. 'You have brought me a great delicacy, but even the grandest feast needs spice; some entertainment to accompany it.' He exhaled a particularly noxious sigh; I found myself gagging once more. 'Let me hear your voice—tell me a story of yourself. I have no interest in green fields or babbling brooks, kind fathers or attentive mothers; nor do I need your fondest memory... No: I want to hear your *shame*. Tell me your sin, so that I might enjoy this sweetmeat all the more.'

It seemed an odd request; but not so odd that I could refuse it. Yet I struggled to think of anything to say. What was a sin? The very word seemed archaic, an idea burdened by outdated morality and religious affectation. However, the more I thought about his request, the more it interested me—not for his benefit, but for my own. Unless

44

I acknowledged the mistakes of my past I would never become whole; I could not truly live again.

But the question wouldn't go away: what was a sin?

'When I was two years old, I went to kindergarten for the first time,' I said. 'I was a solitary child. My mother had kept me largely to herself until the moment she waved goodbye at the school gate; I don't know why and I didn't live long enough to ask her... But the separation was difficult. I was sickly, my attendance was sporadic and I became a target for bullying. Most of it seems harmless to me now—children shunning the stranger in their midst—but there was one boy in particular I remember... He stole things from me. It started with sandwiches and sweets; later, I saw him take a toy from my bag and place it into his own. These incidents continued into the winter of my second year, when I became seriously ill. It began innocently with a persistent cough. I didn't feel particularly unwell, but my mother sent me to school with a security blanket—I remember how thick and blue it was, how safe it made me feel, how it smelled of her... And the boy stole it from me. We were taking our afternoon nap and I was using the blanket for a pillow; but as I was falling asleep, I felt him pulling it from beneath my head—I tried to hold onto it but he was too strong. He didn't run away: he returned calmly to his mat, placed the rolled blanket beneath *his* head, then looked at me and smiled. I was seized by an uncontrollable fury. I leapt from my mat, ran toward him and struck him with my fists—and the agitation and rage I felt brought on a coughing fit. He shoved me away, but I kept coming back, coughing as I threw blows that barely landed, coughing in his face, hating him... A few days later I was hospitalised with pneumonia; a week after that I was back home. But he was not so lucky: he was in hospital for a month. And I felt no sympathy for him when he returned—only loathing.'

The silence that followed was broken by the sound of a demon licking and sucking his fingers.

'A poor start,' he said at last. 'This is a nothing more than a minor offence. A conscious act of aggression, leading to an infection; but mitigated by the fact you were a child, with no idea of the consequences.'

'My anger could have killed him.'

'But it did not. In any case, a disease is not a sin, it is a biological process. If *you* hadn't infected him, someone else would... No, you can improve on this story, Half-life. Tell me a better tale; show me a deeper sin.' He sighed. 'But it must wait until tomorrow. Our meeting is almost at an end.'

My heart pounded with relief; I wanted nothing more than to be free of this creature's presence. I stood up—but he immediately told me to sit down again, and the sense of dread returned.

'Before you leave, I will tell you the truth of the deal you have made. The gift that you gave me tonight was a soul: a frigid, shrunken soul, but no less delicious for that. Now, there are as many varieties of souls as there are people living on this Earth, and you will encounter many more in the next few days; but I only want you to bring me ten. Ten souls for your ten fingers. Ten souls for *your* soul. You have already given me the first; you must bring me nine more.'

PART TWO

Caym the Magnificent

Terrifying but strangely purgative

I am the ghost of myself. I am Death's shadow, following his every move. I search in my dreams for the fragments of the person I once was. But when I wake I forget everything.

I forget everything.

I woke on a bench in Wellington Square, a green secluded park in the heart of Oxford. Frost had entered my bones while I slept. A giant alcoholic bird was pecking at my skull. I remembered that I had helped kill someone last night.

It wasn't a good start to the day.

The sky was dark. There was no one else around. I rose stiffly, checked that the box was still in my pocket, then buttoned up my coat and walked the five minutes to the bus station. I had fallen from a roof here, a long time ago; but it felt now as if another person had done the falling and I was an indifferent observer watching him fall.

I went to the public toilets and washed my hands and face in front of the mirror. The man looking back at me looked like me: bloodless grey skin, broken lips, dark eyes buried in deep sockets, an unkempt beard that concealed an angry scar. But he was different, too. He tried to hide it, and it took me a long time to discover what was wrong, but when I moved closer to the mirror I finally saw it: the faint image of a fiery ring encircling his left pupil. I blinked and rubbed my eyes and washed my face again, but the blemish remained. It disturbed me; but since I couldn't change it, I had no choice but to accept it.

A short, stocky, balding man appeared beside me.

'You okay?' he asked my reflection.

'I'm fine,' it said.

The sun still wasn't up but there was light on the horizon. I left the bus station and cut into Bulwark's Lane, a narrow cobbled backstreet. I saw three large green wheelie bins arranged in a haphazard line. I lifted the lid on the first and found bottles, cardboard, paper and cans. I checked the cans for leftovers but they had been rinsed clean; likewise, all the bottles were empty. The second bin was more promising, however: even without opening it I caught the sharp tang of discarded food.

I pushed the lid upright, clambered onto the edge, then dropped lightly inside, landing with a faint squelch as my feet sank into the soft, wet surface. The smell was intense but I had learned to tolerate it; in any case, I'd eaten nothing since the noodles yesterday. I closed the lid and rummaged in the slop and swill for something edible.

I soon realised that Zoë was sitting in the darkness with me. I couldn't see her, but her voice was unmistakable: 'Why not wait until you get to the workshop? They'll give you breakfast.'

'I don't want to rely on anyone else.'

'Don't you trust them?'

'Of course not. They're devils.'

'Malache seems like a good person.'

'True. But I haven't known him very long.' My left stump struck something firm and familiar. 'Pizza crust. Do you want some?'

'No, thanks. What about the others?'

I pushed the crust into my mouth and chewed awhile. It had a fizzy vinegary taste which wasn't unbearable. 'I can't tell yet. Dumuzid seems friendly. I don't know anything about the other two.'

'You should talk to them.'

'Every time I talk to someone it ends badly.'

She didn't say anything.

'How are you, anyway?' I said.

'The same as always. Why do you ask?'

'I'm trying to remember what it was like to be alive.'

'You just need practice, like everyone else.'

We sat in silence for a while. I was still peckish, so I rummaged in the slime and scraps for another morsel. I caught something soft and greasy, with a firm bony core. I considered telling Zoë that I had watched a demon burn someone to death last night, but I didn't want to spoil the moment.

'I'm glad you came. We should do this again.'

'Shut up and pass me that chicken,' she said.

It wasn't the best breakfast I'd ever eaten—the pizza crust was mouldy and the meat more rancid than I would have liked—but it sated my hunger. When it was over I said goodbye to Zoë and lifted the lid cautiously. The sky was cold and blue now, but the alley was still in shadow. I stood up, hooked myself onto the lip of the bin and rolled out onto the cobbles; but I landed awkwardly, lurched forward and struck something solid. The something was a woman dressed in a long ribbed coat that made her look like a giant worm.

'Look where you're going,' she said.

I apologised, but Zoë had told me I needed to practice my Lifer skills, so I added: 'Do you have the time?'

She answered with a sour expression, and hurried away.

I followed Bulwark's Lane to the end, then headed east to Carfax, where the clock tower told me it was a quarter past eight. I doubled back to the plaza at Bonn Square, found a bench, and sat down.

My mind returned to the early hours of the morning and the meeting with the demon who had taken my hands. The encounter had been terrifying but strangely purgative: I had escaped uninjured and it had felt good to expel, through confession, some of the darkness within me. In contrast, the deal I had agreed to was worse than I thought: I had to assist in the suffering of nine more people before my hands could be made whole. I wanted my soul but didn't want to pay the price; but I had to pay the price if I wanted my soul. It felt like I had placed a noose around my neck and was waiting for someone to spring the trap door.

I was disturbed by a moving object at the edge of my vision. It was large, red and very loud. Out of habit I didn't look up in case I attracted its attention; but it drifted toward me anyway, as if we were connected by a single retracting thread. The object was a portly man in his fifties with a snow white beard and matching curly hair; the face in between was crimson. He was dressed as someone who didn't exist, which made me sympathetic toward him; but as soon as his mouth opened my sympathy waned.

'Merry Christmas!' he shouted. 'Why so glum, young man? This is the best time of the year! 'Tis the season of joy and goodwill to all! Release Your Amazing and join—'

'Release my what?'

'Your Amazing!'

I shrugged.

The first traces of what I'd eaten (and squatted in) reached his nose, which he wrinkled in disgust. But it didn't put him off: 'Yes! Release Your Amazing and join the millions of people around the world whose lives have been transformed by the power of positive thinking! Our two-part, ten-step, self-help programme has only one rule: Embrace Your Happy.' His nose wrinkled again and he took a subtle stride backward, but continued to shout as he rang a little brass bell. I admired his persistence, while rejecting his presence. 'Embrace Your Happy and you embrace everyone around you—family, friends, strangers and brothers! How much is your life worth? Don't answer: every one of you is priceless! For a small fee you get one-to-one coaching—'

'I have to go,' I said, standing up.

He leaned toward me and whispered, 'All right, you miserable sod. You're queering my pitch anyway.' He stuffed a leaflet into my coat pocket and raised his voice again. 'Who else wants to unlock the door to health, happiness and long life? You, madam...'

The ringing continued as I headed toward the workshop, but it had changed in depth and tone. I briefly wondered if I was suffering from a form of undead tinnitus; then I realised it was simply the bells of Oxford chiming nine.

I quickened my step and headed for Babylon Bookbinders.

Vice fills the hole

I didn't want to be late—but what would happen to me if I was? I would feel a passing discomfort, that was all. The world wouldn't end; it wouldn't even pay the slightest attention. So when I arrived at the workshop I took a moment to look at the window display.

I was a keen reader as a child, spending hours alone in my father's study, devouring everything I could find—but I recognised none of the books before me. These were serious, leather-bound volumes with obscure names. Some lay open, revealing arcane illustrations in monochrome or tiny paragraphs printed in gothic script; others displayed the front cover or spine, embossed with titles whose significance eluded me; still more were marked only by a handwritten label beneath the work. What was the *Temple of the Black Light*? Who was the subject of the *Approche Historique d'un Magicien Contemporain*? Why would anyone buy the *(1863, First edition)* of the *Dictionnaire Infernal*? And yet, as I allowed my gaze to roam these treasures, I realised that I had an urge to read them all: I would happily browse their yellowing pages and trace their drawings and photographs with my mutilated hands; and in doing so I would be transported from the ghoulish reality of my existence to a better world.

'Aren't you coming in, Rabbit?'

Ereshkigal's voice disturbed my daydream. She was standing on the threshold; in the winter daylight her hair was black as a raven's wing. She shivered involuntarily, grabbed my arm and pulled me inside; then she closed the door and rushed back to her workbench.

I waited by the entrance, watching. The room and personnel were much the same as yesterday. A narrow disorderly space. Three self-proclaimed devils disguised as ordinary people. A stifling blanket of hot, foetid air, like the inside of a reptile house. Nergal was staring at a laptop and smiling. Ereshkigal had opened a book and was taking notes. Dumuzid was bent over the scroll he had been working on yesterday, his green cap shielding his face from view. In his left hand he held a black feather shaped into a quill which, now and then, he dipped into a pot of ink. More black feathers littered the floor around his desk. I noticed a clear trail of them leading to Nergal.

'Nerg stole some of my quills so he could tickle Resh on the cheek; she responded by sticking two feathers up his nose,' Dumuzid explained glumly. 'Sometimes I doubt their dedication to the cause.'

'Be quiet, old man,' said Nergal distractedly, 'I'm trying to watch a livestream... Zombie, you might want to see this. Come over here. Sit down.' He pulled a step-ladder from beneath his desk and turned his laptop toward it.

'Is Malache around?' I asked. 'He was supposed to be here by nine.'

'No.'

'Then perhaps I could collect the note—'

'Malache has the envelope.'

'Do you know when he might be in?'

'No clue.'

Reluctantly, I crossed to the workbench and sat on the top step of the ladder, my head resting just above the level of the desk. I felt like a child. The desk itself was covered in pencils, wrappers and tools, but the laptop rose above it all like a breaching whale.

The livestream was a local news report from the crematorium. The building was a carcass now: a rotten skin of blackened brickwork surrounding a skeleton of charred beams. The camera panned across scraps of smoking wood, clumps of blackened cloth, pools of dirty water. A Lifer was being interviewed by another Lifer at the scene; both looked unhappy. Neither they nor the scrolling text at the bottom of the screen mentioned the victim or the demon who had killed him.

I glanced across to a sidebar which contained links to further news stories. A cat had been shot with an airgun. A woman had died of a heart attack in a health food store. There were fears of a virulent winter vomiting bug after a man had been hospitalised with an unknown sickness. The Organisation For The Protection of Spiny Mammals had launched a public awareness campaign to prevent hedgehogs from going extinct.

'Seems your first night went well,' said Nergal.

'I wanted to be somewhere else.'

'Demons have that affect on everyone. Noisy, callous, unsubtle brutes—and those are the good ones. Haborym is gentler than most; Alastor and Moloch, on the other hand—'

'Don't tease our guest,' Ereshkigal said.

'It's just words, Resh. Surely your little pet can survive the onslaught of a sentence?'

A brief silence followed. I am normally grateful for silences, but as the subject of their dispute I felt responsible for it. 'Actually, I can survive anything,' I said proudly. 'A few years ago I fell into the River Styx. Nothing can kill me now.'

Nergal smiled. 'Let me explain something, zombie,' he said, stroking his great ginger beard. 'It's true that any mortal who finds himself bathing in our sacred river—inadvertently or otherwise—is afforded certain immunities. For example, his body doesn't decay, and he can't be killed by another mortal's hand; but he can be burned, disembowelled and decapitated, none of which make immortality a particularly pleasant experience... However, this is tangential to my point: the smell of the Styx does not grant you protection from supernatural interference. If anything, the opposite is true: demons are actively drawn to those tainted by its waters. The scent excites them, sometimes driving them to an uncontrollable frenzy—the results of which, as you can probably imagine, are rather gruesome and absolutely terminal—'

'That's enough, Nerg.'

'He needs to know what's out there, Resh.'

'Not from an insensitive dolt like you.' She sighed. 'I'm not sure which reptilian corner of my brain persuaded me to marry you, but hardly a week passes when you don't give me cause to regret it.'

'I love you too, my little meat hook.'

She waved him away, then stood up and offered me her hand. 'Come with me, Rabbit. I need a cigarette. Do you smoke?'

'I don't remember... I don't think so.'

'Well, now would be a good time to start.'

I placed my withered hand in hers. I expected her skin to feel scaly or cold, but it was warm and welcoming, like a human hand. When she led me outside, I didn't want to let go; but she released me to remove a packet of Marlboros from her pocket. She flicked open the lid and raised the pack, so I could grab a cigarette with my teeth. I drew it inward a little. It didn't taste unpleasant.

Ereshkigal took another for herself then struck a match, lighting my cigarette first, then her own. 'Vice fills the hole vacated by the soul,' she said, staring into the distance. 'It's funny. I always think of the Underworld as home, but sometimes I prefer this place—even if it is cold and dreary most of the time... Are you okay?'

I sucked on the cigarette, inhaled the smoke and breathed deeply, drawing a burning coil deep into my chest. At first it felt light and feathery, then the prickling

56

heat stung my throat and picked at the lining of my lungs. My eyes watered, I felt nauseated, and I retched, dropping the cigarette onto the pavement—and in my mind I saw a roiling fire reduce a man to ash, a raging fire burn a building to the ground. When she asked how I was my chest swelled with a cough that shook my whole body, followed by a series of hacks and wheezes that expelled tiny clouds of smoke.

'I'm fine,' I said hoarsely.

She picked up the abandoned cigarette and offered it to me. I nodded my assent and she placed it gently between my lips. 'Take it slow. Keep it in your mouth until it cools.'

The smoke soothed the irritation it had created. I felt calmer, cooler, more important. Why I had waited until after my death to discover smoking? 'All that coughing loosened a couple of my stitches,' I said, out of the corner of my mouth.

She stubbed her cigarette on the pavement. 'Where?'

'On my torso.'

'May I see?'

I opened my coat and lifted my clothes to reveal the wounded skin beneath. There was no pattern to my disfigurement: it simply reflected the jaw movements of the animal that had killed me. Ereshkigal traced her forefinger along one of the lesions that led from my waist to the centre of my chest, then followed another along the line of a rib to my right armpit. I felt an unfamiliar excitement at her touch, a remembered longing for physical contact. It thrilled and agitated me in equal measure.

'Here,' she said, laying her finger on a wound I couldn't see, somewhere in the region of my heart. 'If I pull this end of the thread it should make you whole again.' She didn't wait for my consent but gently tugged the suture and tightened the loops that bound me together. I felt a brief spasm of pain and pleasure.

'Thank you.'

'You're welcome, Rabbit... How about some breakfast?'

I shook my head. 'I've already eaten.'

'And it smells lovely on you... Look, come anyway. Even if you just sit there staring into space, you'll be better company than my idiot husband. '

I took a last drag on the cigarette and let it fall to the ground.

'Okay,' I said.

She walked to the purple Vespa at the kerb. As she disengaged the kickstand I saw Malache approaching from the direction of The Noodle Bar. Ereshkigal saw him too. We both waited in silence until he arrived.

'You're early again,' he said to me.

'You told me to be here by nine.'

'I'm sure I said ten.' He seemed genuinely puzzled. 'I trust the others have been treating you well?'

'I've been teaching him to smoke,' said Ereshkigal. 'Nerg was trying to frighten him. Dum's too busy with his scroll.'

'Well, at least one of you is working... Resh, I'll see you inside: I'd like to talk to our friend in private. We have a big delivery for the grinder later—perhaps you and Nerg could give me a hand?'

'Whatever you want, Mal.' She touched me on the arm as she left. 'See you later, Rabbit.'

Malache watched the door close behind her.

'Is something wrong?' I said.

'Not at all. In fact, quite the opposite. I've just been to the overseer and he gave you a glowing report. We're all very proud of you... I know it's hard—and to be honest, it won't get any easier—but I advise you to persist. A demon's word is his bond; you will get what you deserve in the end.'

I looked down at my gnarled stumps, which seemed more pathetic and useless than ever. 'Ten souls for *my* soul—'

'Actually,' he interrupted, 'I think you'll find the key wording in the agreement was: *ten souls for ten fingers*.'

'Either way, I'm not sure I can continue.'

58

'What's the problem?'

'The work... disturbs me.'

'A little conscience is a terrible thing,' he said sympathetically. 'Look, I'm not trying to make you feel better, but if it's any consolation the people who will die tonight, tomorrow, the day after—they would have died anyway. What you're really doing is *saving* lives: without your help, these demons would kill every stranger in their path until they found the prey they were looking for. That could be ten, twenty, even fifty people, depending on the demon in question and how astonishingly stupid they are. The work you do helps *me* deal with the difficult issues of population growth without distraction, it helps the *demons* find their targets without excessive collateral damage, and it helps *you* unlock that box in your pocket. To be blunt, I don't see a downside to any of this.'

I thought for a while.

'Fine,' I said.

'Splendid! Now, if you would kindly stay here—'

'What about the note?'

'Yes. Of course.' He reached into his pocket and handed me a wax-sealed envelope. 'Read it at your leisure, memorise the contents, study the photograph—the usual.'

'Where are you going?'

'To my office.' He smiled broadly, revealing his pointed feline teeth. 'Listen, I don't mean to be rude, but we like our employees to look presentable when they represent us in the wider community... So to begin with, I'm going to ask Nerg to take you for a haircut.'

Two bits

It was a cool, sunny December morning. I leaned with my back against the plate glass window and gazed at the leafless trees in the garden opposite. The garden belonged to the Oxford Union, a debating society for students attending the local university. The Union didn't particularly interest me—study, debate and the acquisition of esoteric knowledge were about as relevant to my existence as a chicken farm on Mars—but the trees were beautiful.

'Hello again, zombie. Ready and raring to go?'

I had only ever seen Nergal sitting down: standing beside me, he was much shorter than I anticipated, but made up for his lack of height with a muscular frame that seemed to crackle with energy. He looked like he might leap on you, wrestle you to the ground and cuff you about the head, all while laughing maniacally.

'I'm ready. Which is your Vespa?'

'The ginger one, obviously. Why do you ask?'

'I thought you were driving me to the barber.'

He laughed raucously and punched me on the back. 'We're walking, lazy bones. Or would you prefer me to chop you up and carry you there in a wheelbarrow?'

'I'll walk.'

'Great! Nothing like a brisk stroll to get the blood pumping.'

We set off. My blood felt like molasses oozing through my veins, but we headed north along Walton Street until we reached the junction with Little Clarendon Street. The barber lay just beyond, wedged between a charity shop and a grocer. It was called Herbert's Hair, which struck me as slightly insalubrious.

I looked at the prices in the window.

'I can't afford this,' I said.

'Don't fret, paleskin. Business expense. Tax deductible.'

We walked inside. The place lacked customers. I saw three leather barbers' chairs and one barber, who I presumed to be Herbert. He was a tall middle-aged man with a full head of greying hair and pronounced curvature of the spine. His voice was deep and friendly.

'How can I help you gentlemen?'

'Shave and a haircut,' said Nergal. 'Not for me, you understand: for my friend here. He needs tidying up.'

'Please take a seat,' the barber said, indicating the central chair. I did so, and he immediately wrapped me in a protective black cape.

'Pardon my friend's odour. He's had a tough time of it lately.'

'I notice no odour whatsoever, sir. What kind of haircut would you like?'

Several options passed through my mind—Mohican, mullet, Caesar, perm—but Nergal answered on my behalf. 'Number one buzz cut. And take the beard off; it's a filthy-looking thing, don't you think?'

The barber gave a noncommittal response, grabbed a mist spray and hair trimmer, and set about his work without fuss.

'What line of work are you gentlemen in?'

'Again, you'll have to forgive my friend,' said Nergal. 'He was rendered completely mute by severe personal trauma—I won't go into the details for obvious reasons—but we're trying to put him back on track with a job and a little personal care. As for me, I work for Green Devil Recycling. Perhaps you've seen our lorries hereabouts?'

'Can't say I have.'

'I'm pleased to hear it; we pride ourselves on courtesy, efficiency and discretion. Our motto is: *Reducing Human Waste One Piece At A Time...* You really haven't seen us?'

'I work during the day. At night I go home and read.'

'A simple life, but a fine one.'

The barber ignored him and finished shaving the hair from the left side of my head; he started on the right side as Nergal continued his small talk.

'I have a couple of other jobs too, of course.'

'Indeed, sir?'

'Some of my day is spent at the bookbinder on St Michael's Street—so if any of your reading material gets ragged around the edges, you know where to come. In the evenings I create content for an online encyclopaedia, a role which allows me to undermine the truth by countless subtle means: changing a word here, a sentence there, inventing sources and references, reworking established facts and generating new ones, and meticulously erasing anything which might interfere with our corporate agenda. I sow confusion and lies so that eventually no one knows what to trust anymore and the truth is lost.'

The barber turned around. The trimmer buzzed angrily by my right ear. 'I fear that you're teasing me, young man.'

Nergal smiled charmingly. 'I apologise. It's a tiresome habit, but it tells me so much about the men and women I meet... I have a theory that there are two kinds of people: ears and mouths. Two mouths fight for attention and never listen. Two ears shrink from embarrassment and never talk. But a mouth and an ear together can make a wonderful partnership. Case in point: my friend in the chair is very much an ear, so he gets on very well with my wife, who is indubitably a mouth. I am a mouth too, so my wife and I have been in constant conflict throughout our marriage.'

'As you say, sir.'

The barber sheared away the last of my hair, which now lay in a greasy, chaotic circle around the base of the chair. He set about the beard with equal skill and vigour, trimming it with scissors before applying a thin layer of shaving foam and massaging it in. When he drew out a sharp razor and began to scrape away the stubble, I closed my eyes. *Cut my throat,* my brain whispered. *I want to feel something. Anything.*

Why was Nergal lying so brazenly? Clearly, it entertained him. Perhaps he was testing boundaries too, like a teenager trying to provoke a reaction. But as Herbert moved his razor over my sluggish jugular, I realised that he was also lying to deflect attention from an obvious truth: there was a zombie in the room.

Then again, he was a devil. It was in his nature to lie. And he really couldn't help himself:

'Naturally, work isn't the be-all and end-all of my life. In fact, you could say my most important role is that of *creative maverick*. For example, I practically invented the concept of clickbait. And I was the first online influencer, of course. The invisible hand of the market, modern democracy, wasps—'

'Would you mind not talking, sir?' the barber said.

Nergal didn't reply, but I heard him chuckling softly.

A short while later, I felt something hot against my throat. I opened my eyes and saw a clean-cut, clean-shaven stranger in the mirror. A thick white towel was wrapped around his neck.

The barber placed his razor into a jar of pink disinfectant and picked up a small mirror, which he held behind my head so that I might judge the delicacy and precision of his craft. I nodded my approval.

'Smart work,' said Nergal. 'How much?'

The answer would have bought a three-course meal when I was alive. My companion paid it without question.

The barber murmured his thanks, removed the hot towel and gently applied a cooling lotion to my raw flesh. Then he unfastened the black cloak and brushed off the excess hair.

I stood up and offered to shake his hand. It was a spontaneous act—a dangerous move for the undead—but it felt like the right thing to do. He held my shrivelled stump in his soft, doughy fingers and squeezed it lightly; and if he felt any disgust for my deformity, he didn't show it.

The cool December morning was even colder now; my head felt like a billiard ball in a bucket of ice. I pulled my black woollen hat tightly over my scalp and waited for Nergal to decide our next move.

'You're looking better already,' he said. 'Soon you'll look like every other Lifer walking these streets.'

I felt ambivalent about his words. I have grown used to the idea of being a zombie; I feel comfortable in this gaunt sack of skin. My clothes become me—and until now my facial hair had disguised me.

'Why did you make up those stories?' I said.

He punched me on the arm and said, enigmatically: 'Why bludgeon a man with a hammer when you can tickle him to death with a feather?'

Like Dumuzid yesterday, Nergal suddenly realised he was busy and had to get back to work. I wasn't sorry to see him leave.

I walked back into town and sat on a bench in the bus station square. I removed the envelope from my pocket, nibbled at the wax seal and tipped the contents onto the seat beside me.

Zoë leaned over my shoulder and looked sceptically at the note and photograph. 'Walk away,' she said.

'No. I made an agreement.'

'With the demon who melted your hands.'

'I gave my word. I have to honour it.'

'Do you think he'll honour his side, too?'

'It's worth the risk. If he doesn't, I'm no worse off. If he does, I'll get my fingers back. And I'll come and see you again.'

'It's a bit late for that, don't you think?'

I clasped the photograph between my stumps. It revealed a man with a blond beard and long hair, which partially concealed a scar on his right cheek. Eyes as bright as coral. A proud face.

'Well, there's your next victim,' she said. 'Go and watch him die. And think about him every time you look at your new fingers.'

I picked up the note. It said: *Man, woman, whatever. 0112358132134. Hairy pelt, or it might be a suit... Idgaf. I'll find the zombie. Shop closes at 10pm—Master of Flight.*

Death is always on its way

I pulled my hat over my eyes and slumped forward dejectedly. *Walk away.* Malache had offered me that choice, now Zoë was telling me to do it, too. At some point I would have to decide: what did I really want?

I was still slouching when a woman pressed something into my hands. 'Have a drink on me,' she said. It took me a moment to realise that she had given me a bank note. I lifted my head to thank her, but she had already gone.

I stood up and looked around. On the far side of the plaza, people were gathered around vans selling wraps, burgers and baked potatoes; others walked here and there, spinning intricate patterns across the square, like spiders weaving invisible webs.

I turned and entered a narrow passageway. Halfway along I stopped at a café, a place of small windows and subdued lighting. I ordered a black coffee and a cinnamon Danish and retreated to a wooden table in the corner.

Nearby I found a bookshelf stacked with a generous selection of books. I selected one at random: *The Abyss and Other Stories*, by Leonid Andreyev. I laid it flat upon the table and began to read, turning the pages ham-fistedly at first, but soon finding a rhythm that allowed me to forget who I was. I discovered I had enough money for a second coffee, then a third, and I made them last until I had reached the end of the book.

And when the café closed at six, I thanked the barista and said goodbye, just like everyone else.

I spent the next three hours browsing the Christmas displays on Cornmarket. The caffeine in me made the lights brighter, the colours more intense, the products and foodstuffs more attractive. I had no hope of owning anything, but it felt good to stand still, to look at everything, to be a part of this dazzling life.

And I wanted this sensation to continue: I would honour my agreement, I would free my soul from its prison!

I reached the workshop at nine. Malache was standing by the entrance. 'You're too early,' he said. 'The prey is literally five minutes away.'

'I'm sorry. The note didn't say much.'

'Demons prefer to express themselves by ripping someone's head off... Anyway, come in.' I followed him inside. The lights were dimmed, the workbenches empty. We entered his office and sat down. 'By the way, Resh left you this.'

He offered me a cigarette; I accepted gratefully. He placed it between my lips and clicked his fingers: a flame extended from his thumb and lit the tip. *Slow breaths, cool the burn.* It tasted like nothing much of anything, but it made my brain purr with pleasure.

I looked around coolly, like a resurrected James Dean. The room was much the same as yesterday, but its geometry wasn't distorted by alcohol. The machine noise was still there, too. Whirring, snapping, shredding.

'What's that sound?'

'We call it the grinder,' said Malache. 'The pride of Green Devil Recycling. It converts organic waste into fertiliser.'

'Can I see it?'

'Another day, perhaps. Finish your cigarette, then we'll leave. If you're lucky, Caym will arrive early.'

The Master of Flight had a name. The name told me nothing. The nicotine in my cigarette didn't care either way. Maybe this victim wouldn't feel as bad as the last. Maybe the demon would be killed by a cat before I arrived; or it would kill the cat and draw nine souls from its carcass and my agreement would end... But these fantasies ran counter to everything I had ever experienced: life means death, and death is always on its way.

The room reeked of smoke. Malache watched me casually, without seeming to watch; his eyes gleamed with unspoken thoughts, his body glimmered with energy. I leaned across the desk and let the cigarette fall from my lips.

'I'm ready,' I said.

'Yes,' he replied. 'I believe you are.'

I sat on the back of the Vespa and put my arms around his waist. He turned on the ignition, pulled in the brake lever and pressed a button on the handlebar. After revving the engine a couple of times, he drove north along Walton Street—past Herbert's Hair, the Phoenix Picture House and the Jericho Café, beyond the street where the Four Horsemen had once lived, and still further, until we stopped at last by a modest shopfront.

At first glance, it was hard to tell what kind of shop it was. The window display featured two poorly lit bookshelves, and the sign above the door consisted of just three letters, written in florid scroll: RVE. It looked like an exclusive club for socially-challenged bibliophiles.

Malache stayed on the scooter. 'This is where you and I part company. Are you allergic to feathers?'

'I don't think so.'

'Good. The demon will be here shortly; she may already have picked up your scent... Any questions?'

I had too many to ask. When was he coming back? What would happen if I walked away? Who was the person inside this strange shop? And did they deserve what was coming?

'No.'

'Fine. I'll pick you up when she's finished. Good luck, and try not to be rude. Demons are spiteful, stupid, vicious and narcissistic, but they don't have it easy.'

I watched from the pavement as he rode away. After a hundred yards he performed a screeching U-turn and headed past me in the opposite direction.

I waved, but he didn't wave back.

When I reached the entrance, the shop's purpose became clear. Directly beneath the RVE lettering I saw the words *Retro Video Emporium*; and the window display didn't contain books, but shelves of DVDs, laserdiscs, video-CDs, Super-8 film and videotapes, as well as the machines to play them on. I opened the door slowly and sneaked inside.

The interior was an extravagant reflection of the exterior: shelves of movies, arranged alphabetically and divided by format; glass cupboards containing antique video recorders and cameras; locked cabinets showing off oddities and rarities; a few consoles and games; a dozen books. Most of the prices made no sense, and a couple of items were marked *Not For Sale*, but everything I saw inspired in me a melancholy yearning for the life I had once lived. I ran my damaged hands over the spines of familiar VHS boxes and stared in wonder—

'Do you need help?'

I turned in panic. I hadn't expected to be seen. This encounter could ruin everything. *I should run.* I stood still. *He knows why I'm here.* How could I be so stupid? *Maybe he's the demon...* But there was no stench, no wings or claws. Just a middle-aged man dressed in a white shirt, a red tie and a tweed three-piece suit. A man who looked like his photograph.

'I'm just browsing, thanks,' I said, too loudly.

'Looking for anything in particular?'

'Not really.'

He came closer, until he was standing beside me. His nose twitched as he smelled the faded remains of my breakfast, but his instinct for a potential sale overcame his disgust. 'What's your favourite genre?'

I said the first thing that came to mind: 'Horror.'

'An excellent response! We have all kinds here: apocalyptic, vampire, zombie, slasher, body horror, low-budget, high-concept, sci-fi, psychological and supernatural. All the great directors, too: Carpenter, Cronenberg, Craven,

Raimi, Argento... Or are you looking for something a little more exotic?'

'I'm not sure.'

'Probably not, then. How about the complete Hammer House of Horror on VHS? Or Roger Corman's *Masque of the Red Death*? You haven't lived until you've seen Corman's take on the macabre.' He stepped back and framed my head with the thumb and forefinger of each hand. 'You know, you have quite the face. Lean and pale, with a hint of menace; it would look wonderful on the big screen. Nosferatu, Bela Lugosi's Dracula, one of George Romero's undead—you could play them all.'

'I couldn't play a zombie in one of those movies; they're just not credible. In fact—'

'Surely you're joking?' he interrupted. 'Even the modern examples—*28 Days Later*, *Train To Busan*, *Planet Terror*, *Rammbock*—have something to offer the genre; but let's go back to basics... You're telling me you don't think *Night of the Living Dead* is a classic?'

I shook my head; he had misunderstood. I didn't know the other movies he had mentioned, but I had watched Romero's undead nightmare many times in my youth. 'It's a good film. Exciting, horrific, tense... But the zombies in it aren't real. They shuffle around like idiots; they moan like cattle. I want them to come back from the dead like Lazarus, with a head full of terror and disbelief. I want to be afraid of what they've seen, not of what they do. And why would they eat other human beings anyway? The undead aren't cannibals! But every film maker treats them like blood-crazed lunatics with a terrible, irrational grudge against the living...'

I stopped. I saw the old fear in his eyes—the same fear I had seen in many Lifers, again and again, over many years. He had identified me as *different*.

'An interesting viewpoint,' he sniffed, 'but one with which I profoundly disagree. And though I hate to pass up a sale, I will not compromise my beliefs—I can lose one, but not the other. So I'm going to have to ask you, very politely, to leave my shop.'

My heart sank. I had alarmed and offended him. My appearance was too abnormal, my manner too strange. How could I ever hope to interact with Lifers? Why had I even opened my mouth? Romero was right, after all: a zombie should shuffle aimlessly through life, moaning quietly, until he gets his head blown off with a shotgun.

I nodded regretfully and turned around to leave—and felt a cold blast of air on my face.

Bad Liver and a Broken Heart

A tall, confident woman walked through the door. The store owner quickly recovered his composure, dismissed me with a curl of the lip and addressed the newcomer directly—formally at first, but with increasing delight as his eyes drank her in.

'Welcome to my humble abode, madam. And if it's not too bold of me, might I compliment you on your outfit?'

The stranger was dressed in almost exactly the same clothes as the proprietor: brown tweed jacket and trousers, white shirt, red tie. Her bald head merely accentuated the similarity: when I looked from one to the other I saw no difference other than gender, and that was marginal. The shop owner realised it, too: for him, it was like gazing at his own reflection.

'I'm sure a lady of culture such as yourself won't be interested in the same base subject matter as my friend here. Horror! I think not. So what can I unearth for you? I have a wide collection of Criterion DVDs... Jacques Tati's short films, perhaps? Something by Tarkovsky? Or—and I mean no offence—perhaps you would prefer one of the more mainstream classics. *Twelve Angry Men*, for example?'

'Have you got any snuff?' she said harshly.

'Snuff? I'm not sure what—'

'Snuff!' she rasped. 'Where people kill each other and it's not acting it's real.'

'I'm afraid those kind of films are illegal, and I can't— I *wouldn't*—stock anything of that sort. However, if you tell me the name of the particular video you're looking for, I could perhaps recommend—'

'Fuck off. What about *Driller Killer*?'

'There's a VHS recording somewhere in the back.'

'I want Betamax. VHS is bollocks.'

'While I agree with you on the relative merits of the two formats, VHS is far more versatile and did after all "win" the video format wars of the nineteen-eighties—'

'Oh, fuck this,' the woman said, spitting heavily on the floor. She turned to me. 'Is this thing him, or are you him?'

'It depends what you mean by *him*,' I said cautiously.

'The meat. The offal. The liver and lights. I'm fucking hungry. Don't waste my time with this semantic shit.'

'If you're hungry,' the shop owner said, 'there's a lovely Japanese restaurant on the next block. They welcome all sorts of people—'

'He is him,' I said.

'I thought so. You stink of the black river. If this skinny little twat doesn't satisfy me, I'll have you for dessert.'

I glanced at the proprietor. The night had taken a direction he had not anticipated. His whole body slumped in resignation, but his mind tried one last verbal gambit. 'I'm sorry,' he said haltingly. 'I have a dreadful headache and I must close early. Please do come again—'

'Will you shut the fuck up?' the woman cawed. 'I'm trying to focus on this fucking transformation.'

The man sank to his knees, bowed his head and clasped his hands together, muttering some quiet prayer to himself. He didn't see the woman's outline shimmering; he didn't respond to the eruption of blood and bone from her flesh; he paid no attention to the gigantic torso that emerged or the feathered wings that burst from its sides;

he was oblivious to the clawed feet, the gangling legs and the cruel beak; he did not gaze into those black, frenzied eyes. But some small part of him must have been aware of the grotesque, bird-like creature that now stood as high as the ceiling.

The demon opened her curved bill—and the vulgar human that had cawed like a crow was now an aesthete speaking with effortless condescension.

'This simply won't *do*,' she said. 'How am I expected to perform in these conditions? There's absolutely no room whatsoever... You, undead thing, come over here. Chop-chop! Put those stubby little lumps you call hands around my waist—be gentle, I'm frightfully sensitive in that area. Now, beneath the feathers you should find a belt... Yes, that's it. I'm a southpaw, so if you feel your way around you'll come to a leather scabbard on the left side... *Wonderful*. I believe you have it. Now, you should find a scimitar within—I want you to place it into my left hand.'

I removed the sword with hooked stumps and squeezed through a wall of feathers to the creature's front. I saw two taloned hands at her wingtips; I raised the scimitar to her outstretched fingers.

'Lift it up a little more... There. Now, if you would kindly kneel beside your friend here, I will deal with both of you at once. Half the effort, twice the reward—'

'No,' I said.

'You'll do exactly as I say. Or would you prefer a slow and agonising death?'

'I need to take this Lifer's soul to your superior.'

'Superior? What are you talking about?'

'The overseer.'

She flapped her wings wildly for a moment; then became very still, until only those tiny black eyes moved inside her skull. 'I see,' she said softly. 'In that case, I advise you to stand well back. Once I start I find it rather difficult to—'

Her words were interrupted by a loud roar, as the shop owner charged the demon with his head down and his fists extended. The force would have knocked me off my feet, but he simply bounced off her plump belly as if it were made of rubber—then fell backwards on the floor, where he sat with his head bowed once more, whimpering.

I admired his resistance. I thought, *This is what it means to be alive: to struggle against the inevitable with every last ounce of your strength.* What would I have done in his position? I did not know. If you were to ask a zombie what he wanted more than anything else, he would say:
'I want to live. I want to die.'

I stepped back as the creature clawed her way forward and raised the scimitar above the man's head.
'I am Caym the Magnificent, from the venerable and ancient Bureau of Infernal Affairs. I have come to kill you and devour your remains. You should feel honoured. However, if you would like to beg for your life I will listen to your words without prejudice.'
The man said nothing; and I watched numbly as the scimitar cut an invisible arc through the air and sliced cleanly and swiftly through his neck. His head remained in place for a moment then toppled sideways and rolled along the floor; blood bubbled and spurted from the open wound. The demon leaned forward quickly and pierced the stump with her beak, keeping her victim's body upright as she greedily drank his warm lifeblood with her tongue.
I listened impassively to the wet lapping sounds. I watched flecks of blood spatter the floor all around. I saw the severed head resting in a crimson pool beside the demon's feet. At last the beak released its grip and the body flopped backwards like a half-empty sack; but the neck continued to ooze blood, which flowed in a slow congealing trickle toward me.

'Now for the main course,' said Caym. 'It may seem indulgent, but one must take one's time with such delicacies.'

She began to peck at the torso.

I felt an overwhelming urge to leave. I wanted to breathe air that did not smell of offal and new death. I wanted to escape this horror and grief.

I made a move for the door—but I was careless. I slipped on the pool of blood by the stump, lost my balance, fell heavily on my back, cracked my head on the ground—

And lost consciousness.

When I awoke, my clothes were matted with flesh and blood. Caym was tugging at the corpse's intestines; the effort sprayed clots and gobbets of viscera in my direction. I sat up and slid away, fighting a wave of nausea.

'You're awake, I see. But you don't have the stomach for this. Why our mutual friend chose you to be his delivery boy is beyond me.'

'Have you found the soul yet?' I said flatly.

'Of course not. Frankly, I'm not even looking. This body has plenty of other delights to keep me occupied.' She assaulted the abdomen once more and picked up a chunk of some yellow-brown organ—then spat it out immediately. 'No, no, absolutely *not!* This is terrible! I've never tasted so much *fat* in one liver; this thing was practically an alcoholic... These kidneys, on the other hand—but no, I shan't eat another morsel until I've cleansed my palate.' She turned toward the severed head, hopped forward and pecked at the eye sockets, cutting the fibres and sucking the eyeballs into her hooked beak; then she stumbled backwards in the gore and cracked her victim's ribs. 'Now I've trodden on the heart! It's ruined! This night goes from bad to worse!'

'Haven't you eaten enough?'

'Your attitude stinks, undead. I feel a horrible mood coming on. I suggest you leave me in peace.'

I did so. I turned away from the disembowelled corpse and shuffled across to the severed head. I gathered it up and cradled it gently in my arms, looking into the sockets that saw nothing, whispering comfort to the ears that didn't hear. There was no more resistance inside that skull: the end had come. I felt sorrow for the manner of his death, and though it did him no good and he could not feel it, I kissed him lightly on the forehead.

'Sleep the long sleep,' I said.

After gorging herself further, Caym appeared to rediscover her humour. 'That's better: a little arterial furring, but overall rather good. A frothy pair of lungs and a juicy spleen. You're welcome to share what's left.'

'No thanks.'

'I thought your people liked this sort of thing?'

I shook my head. 'My *people* hardly eat anything.'

'A pity. You're missing out... Still, that means more for me.' She snapped at a finger and cut clean through the bone, then raised her head and swallowed it in one gulp. 'Don't you feel the need to keep me entertained, undead? It's rather boring having to stare at your glum little face while I eat. Tell me something about yourself—how did you die, for example?'

I looked again at the eyeless sockets in that severed head. How would it feel to see nothing? To grope your way around the beauty and ugliness of the world; to taste the breath of your beloved in the darkness; to smell the invisible flowers and grass, and listen to the sound of birds you would never see? A world filled with everything, blinded.

'I was mauled by an alligator.'

The demon tore something small and slippery from the man's abdomen. 'That must have impressed your neighbours in the soil.'

'I never told them.'

'No matter. Every night I gift a death to a Lifer that exceeds yours in prestige tenfold. This creature before us, though it doesn't know it yet, will spend *years* in the grave boasting of the time it was pecked to death by a giant demented bird.'

She was right. The corpses in my graveyard had all suffered relatively commonplace deaths; they would have killed for an ending like this... However, I didn't share her pride. Every death was melancholy. It was numbness and forgetting. The moment when something became nothing.

Caym burped loudly and took a few listless stabs at the man's thigh. Her breath was damp and reeked of offal.

'Are you sure you won't join me? I'm getting rather full.'

'I'm fine.'

'As you wish. But if you want my advice, you should try to enjoy yourself. There's more to life than weeping and wailing... Wait—how could I have missed this luscious little pancreas?' Her beak dipped quickly into the wounded belly, extracted a fleshy, elongated lump and swallowed it whole. 'Now, one last thing before I go.' Her beady little eyes darted from the severed head in my arms to the neck stump, and back again. 'What's the ID?'

I put down the head and worked the envelope from my coat pocket. It was stained with blood, but the note inside was legible. I read out the thirteen digits. She shambled forward, her three-toed feet squelching and slapping through the Lifer's remains. Then, with a long black talon, she scratched the first digit into the skin of the headless stump.

I couldn't watch the rest.

When she was done, the demon stared at me with her beak open, like a thirsting blackbird on a hot summer's day. For a moment, I wondered if she might attack me after all; then her outline began to shimmer and her body underwent a reverse transformation. Her cramped wings withered and retreated into her torso, the beak withdrew into the head, the head sank into the neck, and her legs receded as if someone was pulling them from the inside. Finally, the fat body of the bird drooped and shrank and

76

shifted—until it found the form of a woman dressed in a smart tweed suit.

'What the fuck are you looking at?' she squawked.

I lowered my gaze.

'I suppose you want this fucker's soul now?'

I nodded.

'Well you'll have to find it yourself.' She took a mobile phone from her jacket and snapped some photos of the scene. 'I've got to get off. My editor needs five hundred words on her desk by morning. What a fucking scoop!'

'Wait,' I said.

'This had better be good.'

'Where should I look for the soul?'

She laughed—a crow cawing hatred at the dawn. 'Stick your hand up his throat and pull out the first thing you touch.' She turned abruptly and strode toward the exit. 'Pray you don't see me again, undead. I won't be as kind to you next time.'

The severed head lay on the ground before me. Its expression was neutral. I felt sorry for it, and for what I was about to do.

I attempted to squeeze my stump up the severed windpipe, but it was too narrow, so I pushed it into the mouth instead, and hooked it upwards past the uvula. I felt something firm there, like a rubber ball. I pressed it gently, but it didn't move; I tried to pry it out, but it wouldn't come loose.

I looked toward the door, but the demon was gone.

I removed my hand and rested the head on my lap. I didn't know what to do. I was steeped in blood. Overcome by the misery of existence. Depressed by the futility of hope.

I stood up and tucked the head under my arm. The least I could do was find a grave for it—perhaps in one of the college gardens, or somewhere by the river. And afterward I would break this monstrous agreement, forget about my lost fingers and accept that the box in my coat contained a soul I would never see.

As I was leaving, I met Malache on the threshold. He ran his fingers through his golden curls and frowned.

'Where are you going with that head?' he said.

A heap of junk wrapped in shabby cloth

'I want to bury it.'

'Why?'

I gestured toward the carnage behind me: the decapitated corpse, the viscera and blood, the destruction of a life.

'Let's go back inside,' he said.

It was the last thing I wanted to do, but his tone was firm. He closed the door and led me to the counter at the rear, where we found a solitary chair.

'Please sit.'

I did so gratefully, still hugging the severed head in my arms. Malache stood by the till with his hands in his pockets.

'Tell me what's wrong.'

'I can't do this,' I said. 'I thought I could but I can't. It's been a long time since I worked for the Agency, and that work was different, I made a connection with those people. Now I'm nothing more than a butcher in a slaughterhouse.'

'Killing is more efficient if you don't waste time on sympathy; but I acknowledge it isn't easy for you... Even so, you are obligated. It is difficult to extract yourself from this situation.'

'You told me I could walk away.'

'And you still can, absolutely.' He stroked his chin broodingly. 'However, there are consequences to disappointing the overseer, particularly at this early stage, so the more you do for us the less serious those consequences will be. Nonetheless, should you choose to end our deal here,

78

I'll be right behind you, one hundred per cent.' He crouched down and put a reassuring hand on my shoulder. 'All I ask is that you sleep on your decision. Consider the many lives you will save rather than the few you will bring to an end; focus less on the manner and morality of killing and more on your ultimate goal. In the end, a death is a death: in style they may be radically different, but in substance they are all the same.'

'You should have left the demons in the Underworld.'

'We have to make the best of it,' he said softly. 'Listen, I have no great love for Caym, or Haborym, or any of them, but the fact is they need to feast regularly, and our job is to make sure they don't do it excessively or publicly. You're helping us achieve that goal. You should be proud of your work.'

'It's hard to feel pride in something so gratuitous.'

He nodded, but let the subject slide. 'It's time to visit the overseer,' he said.

We walked outside to the waiting Vespa. I was about to get on, but Malache stopped me. He looked at my blood-soaked body, then removed a plastic sack from his jacket pocket. He took the severed head from me and dropped it inside.

'On second thoughts, let's walk,' he said.

I had no objection: the streets were deserted and the night air was cool and fresh. Thick grey clouds moved slowly overhead, promising snowfall.

I thought about the soul inside the head inside the bag. It had felt firm and rubbery, like the one I had held at the crematorium. Were all souls the same? Were they even souls? Or were they something strange and unique encountered only at the moment of death?

I tried to remember what my own soul had looked like in that fleeting glimpse by the river, so long ago. All that remained were impressions: *weak, small, glimmering, chaotic*. I could reconstruct an image in my mind from those words; but I wouldn't know if it was accurate until I opened the box.

I have attempted to do so many times over the years: I have examined every inch of the exterior, pushed and prodded it with my shrivelled hands, looking for the secret key, the hidden button, the magical combination that would lift the lid; but without success.

And perhaps it isn't important. Whether you have a soul or no soul—whether you are a corpse, a zombie or a Lifer—you have no choice. You carry yourself everywhere with you, like a heap of junk wrapped in shabby cloth.

Malache handed me the sack when we arrived at The Chimera. I don't know why he had carried it; the burden was meant for me. Maybe he was being kind, and he just wanted to lighten my load. Or maybe he believed I would quietly drop the head in the shadows when he wasn't looking. But I wouldn't have done that: I wouldn't have wished the finding of it on anyone.

I expected him to deliver another speech, but he simply unlocked the door to the pub, patted me on the back and turned away.

I wanted him to stay a little longer.

'What was the old name for this place?'

He turned around. 'It's always been The Chimera.'

'No. When I was alive it was called something else.'

'It's operated under that name since the takeover.'

I shook my head. 'It's on the tip of my tongue.'

'What came before is no longer germane. As far as the Bureau is concerned, the past is trivial.'

He turned back, climbed on the Vespa and puttered away; and even though he couldn't see me, I raised my hand to wave goodbye.

Then I walked inside.

Confessions of a zombie

How long had it been since the citizens of the Underworld had replaced the Four Horsemen of the Apocalypse? I couldn't remember; like everyone else, I hadn't noticed the transition. People continued to die, as always, and I had never given a moment's thought to who or what was doing the killing. Until yesterday, I hadn't even known there were devils walking the Earth or demons feasting on the unfortunate. Perhaps Malache was right: a death was a death and my outraged sensibilities were misplaced. Everyone ended up in the soil or the flames; how they got there was irrelevant.

These thoughts relieved my despair. I had been shocked by the Caym's visceral assault and repulsed by her profane disregard for her victim. But ultimately, what did it matter?

What did anything matter?

I sat in the courtyard with my back to the grille, waiting for the stench that would mark the demon's arrival. It came soon enough.

'How was your evening, Half-life?'

'Not good.'

'A pity. Caym is a favourite of mine; her methods are delightfully antiquated. She reminds me of the old days: razing cities to the ground, watching my servants ransack, pillage and violate... But those times are gone. It was our own fault: we were so proud of our achievements we thought we were invincible. Complacency set in. Our power weakened, our influence waned, our role was usurped.' His ramblings irritated me; I clutched the severed head for comfort. 'So the Four Horsemen took control—and, of course, they couldn't handle the numbers. They were crushed by bureaucracy: contracts, Life files, death codes, storage problems, procedural recommendations, paperwork up to their bloodless eyeballs... We all knew they would make a mistake sooner or later, but even I didn't foresee how grave that error would be.' I felt his warm breath on the back of my neck and shuddered. 'They killed Hades. No one knew for sure who did it, but he died on their watch—and that infuriated the Boss. Grievances were aired, the takeover was negotiated and I was dispatched to relieve them of their duties... And you, in your foolish ignorance, brought me the key that eased the transition.'

For a brief, blissful moment he paused; but I was an ear, and he was a mouth, and the mouth couldn't contain itself for long.

'Do you have my second gift?'

'It's stuck inside a severed head.'

'And?'

'I brought you the head.'

'Wonderful! I should give you *twelve* fingers—perhaps even an extra hand! Would that gratify you?'

'Two hands will be fine.'

'Your lack of ambition saddens me; but it is not a surprise. Hold the prize before the grille, and know that you are forbidden to look upon my face.'

I stood up, offered the severed head to the lattice and closed my eyes. I heard a faint squeal and felt a change in the air: the darkness seemed to press upon my face and the demon's foul stench congealed in my nostrils. His shifting bulk disturbed something else, too—a swarm of tiny wings that hummed and chittered before settling once more. Then the head was gone, lifted clumsily by a hand whose claws and scales I was meant to feel, followed by a second squeal as the grille closed.

Then the crunch of teeth on bone.

'Yes, I see it,' the demon said. 'A rare delicacy: swollen like a cyst and juicy as a peach. You have done well.'

I said nothing. I longed for Malache and his calming words, not this boastful, hideous monster... Then, to my horror, I heard a second voice from behind the grille—a softly-spoken, sycophantic stranger:

'How does it taste, sir?'

'Delicious.'

'Would it be impudent of me to request the smallest morsel? Only when you've eaten your fill; and even then, I suggest a portion infinitely less appetising than any other.'

'Such a request would be grossly impertinent.'

'My apologies, sir.'

'Be quiet. I'm eating.'

'Naturally, sir. And I don't mean to disturb you further, but perhaps now would be a good time to hear this zombie's confession? Merely for the enhancement of your pleasure, of course.'

An unpleasant combination of crunching, munching and spitting punctuated the demon's contemplation of this question; after a particularly disagreeable *slurp*, he said: 'Worm, if you interrupt me again, I will strangle you for a thousand years... Nevertheless, your advice is sound.' He sucked his fingers as he added: 'Tell me your sin, Half-life. And don't spare the details.'

So I began:

'When I was a child—seven years older than my last confession—I had a good friend. I don't remember his name now, because I've forgotten almost everything about my life; but we attended the same primary school and our houses stood no more than a hundred yards apart. He was a gentle boy with a good sense of humour, but there was a sadness about him I didn't understand, an impression that he lacked something because of some personal tragedy he never discussed. However, he was the first real friend I'd ever had—'

'Get on with it!' said the sycophant. 'My master doesn't have all night!'

'Fine. So, we always walked home together from school, on a path that took us through woodland. And one day, after a storm, without thinking or knowing why, I picked up a fallen branch and hit him with it. He flinched, so I hit him again. He asked me why I was doing it, and instead of answering I hit him a third time, and a fourth—and I kept on hitting him until he burst into tears and ran away... I think the animal part of me sensed the weakness in him and wanted to punish it, to exert my dominance over something that I feared in myself—'

'Spare us the amateur psychoanalysis,' the sycophant said. 'Is that the end of the matter?'

'Almost. I lost touch with him when my family moved to Oxford; but many years later, when I was an adult, I read about him in the newspaper. I learned that he had hanged himself from a tree in some village graveyard. It stung me a little, and I felt guilty for a long while afterward, because in my mind's eye I imagined him swinging there—not as the young man he would have been, but as the nine-year old boy I had known—and I saw myself running toward his corpse and beating him with that branch again and again.'

'Not bad,' said the demon. 'A thrashing and a hanging in the same story. But nothing you describe is particularly immoral. The weak deserve to be punished; it is their due. And your friend's suicide could hardly be laid at your door.'

'But did my actions undermine his trust in people? Did it start him on the path that led to his death?'

'Perhaps you'd like to believe so, but I doubt it. If you're guilty of anything, it's vanity. You overstate your importance in the lives of others.'

'But the cruelty inside me, the desire to punish him, the irresistible power I felt—these things are shameful.'

'On the contrary, they are a natural and inevitable part of human nature. In any case, I've heard worse: you didn't stab him, or push him off a cliff, or drown him in a quarry. You didn't even break his arm! What you did wasn't a sin, it was a negligible offence; and frankly, it scarcely piques my interest.' He sighed heavily, and his rotten odour hit me like a slap. 'You disappoint me, Half-life; I expected more from you... Leave me now—and tomorrow, tell me a better tale, show me a deeper sin.'

Outside, the temperature was dropping rapidly and the grey clouds had thickened into a white blanket that smothered the whole sky. I needed to hurry before the snow came. I headed south along the river, then followed silent paths until I reached Hinksey Park. It was a public space, but there plenty of shadows to hide in. I would be safe here until morning.

I concealed myself in a clump of bushes, between a lake and a row of allotments, and settled down for what was left of the night. I patted my coat to check that the box was still there—and discovered the leaflet I had been given this morning by the man in the Santa Claus outfit.

I removed it from my pocket. It was smeared with blood but the message it contained was still legible. It said: *You Can Change Your Life*.

I screwed it up and threw it away.

PART THREE

Alastor the Lustful

Snow on silver birches

I woke to sunlight and whiteness and the sound of children screaming. My limbs had turned to ice and my face had been punched by a Brutalist snowman. I wanted coffee and a cigarette, or to be dead, whichever came first.

I sat up slowly, disentangled myself from a mass of argumentative foliage, and found a world of snow. Snow that lay thick and drifting on the allotments and tennis courts, powdery blankets of snow spread across the grass, small clumps of snow sprinkled over trees and bushes. There was ice on the duck pond and the lake, and snow on the ice, and a light snowfall in the air.

But on me, there was only blood.

I needed to wash my clothes, but there were others in the park: solitary adults walking their dogs, groups of children throwing snowballs at each other, a couple of teenagers testing the ice. I used the snow to remove the more obvious stains from my coat and to clean the matted blood from my hair, face and hand stumps; but it wasn't enough to let me walk around freely. I had to find a source of water far from hostile eyes.

I buttoned up my coat, kept my head low and followed the curve of the lake southward until I reached the path to Hinksey village. There was a bridge over the lake, followed by another over a railway line, descending to a winding path at ground level—a route collectively nicknamed the Devil's Backbone. I navigated it without incident.

Where the path wound through trees on its approach to the village, I found what I was looking for: Hinksey Stream. It was frozen over but I saw water flowing beneath, so I turned aside and followed its course northward. In a copse of silver birches I undressed, until I stood naked in the snow with a pile of bloodstained clothes beside me. I carried them to the bank of the stream, broke a hole in the ice and began the painstaking task of scrubbing each item by hand. My hat, socks, boxer shorts and tee-shirt yielded quickly, but my shoes, sweatshirt, trackpants and coat took much longer, and a few faint bloodstains remained. I hung the clothes to dry over a low branch, then found a space in the undergrowth where no snow had fallen. I lay down and curled into a ball.

Malache had asked me to sleep on my decision. I had slept, and I had decided: I would not break my agreement. Even if everything he had told me was a lie—that I was saving lives, that I would get my hands back, that I could open the box—I wasn't sure it mattered anymore. At least I was feeling something again, making myself useful, doing more than just walking the streets and waiting for scraps.

Besides, he had used that ominous phrase: *there are consequences to disappointing the overseer*. I shuddered to think what he meant, but it was clear that if I stopped now I would be worse off than before I had started.

I closed my eyes, and tried to forget that I was nothing more than driftwood afloat an alien current, in an unfamiliar ocean, on a world I no longer knew.

When, pale and shivering, I finally stood up again, I discovered that my clothes were still damp. However, I needed to be at the office by ten, so I began to dress quickly.

As I was pulling on my trousers I noticed a burn or a tattoo in the centre of my chest, just below the collar bone. Examining it more closely, I saw a stylised image of a heart broken into two pieces, created from hundreds of miniature puncture wounds; and though it looked a little kitsch, it was clearly fashioned with care and skill. I suspected it was Caym's work: she must have seized the opportunity when I passed out last night. Or perhaps this wound had somehow manifested spontaneously, like the ring of fire around my pupil. In any case, it seemed that my complicity in these killings brought its own payment: a permanent stain on my flesh.

I ran my fingers over the design one last time with a mixture of pleasure and regret; then I put on the rest of my clothes and returned along the Devil's Backbone to the park. My skin felt clammy and bitterly cold, but I no longer looked like a murderer, which gave me the confidence to hold my head up and look strangers in the eye. There were more people around now, and I even wished one of them good morning in an attempt to appear normal. They responded with a look of hostility.

I skirted the lake once more until I reached the duck pond. I saw children throwing chunks of bread onto the frozen surface; ducks and moorhens skittered uncertainly between them, pecking at the crumbs. I was famished—I hadn't eaten much yesterday—so I walked out onto the ice, picked up a couple of chunks and started to eat them. The bread was satisfying, fresh and chewy; but I heard a small voice crying nearby. A group of children were pointing at me with varying degrees of amusement and distress; their parents, gathered around them protectively, were giving me the pitchfork glare.

I panicked and ran. It was a mistake: I slipped and crashed to the ice. I got up slowly, bolted for the shore, felt air beneath my feet and fell flat on my face. The glares were replaced by a combination of pity and disgust. With what was left of my dignity, I raised myself upright, shuffled carefully across the frozen pond, climbed the bank and walked away.

I left the park and headed toward town. The road was awash with black and grey slush carved into ridges by passing cars. On the pavement, dirt and snow had hardened into patches of ice.

As I approached Carfax I noticed a vehicle marooned on St Aldates. It was a waste van emblazoned with the same lettering and emblem I had seen in Malache's office: Green

Devil Recycling. It lay at an angle in a drift of snow; pedestrians gave it a wide berth. I soon realised why. Even though the container was sealed and the tailgate lowered, the stench was overwhelming: a pungent mixture of waste, butchered game and rotting flesh. I am normally tolerant of the smell of death—in the right circumstances, I even find it comforting—but the foul, acid and putrid undercurrents of this wretched odour repulsed me. I held my breath and hurried up the slope to Carfax, then walked carefully down Cornmarket toward the bookbinder.

By the time I reached the entrance, the odour had faded to an unpleasant memory, usurped by the fear of a new day.

Blackjack

I walked inside. The room temperature was stiflingly hot. I saw three minor devils sitting around Nergal's desk, playing a game of cards.

Dumuzid looked up. 'Have you been swimming?'

'It's a long story,' I replied. 'Is Malache around?'

'He stayed until nine,' said Nergal, dealing a new hand. 'But he left when you didn't turn up. He said he'd see you tonight.'

'Never mind, Rabbit,' Ereshkigal said. 'There's a heater beside me. Come and dry yourself off.'

She cleared a space between herself and Dumuzid, pulled out the same two-step step-ladder I had used yesterday, and positioned it in front of a large storage heater. I felt the warmth immediately, and as the minutes passed I started to sweat and my clothes began to steam. I removed my coat and hat and placed them on top of the heater.

'Did Malache leave a note?'

'Don't interrupt,' said Nergal. 'This is an important hand.'

They were playing pontoon with a company pack: the back of each card was adorned with a dancing green devil wreathed in flames. Nergal dealt the second round face up: he got the five of hearts, Dumuzid the ace of spades, Ereshkigal the ten of diamonds.

'I'm sticking,' said Dumuzid, smugly.

'You're bluffing,' said Nergal. 'You've got seventeen at best.'

Ereshkigal bought three more cards.

'You're bluffing, too. No way you have a five-card trick.'

She smiled inscrutably.

'Fine. You're both going to lose.' He flipped over his unseen card: a nine to go with the five. 'Seven for blackjack,' he said, blowing on the pack for luck. The next card he turned over was a six. 'Twenty—that'll do. You two are full of shit. Victory is mine!'

Dumuzid flipped his cards: a king to go with the ace. Resh's hand added up to nineteen.

'Fuck this bullshit,' said Nergal. 'How much do I owe?'

'Eleven hundred,' said Dumuzid.

Nergal's shoulders slumped.

'Forget it,' said Ereshkigal. 'We're family.'

'I'm not family,' said Dumuzid. 'I want my money.'

'You married my sister, you old goat.'

'Fine. We'll split the difference.'

Nergal recovered his composure, shuffled the cards for the next round, then glanced at me. 'Want to join us?'

I shook my head. 'Solitaire is more my game.'

'Sure. But how about this: if you win three of the next five rounds, I'll ask the overseer to give you your fingers back *immediately*.'

'And if I lose?'

'You're my slave for the afternoon.'

'Stop teasing him, Nerg,' said Ereshkigal.

'It's a fair offer, my little guillotine.'

'It's no offer at all. You don't have the authority.'

'I have some sway with Mal. It's not impossible.'

'Don't be a creep... Ignore him, Rabbit.'

The game continued but I stopped paying attention to the details. I was half-aware that Nergal won some of his money back from Dumuzid, and I heard someone shout 'You stitched me up!' and someone else ask 'How can you have five aces?'; but everything else was lost in the fog of my own concerns.

The first of these was physical. The air was humid, I was sitting in damp clothes and my face and arms were bathed in sweat. I wanted to throw off my outfit and lie naked in the snow again; but I stayed where I was, fidgeting uncomfortably. On top of this I wanted to know if Malache had left me the note from tonight's demon; but there was barely a pause in the game and I didn't know these strangers well enough to interrupt. Finally, I wondered if Malache was angry with me for being late. Was his departure a sign that I had committed some grievous error?

Would I be punished?

'What did you think of our feathered friend?'

I looked up. Nergal was speaking to me as he dealt another hand, but I was too distracted to grasp his meaning.

'Caym,' he explained. 'The creature you met last night.'

'I don't want to think about her.'

'Tell us about the victim instead,' said Ereshkigal.

'A man. He ran a video store. She cut off his head then feasted on his insides.'

'That reminds me,' said Nergal. 'We should organise another movie night soon. One of the old favourites: *Errementari*, *The Devil Rides Out*, *Night of the Demon*—'

'No. It has to be *The Exorcist*,' said Dumuzid. '"Your mother sucks cocks in hell!"' he added with a chuckle.

'Could you two be any less sensitive?' Ereshkigal said.

I lowered my head. I felt like a raw onion in an apple tart: unwanted and completely out of place.

My misery was interrupted by the tinkle of the doorbell.

'Is that a customer?' whispered Nergal in astonishment. 'Dum, you know how to handle these people. Go and see what they want.'

Dumuzid acquiesced and shambled toward the displays, where a young woman was standing. 'Welcome to Babylon Bookbinders,' he said dourly. 'We bind books of all shapes and sizes. Your words are our business...'

Nergal furtively put away the playing cards; Ereshkigal returned to her workbench and acted busy.

I looked at the woman. She was dressed sombrely; dark hair framed a gamine face. Dumuzid bowed his head and adopted a flattering tone, but I couldn't hear what he was saying. After a few brief exchanges, they traded polite goodbyes and the woman left.

Dumuzid returned to his table with a large plastic bag. He removed a package and unwrapped it slowly. It contained a thick, heavy book with a few loose pages, a broken leather binding and a large water stain on the reverse. 'A Bible,' he said, wincing. 'It belonged to the client's great-grandmother; she died a few months ago. It needs new boards and endpapers, and I'll have to sew back the loose leaves; it shouldn't be too onerous.' He ran his fingers along the spine. 'It's a beautiful book, but—well, it's not one of ours, is it?'

'Have some fun with it,' said Nergal. 'Draw a cock-and-balls in Matthew's Gospel. Erase the Four Horsemen from Revelations. It'll cheer you up.'

Dumuzid ignored him and set to work, carefully opening the inner part and easing out the loose leaves. I watched him awhile, surprised by the care and attention— the *love*—he devoted to his task. After a few minutes he looked up and summoned me toward him.

'Mal asked me to give you this,' he said. He patted the right pocket of his jerkin and removed a white envelope with a red wax seal. 'Today's note... It slipped my mind earlier. My apologies.'

He said no more and returned to his work. I looked around. Everyone appeared busy; I had no reason to stay. I collected my coat and hat from the storage heater, put them on and walked outside. The snow had stopped and the air was clear and crisp.

I closed the door quietly, but the door fought back. I tried again but it refused to yield. I realised belatedly that someone was trying to open it from the inside. It was Ereshkigal.

'Wait!' she said. 'I almost forgot. You and I have a date.'

Pretending you like the taste

She went back inside momentarily. When she returned she was wearing a long black coat, heavy black mittens, a thick multicoloured scarf and a pair of fluffy black ear muffs.

'I'm taking you to see a friend of mine,' she said. 'But before we go, I have a request: I want you to call me Resh from now on. My formal title is a bit of a mouthful: Ereshkigal, Queen of the Great Below, Ninkigal, Lady of the Great Earth, Irkalla of the Underworld, Ruler of the Dark—'

'Okay,' I said. 'Resh it is.'

'That's better. We can be friends now.' She leaned across and sniffed my scalp. 'Good. You smell fresher today. Promise me you won't climb into any more food bins.'

'I'll try.'

'If you get hungry, I always have a snack or two on my desk. Nerg says I eat like a tapeworm, but he eats like a pig, so I guess we're even.' She sighed. 'Have you ever been married, Rabbit?'

'When I was alive. But it didn't last.'

'A pity.'

'We were too young. We grew apart.'

She nodded in sympathy. 'Nerg and I have become inured to each other over the years. But it's not been easy.

96

Sometimes it feels like we've been together forever.' She smiled. 'You know what I think the secret of a long-term relationship is? Eating shit and pretending you like the taste.'

'Whatever works,' I said.

She took my arm and we walked together, sliding over the hard snow. I stopped outside The Noodle Bar. The mere thought of a bowl of plain noodles made my mouth water, and I tried to go inside, but she steered me toward The Oxford Manicure instead.

'Show me your nails, Rabbit.' I held out the shrivelled balls of melted flesh and fused bone that passed for hands. She frowned. 'I thought the overseer might have given you a couple of fingers by now.'

'That wasn't our agreement.'

'That's not the point. Any contract can be negotiated. You should have asked for five fingers after the first night; you might have ended up with three, but that's still better than none.'

'Sorry,' I said.

'It's not your fault. They took advantage of you.'

I didn't feel as though anyone had taken advantage of me; I believed my contract was a good one. Even if I was wrong, the mantra of the zombies' creed offered some consolation: *I will accept whatever befalls me.*

'What about your feet? Do you have toes?'

'Eight,' I said. 'Four on each foot.'

'That's plenty. Let's go inside.'

The salon was a short narrow room, brightly lit and minimally decorated. The walls were white, the boards wooden, the ceiling tiled. Three chairs, three foot rests and three free-standing lamps were arranged on the right; on the left stood three tables, each with two chairs, a desk lamp and a large wall-mounted mirror. A simple window display contained lotions, nail varnishes and various pieces of equipment relating to manicure and pedicure.

There were no customers. The only other person in the room was a woman of medium height with a kind face. As soon as she saw my companion she smiled broadly.

'Hello, Resh,' she said chirpily. 'Is it the usual today?'

'Nothing for me, thanks. I brought a friend, though. He doesn't say much but he needs a major overhaul.'

The manicurist grinned at me and approached at full throttle. I stood still, paralysed by the brightness, which I was convinced would reveal every blemish and scar on my bloodless skin. 'May I...?' she said, lifting my hands and scrutinising them for anything that might resemble a fingernail. Finding nothing, she added: 'Just a pedicure today, then.'

'Give him the full treatment,' Resh insisted. 'I want him to walk out of here feeling like a new man.'

'Right. So that's a foot bath and massage, repair and trim, file and buff—and whatever else you might need. What about nail polish?'

'The works,' Resh interjected. She turned to me. 'I recommend a glossy black varnish and a skull tattoo. A little *memento mori*.'

I nodded in agreement—but I felt like a stranger in my own body, playing the role of me.

'What's your name, sir?'

'Sore point,' Resh interrupted again. 'He can't remember. I just call him Rabbit because he's harmless and very quiet.'

'Okay, Mr Rabbit, would you like to take a seat? Any of the low chairs by the wall. I'll be back in a moment.'

She retreated to a room at the rear of the salon. I heard objects being moved around, water running. I took off my hat and coat, sat down and looked around anxiously.

Resh sat beside me and touched me gently on the arm. 'I'm sorry I spoke on your behalf. It's just that you looked so startled when we came in.'

'I'm afraid,' I said hopelessly. 'She'll see my wounds—she'll know I'm a zombie!'

She moved her hand to my head and stroked my shaven scalp softly. 'Don't worry. She's very discreet. Professionally, she won't even notice; privately, she'll never tell... In any case, you are who you are. That's a cause for celebration. If everyone was the same, this world would be a terribly boring place.'

The manicurist returned with a bowl of steaming water that smelled of Epsom salts. She removed the foot rest in front of my chair and replaced it with the bowl. She glanced at me, then at my companion.

'Take off your shoes and socks,' said Resh.

I pushed off the left trainer with my right foot, then the right with my wrists. I repeated the process with my socks, exposing my feet: two wounded wedges of waxy flesh with cracked heels and stubby toes. The big toe on my left foot and the little toe on my right were missing.

I smiled inwardly: I realised that the reptile that took those toes from me would likely be dead by now. How many people could say they have outlived their killer?

The manicurist didn't gasp or shriek. She didn't hit me over the head with a club and call the police. She simply lifted my feet into the bowl, let them soak for a moment, then began to wash them.

I closed my eyes.

The room was filled with the odour of salts and the sound of splashing water. I felt the gentleness of her hands on my skin, the roughness of the cloth on my skin, and it felt so good and so holy that I wanted to weep, I wanted to weep because I had forgotten what it was like to be alive, I had forgotten that the touch of another living being could soothe and comfort, could make me believe that I was loved, and I was exalted by the dignity in her tender fingers, the love in her gracious hands, and before she was done I felt tears streaming down my face; and I wept, and I was not ashamed.

'It's all right, Mr Rabbit,' the manicurist said, handing me a tissue. 'You let it all out. You'll feel better for it.'

I wiped the tears from my cheeks and felt grateful to be alive—because there is neither love nor dignity in the grave, and only worms can touch you.

The manicurist dried my feet thoroughly with a towel, then began to massage them. I felt life returning, knots unravelling, the hardness become soft. I felt the tension drain from the rest of my body too, and when my companion and the manicurist spoke, I listened without anxiety.

'How's business, Resh?'

'Good, thanks. We're trying to raise brand awareness right now, so we've just launched an online store: tee-shirts, trainers, hoodies, bags, themed food and drink—all with the Green Devil branding. We've bought some magazine coverage too, persuaded a few influencers to review our stuff, and we're running an offline ad campaign. It's pretty catchy... But the Boss is looking even further forward. Ultimately, he wants to rebadge himself as Devil Joe, the friendly neighbourhood guy who's just here to help. All the horns and tails stuff, the fire and brimstone, the fangs and goatee—it's passé now. So we're going to paint him in a softer light: an avuncular figure who's come to solve your problems.'

'We all need someone like that.'

'Exactly. And we think the campaign will work on that basis. Not just on a micro level but on the world stage, too. Obviously, one of the biggest issues we're facing is over-population, so alongside the recycling and disposal efforts, Green Devil is running an education campaign in schools: leaflets, illustrated books, visits from our PR team, and so on. If people have fewer children that's going to be less work for all of us; but in the meantime we have systems in place to deal with the surplus...'

The manicurist continued to listen, with occasional feedback, but was more focused on her work. After the massage she trimmed my nails, filed them to a smooth curve and cleaned them with alcohol. She removed the hangnails and rough skin, applied lotion to my cracked heels, and rubbed perfumed unguent into the soles, balls and bridges of both feet. Then, with care and precision, she applied black nail polish to all but my remaining big toe—onto which she outlined a death's head using a red marker pen. Finally, she took a tattoo gun, dipped it in black ink and traced the needle over the outline to create a perfect miniature skull.

When every inch of my feet was clean and dry and buffed to perfection, she handed me a small bottle of nail polish. 'If you don't like the tattoo, you can hide it with this. Either way, it'll grow out in a couple of months.'

'I like it very much. Thank you.'

'You're welcome, Mr Rabbit.'

She put my socks back on and I pushed my feet into the trainers; then, silently, I stood up and gathered my belongings. Resh paid the bill and accompanied me to the door.

'Come back any time!' the manicurist called as we left, in a voice so innocent it made my heart sing.

I felt as pampered as a prince and as powerful as a king. My feet were silk-skinned and sweet-scented; I walked on spun sugar and warm clouds. My haircut had been a utilitarian experience; this was a work of beauty and indulgence. It made me feel so good about myself I believed I could do anything. I could talk to the living with or without my soul, I could find a job, a house and a partner, I could live out my days at peace with this alien world—

But who was I kidding? I could barely speak to Lifers, and my attitude toward my employers was ambiguous at best. Malache was kind and friendly, but secretive; I couldn't tell when Nergal was teasing me, and didn't understand why; Dumuzid was an admirably diligent old man, but we had nothing in common. And Resh...

I put on my hat and coat, then stood on the icy pavement staring into space, not knowing how to act.

'Thanks for the pedicure.'

'Don't mention it.'

I rocked backwards and forwards on the soles of my feet.

'I like your scarf.'

'Thanks.'

'And your ear muffs are... good.'

She nodded. I hoped she would take my arm, and we might spend the afternoon together, wandering the parks and pathways of Oxford, until we grew tired and found a café, where we could talk.

But she blew on her cupped hands to keep warm and said: 'I should get back to the workshop; I have deadlines to meet. The Boss wants everyone to think he's changed, but underneath it all he's still the same vicious, malicious, vindictive little shit he always was.'

'Okay,' I said quietly.

'I have another cigarette, if you'd like one—'

'I'll pass this time. But thanks.'

'No problem, Rabbit.'

She walked away. I watched her leave, hoping she might look back, but she didn't; and when she reached the bookbinder I turned around, and my life resumed its habitual drudgery.

I wanted to get away from people and my perpetual sense of inadequacy. But only the former was possible: I carried my failures with me everywhere. And the biggest failure of all was my inability to connect with others.

During my lifetime, all of my relationships had ended in disappointment. Friends, lovers, parents, it didn't matter: everything I touched turned to ash.

102

As a zombie, the only meaningful connection I had ever made was with a woman called Zoë, a co-worker and friend. But that, too, had crumbled to dust.

Sometimes the pain of these failures is intolerable. This is what Lazarus knew: once you have been dead you can't come back. You live and breathe and walk around, but the world rejects you at every turn.

You are forever hollow.

A quickening breeze picked up the loose snow and blew it into shallow drifts. I walked down George Street and continued west to Hythe Bridge, where I descended the steps to the southern end of the Oxford Canal. I followed the towpath north for a while, between narrowboats and the backs of houses, until I found a secluded space beneath the railway bridge. I sat with my legs hanging over the water and took Malache's envelope from my pocket.

I tore open the wax seal and tapped the envelope against the heavy stones on the bank. A photograph and letter fell out.

The photograph showed a smartly dressed couple at a gathering of other smartly dressed people; a wedding or conference, perhaps. But the fact that there were two of them alarmed me. Which was the demon's prey? I didn't want to make a mistake—it was literally a matter of life and death—but there was no way of knowing.

I looked to the note for help. It said:

Some think the hunt is a brutal throwback, that we're nothing more than beasts sating our lust for blood—but they couldn't be more wrong. It is an act of worship, an exhibition of skill, the seamless union of desire and need; dissolute in style, pure in execution, divine in nature... Details are trivial: the tracker will bring us together, the ID will flow from the work. Is eleven o'clock good for you?—Master of Pain.

I dropped the note and the photo on the towpath, and the wind took them and carried them into the water, where they floated among the islands of ice and the last of the autumn leaves.

The man who didn't shimmer

The afternoon passed. I sat under the bridge with my back to the wall. A woman tossed me a couple of coins. A stray dog licked me, mistaking me for a side of beef. A college student wanted to discuss my life story, but I didn't feel like talking, so I pretended to fall asleep. Then I lay down and fell asleep for real.

When I woke it was dark. I had drooled on my stumps, so I used my sweatshirt to wipe my mouth and hands.

My eyes adjusted slowly to the boundaries of light and shadow, but at last I got up and shuffled toward town. I saw a young couple out for a romantic evening stroll. They didn't see me.

The sky was thick with cloud and the snow was beginning to melt. Water trickled free in glistening rills, turning the path to slush and mud, creating holes and troughs in the drifts. I trudged through it all, half-asleep, mentally exhausted. In the space of two days my life had been turned upside down by the promise of something better and the certainty of something worse. And tonight was only the third of ten.

The coins the Samaritan had thrown to me were enough to buy a drink. I thanked her silently for the gift and trudged along St Giles to the Lamb and Flag pub, where I ordered a coffee and sat at a table by the window. I remained there until ten o'clock, then returned to the office.

There was a newspaper on Malache's desk. The front page featured a prominent colour photograph of the Retro Video Emporium. The headline above it read: MAN HACKED TO DEATH IN NORTH OXFORD. The subheading below said: Giant Feathers Found At Scene. The article was written by *Our local correspondent, Norma Bidde*. Norma, in brown tweed jacket and trousers, who led a double life as a demon bird.

'Congratulations on your success,' said Malache. He was sitting behind the desk, watching me keenly, evaluating my state of mind.

'I was a bystander. I did nothing.'

'You underestimate yourself. Without you, the story would have been much worse: dismembered corpses in the street, blood flowing in the gutters, cars and buildings on fire—'

'Okay,' I said.

'All I'm saying is that we continue to value your contribution. Speaking of which, did you give any more thought to what we discussed last night?'

'Yes.'

'And what did you conclude?'

'I'll see it through to the end.'

'Glad to hear it.'

'But I have a question first.'

'Fire away.'

I framed the problem in my mind before speaking. 'Many years ago, your superior returned my soul to me, in a box that only I could open; at the same time he took away my hands, which made opening the box impossible. My question is: when our current agreement ends, what is to prevent him taking something else from me, on a whim or out of spite?'

'How can I reassure you that he will not?'

'You can tell me the truth.'

'The truth is as it always has been: bring him the souls you promised and he will take nothing more.'

He sounded convincing, but I didn't trust him... And yet, in a rare moment of insight, I realised that trust wasn't the problem—it was self-belief. *I doubted Malache because I doubted myself.* I couldn't bear the hope of success. By assuming the overseer would betray me, I had given myself an excuse to fail; and if I failed, I stayed the same. Unburdened by responsibility. Safe.

'So. Are we good now?'

'We're good,' I said.

'Fine. Let's get down to business—'

'I'm sorry I was late this morning.'

He waved away my apology. 'I would have waited but I had to be somewhere else. Did Resh take care of you?'

I nodded. 'I have the smoothest feet in the west.'

'Excellent. We'll do something about those clothes of yours in the next couple of days, too. In the meantime, we have to deal with Alastor.'

'Who's Alastor?' I said.

The black Vespa buzzed irritably along St Giles, spraying slush and grime in its wake. It wasn't far to the hotel, but Malache had insisted on taking the scooter, claiming he enjoyed the thrill of driving on ice. So I clung to his waist, feeling the silk of his jacket beneath my hands and the warmth of his back against my face.

We stopped on the Banbury Road beside a low stone wall. The wall guarded an old two-storey house with lights in every window. I had been here often when I was alive, spying on wealthy targets for my clients, eavesdropping on their secrets and lies. It was an amiable, generous kind of place, where even a zombie and a demon might find welcome.

We dismounted, then Malache pulled the Vespa onto the pavement and lowered the kickstand. The entrance to the hotel garden stood before us—an archway crowned by a stone lion—but my companion's attention was drawn elsewhere. He was looking south, toward a Norman church and a triangle of land marked with gravestones.

'That's where you were buried, isn't it?'

'Yes.'

'Ever wanted to go back?'

'Sometimes. But not right now.'

'If you change your mind, I can arrange things.'

'Thanks.'

We walked through the archway to a paved courtyard blanketed by snow. Tables and chairs rose from the whiteness like hardy spring flowers.

Malache escorted me to the entrance.

'The prey is waiting inside, so I'll leave you here. Alastor will be along soon. Do as he asks and everything will be fine.' He patted me on the collar: I felt the pressure of his fingers on the back of my neck, as if he was checking I still had a spine. 'Keep up the good work, friend.'

He turned and left. I waited until the drone of his Vespa had faded to silence, then walked inside.

I removed my hat and looked around. The décor had changed since my lifetime, but the atmosphere was still the same. It was a perfect fusion of ancient and modern: bold colours and contemporary furniture blended with leaded windows and portraits in classical frames; the tables were small and cheerfully lit but the overall ambience was tastefully restrained; the bar had a bright metallic shine, but the bar staff and waiters could have stepped out of a P.G. Wodehouse novel.

One of the Wodehouse waiters offered to take my coat. I acquiesced; he hung it on a peg by the door. 'Are you a guest or resident of the hotel?' he said.

'I'm waiting for someone.'

'May I offer you a drink in the interim?'

'A Southern Comfort. No ice.'

'Of course.'

He gave instructions to the barman and faded into the background.

I scanned the room for either of the people I had seen in the photograph, hoping to establish which was the victim. Unfortunately, I saw both of them, sitting together at a table by the far wall: a brunet man and a blonde woman, dressed in smart-casual clothing. I took a seat at a discreet distance, which also afforded a view of my coat and that small, precious box within.

The Southern Comfort arrived, served on a silver platter. I had no means of paying for it, but I suspected that money would be the least of my concerns in the next couple of hours. I thanked the waiter, took a sip of nectar and let my ears do what they did best.

'I can't wait,' the man said. 'Let's go up to my room.'

'You're a naughty little boy, Tom,' the woman teased. 'And naughty boys have to wait for their pleasure.'

'I prefer my pleasure in the here and now.'

'Don't peak too early. I want this evening to last.'

'Have I ever disappointed you before?'

'Not yet.' The woman leaned across and kissed her companion on the cheek. 'Are you going to film us again?'

'I need something to keep me entertained when you're not around.'

'I know. But one day she'll look through your phone and see what you've been up to. Then mummy will be cross with you.'

'I don't care. We should bring this whole affair to a head—'

'Don't be silly. We both know how it works.'

'Then let's get started.'

'Five more minutes. Surely you can wait that long?'

I had forgotten how to love, but I remembered the language: simple, playful, mutually understood. Words of power that augured the physical struggle to come. Words that defined boundaries, requested permission, threatened retribution. Words that floated somewhere in the banal chasm between the poetic and the explicit.

'I feel like I'm dying when I'm not with you.'

'Go ahead and die, then. I'll piss on your corpse.'

'Don't encourage me. I'd do it, for you.'

'No,' she pouted. 'I prefer you warm.'

'Do you think anyone suspects at the office?'

'Of course. You're so transparent.'

'I can't help it. When I'm with you I turn into—'

'Shh!' she hissed. 'We don't want *everyone* to know.'

'There's one way you can shut me up.'

'And what way is that?'

'It's a surprise. I've hidden it in Room Seven.'

'Now I'm intrigued... Whatever could you mean?'

I heard giggling, or it might have been the sound of two rats arguing over a bone; in any case, I watched them rise from their seats and heard them pass through the door behind me.

I took another sip of Southern Comfort. I didn't want to get drunk, but there were plenty of stations between drunk and sober and who the hell cared anyway? So I waited there, steeping in alcohol, bait for a demon—

Something about that last phrase didn't feel right, but my brain was too slow and stupid to figure out what. I scratched ineffectually at the surface of its wrongness for a while, until my mind was distracted by a shifty-looking individual at the entrance. He was bending over my coat, simultaneously groping it with his fingers and sniffing it in a shameless manner. I stood up immediately and walked rapidly toward him, calculating that he was more thief than demon, because his body lacked that elusive shimmer. But as I approached he turned around, and I realised my mistake:

He wasn't human after all.

Bits and Pieces

'Hello,' he said lasciviously. 'Are you amuse-bouche or aperitif? Come, let me inhale you.' He leaned forward, pressed his nose against my neck and sniffed a couple of times. 'Oho! You're definitely the one.'

He was almost human. Everything fitted in number and proportion: arms, legs, head, torso. His face, while it wasn't quite *right*, wasn't particularly *wrong* either: the nose was too long, the chin too pointed, the mouth too wide, the eyes too large and the ears too thick—but all the elements were there, after a fashion. His high-pitched voice wasn't totally outside the range of human experience either, and with the right comb and a patient barber his hair could have passed for eccentric. And yet, he wasn't human.

'Forgive my rudeness, but I had to be certain,' he said, extending his long, slender fingers. 'My name is Alastor, and you are—? Oh, but we've met before, haven't we? I'm almost certain of it. Let's find somewhere private to discuss our mutual interests.'

I didn't believe I shared any interests with this creature, but I escorted him to my table, sat down and waited for him to speak.

'Yes, I *think* I remember you. A stone slab, a pure blade—a slice and dice!' He moved his fingers rapidly, as if wielding a knife. 'But there were so many of you back then, it's hard to be definite... May I see it, by the way? I know it's hiding in your coat. They're such delicious little things, aren't they?'

'It's inside a box. I can't open it.'

'A pity—it would have added flavour to the evening... But never mind. Where is my prey?'

'There are two of them. I don't know which is which.'

'No matter; I intend to take them both. Two for the price of one, as they say. I can't wait to see the look on their faces!'

'The note didn't mention two victims—'

'I *said* I will take them both, undead. It is decided. The only question that remains is how.'

He tapped his teeth with a fingernail. That was something I hadn't noticed in my initial appraisal: he had far too many teeth. How could I have mistaken him for a man?

'Eureka!' he said excitedly. 'Oh, that's *perfect*. I had intended to beat them about the head and cut them into little pieces—well, I'm still going to do that to some extent, of course—but I've found the missing *je ne sais quoi*. This union of bodies, this bonding of flesh! It's time, my pallid little friend.' He turned around and snapped his fingers. 'You, waiter-thing, over here!'

The man who had helped me out of my coat glided into view. If he was irked by the demon's tone he disguised it beautifully. 'Can I help you, sir?'

'I need a sewing kit.'

'If you're staying with us, you'll find one in your room.'

'Yes, yes—but I need something stronger. A reel of thick cord and a needle to match. Is there something in your kitchen, perhaps?'

'So that I can meet your requirements more readily, may I ask what you need it for?'

'No, you may not!'

The waiter was unperturbed by the demon's outburst. 'My apologies. But it would help us—'

'A canvas bag.' Alastor waved his hand dismissively. 'The canvas is torn; I need something to hold it together until... whatever.'

'Thank you, sir. I'll ask the chef.'

He slid noiselessly into the kitchen. Alastor grumbled to himself and rapped his knuckles impatiently on the table; then he looked me in the eye. 'Admit it,' he said. 'You exude that aroma merely to tempt me. Well, I refuse your advances; I have work to do. However, when the work finishes...'

'They're in Room Seven,' I said, ignoring him. 'Would you like me to describe them to you?'

'No need. I know *exactly* what they look like.'

This surprised me, but before I could ask him about it the waiter returned with a reel of cooking twine and a long needle, both arranged on another silver platter. 'Will that be all, sir?'

'I want more,' Alastor said grumpily.

'More twine?'

'It's a big bag.'

'As you wish, sir.'

'And bring me a Magnum of champagne. My friend and I have something to celebrate.'

The waiter left; a short while later he returned with a second reel and a large, green bottle. 'Is there anything else I can do for you?'

'Are you free later? Perhaps you could join us.'

'I'm afraid not, sir.'

'Shame... Well, run along.'

The waiter turned and walked away.

'Right,' said Alastor. 'Let's get started.'

He stuffed the needle and twine into my trouser pockets and grabbed the champagne bottle by the neck. I led him through the door behind me, and as we walked up the stairs to the guest rooms he pinched my right buttock. 'It called to me,' he said. 'I can't help myself. But I won't do it again, not even if you beg me.'

The stairway took a couple of strange turns, and the corridor at the top seemed to double back on itself, but a tiny sign at ceiling height eventually pointed us in the right direction, and we soon found ourselves outside a white wooden door inlaid with a black number seven. A discreet Do Not Disturb sign hung on the doorknob; Alastor removed it and tossed it aside. He put his ear to the wood a moment, then knocked politely.

'Room service!' he trilled.

There was no answer, so he knocked more loudly.

'Didn't you see the sign on the door?' a man shouted.

'Go away!' a woman said.

Alastor grinned. 'Tom? Karen? Is that you?'

Tentatively, the man replied: 'Alan?'

'Indeed it is. Sorry to disturb you, but I have a little gift, and I'd love to share it with you.'

'Leave it outside the door,' said the woman.

'Yeah, just... leave it,' echoed the man.

'I absolutely would, but I'm celebrating a promotion, which technically makes me your boss, and I have a bottle of champagne right here, it's far too much for one person to drink, and it would be lovely—'

'All right,' the man sighed. 'Give me a minute.'

Muffled noises came from the room, some of which I was able to identify: bedsprings, angry muttering, zips, hissed whispers, a door closing, water running. After a couple of minutes, the man I had seen earlier opened the door, revealing a stylish bedroom with a bed that looked freshly made. As we walked in I saw the woman too, immaculately attired and sitting in a purple armchair by a leaded window. She was reading a book. The book was upside down.

'Good to see you, Alan.'

'You too, Tom... Karen, how are you?'

'Absolutely fucking great, Alan.'

'Glad to hear it. Tom, would you do the honours?'

Alastor handed him the champagne bottle. The man cut the foil with a pocket knife then eased off the cork with a pop. He poured the champagne into two wine glasses and a tumbler. 'What about your friend?' he said.

'My new assistant. No drinks—he's just here to observe.'

'Is he all right?' the woman said. 'He doesn't look well.'

'Nothing a cuddle and a coddle won't cure.'

They raised their glasses to Alastor's fictional promotion and toasted him by his fictional name. His fictional assistant looked on, wondering how this fiction would end.

'How's your wife, Tom?'

'Be fair, Alan. She doesn't need to know.'

'And your husband, Karen?'

'None of your business, Alan.' The woman turned to me. 'I haven't seen you before. How long have you been with the Tax Inspectorate?'

'He's new here,' Alastor interrupted. 'But let's not talk shop anymore. I have something much more interesting to discuss.'

'I'm all ears,' the woman said irritably.

Alastor placed his glass on the floor, smoothed his clothes with his hands and addressed his colleagues directly: 'Very well. The subject of our discussion is: your death.'

The man backed away slightly. 'I know you like a joke, Alan, but that's a bit much.'

'Cheap and tasteless,' the woman agreed.

'Nevertheless,' Alastor continued, picking up the champagne bottle, 'you are about to die. However, I want you to know that I'm going to transform the two of you into a wonderful work of art. Your fame will outlive you.'

The woman stood up angrily and crossed the room toward us, perhaps intending to leave, but Alastor stepped forward and swung the bottle quickly and precisely, dealing her head a heavy blow; the deflection diverted the bottle directly onto the man's temple, as neatly as if the demon had calculated everything beforehand. Both victims collapsed to the floor, but Alastor knelt down and struck them several more times, just to be sure.

'Should we wait for them to wake up?' he said. 'It will prolong the performance: I take a finger here, a hand there—sorry, that's a sore point for you, isn't it?—then we hit them again and the cycle repeats. We'd need to gag them too, obviously. We don't want screamers in the house.'

'Just get it over with,' I said.

'You disappoint me, undead. Where's your sense of adventure? I'm actually rather tempted to do something particularly vile... However, perhaps you're right. Gross acts of depravity would ruin the purity of the piece.' He stood up. 'Now, take your clothes off—and don't give me that look, I've seen it all before. I'm not going to touch you; it's simply more practical for this kind of work.'

I kept a watchful eye on him as I stripped down to my boxer shorts; then I left my clothes in a pile by the ensuite bathroom and went to stand by the door. Alastor removed his brown slip-ons and white socks, followed by his leather jacket, skinny blue jeans and white tee shirt.

114

Underneath I saw a creature of volatile energy and terrifying malice, a wiry, muscular, powerful demon—all in a loose-fitting, filthy loin cloth.

'Oh, that body of yours!' he cooed. 'The wounds, those stitches, the missing pieces! My little jigsaw man. All I want is to nibble those threads... But I promised I wouldn't lay a finger on you yet.' He smiled mischievously. 'However I am not forbidden to look, so I beg you—please stay out of my sight. I don't want anything to distract me!'

He rummaged inside his discarded jeans and drew out the most unsettling blade I had ever seen. It was long and wide with a razor-sharp point, serrations along both sides and two cruel spikes attached to the hilt. Its eclectic design seemed to encompass all the purposes of a knife: stabbing, slicing, sawing, carving, cutting, filleting and frightening. He caressed the tapered point lovingly. 'Just like the old days,' he sighed.

Then, with two quick movements of his agile hands, he slit his colleagues' throats.

Blood flowed. It spurted from the holes in the victims' necks and sprayed Alastor's face. It soaked the clothes he tore from their bodies. It seeped and gushed from the wounds he made in their flesh. It turned from a hot, bright liquid to a dark congealing mass.

The demon worked quietly, with a keen eye, like a butcher carving cuts of meat from a carcass. He removed the extremities first, the hands and feet, using the serrated edge to saw through the bones. Next he split their mouths, cheeks and tongues, sliced open their bellies and backs, ruptured their internal organs. Finally, he made what appeared to be random slits in their arms, legs and torsos.

'How can you stand it?' Zoë said.

'What can I do?'

'Something. Anything.'

'Nothing,' I said.

115

The hotel room was an abattoir. Alastor stood at the centre of the carnage, among pools of blood and piles of severed limbs. It was all too strange to take in: individual parts of the scene made sense, but I didn't know what the overall picture was. It was too grotesque.

'You'll want these,' he said, throwing me a couple of knobbly, tumescent knots of meat. 'Essence,' he explained. 'All part of the deal. Give them to Abe with my love.'

Two souls, two random blubbery nubs of flesh, or two cancerous growths pickled in blood; the truth didn't matter anymore.

'Now bring me the needle and thread.'

I edged around the scene to my clothes and placed the souls in my trainers. Then I removed the needle and two reels of twine from my trackpants, clasped them between my stumps, stepped over a pair of amputated feet paddling in a red puddle, and handed them to the demon.

'Nice nails, by the way. Where did you get them done?'

'A place on St Michael's Street,' I said flatly.

'The Oxford Manicure? I know it well.' He stuck out his tongue and began to rearrange the bodies and their various parts. 'I'll pay them a visit this weekend; I really need to get my feet sorted. It's hell wearing shoes with these claws.' He placed the torsos on their sides, facing each other, then tapped me lightly on my big toe. 'The varnish is a nice touch, but I *really* like that skull.'

I said nothing.

'So, this is where I need your help. If you kneel down next to her thigh—don't mind the intestines, I'll put them back later—and put your hand on that flap of skin... That's it. Hold it there while I make some adjustments... Excellent. Now, whatever you do, don't move.'

His hands were quick and skilful: he inserted the man's leg into the woman's calf and attached the foot to her shin, then he thrust the woman's arm into the man's back and sewed her hand to his chest—and he repeated this interpenetrative theme over and over. He joined their

116

faces at the forehead and lips, and slotted their split tongues together as neatly as a mortise joint; he wound their intestines into an intricate, inextricable tangle, so that it was impossible to tell which piece belonged to who; then he opened their hearts and fashioned one giant organ with four silent chambers and a single thick septum.

After repositioning a couple of limbs and making a few finishing touches, he stood up, stepped back and scrutinised his work. I didn't know what he had envisioned but he seemed pleased with the result. To my mind, it looked less like two people who had become one and more like a single entity that was tearing itself apart.

'It is done,' he said with satisfaction. 'I won't ask your opinion, because you'll say something you don't mean and I'll be disappointed in you again, and that will taint our little dance a few moments from now.'

I shuddered. I didn't know if he intended to fuck me, cut me, kill me, or all three; but I didn't want any part of it. I glanced toward the exit, but any thought of escape was futile. I was almost entirely naked and covered in streaks of blood: fleeing to the lounge would cause more problems than staying put.

'Do you want to hear something strange?' he said wistfully. 'I sincerely wish I could bring them back to life right now. I'd like nothing more than to see their lungs breathing in harmony and their hearts beating as one. I'd love to watch those displaced limbs writhing inside their tortured bodies. But I suppose it's foolish to imagine such delights. They would probably just scream in agony...'

Without warning, he leapt toward me, teased the stitching on my right thigh and traced his fingertip along the ragged gash that ran from my hip to my knee. Then he put his lips to my ear and whispered breathily: 'I want to stick my tongue into that wound and tear out your stitches with my teeth—but duty calls, and we must delay our desires.' He turned to the conjoined bodies and addressed them directly. 'I am Alastor, from the Bureau of Infernal Affairs. Thank you for your cooperation. I name this masterpiece in your honour: The Beast With Two Backs. And on a personal level, Tom, Karen... I miss you already.'

'You also missed a hand,' I said.

'What are you talking about, undead?'

'Beneath the bed. There's a spare.'

He lifted the valise, saw the woman's amputated left hand and pulled it free. 'That's annoying,' he sighed. 'Do you want it? You're looking for a new set, aren't you? Take this and you're halfway there.'

'I don't think it works like that.'

'Never mind, then. Perhaps I should attach it to one of the shoulders and make it flap like a chicken wing... No, that would ruin the aesthetic.' He cracked his knuckles irritably. 'Fine. I'm not normally one to take trophies from my prey, but I suppose I have no choice. It can wait, however; right now, you and I are going to have a little *tête-à-tête*—well, we can *start* with the head, anyway...'

'I need to shower first,' I said, stalling for time.

'You're quite the innocent little cherub, aren't you? I *prefer* you bloody, you silly man. Touching and licking are so much more pleasurable with a little lubrication.'

I was trapped. I had run out of words. He was too strong to resist. So I would not resist. It wasn't what I wanted, but it was what I had been given. *I will accept whatever befalls me.* And I didn't need to react negatively to it. I was always looking to feel something, after all. And I would be the envy of the graveyard! If only my neighbours in the soil could see me now... But I couldn't—

'I can't—I won't,' I said.

'Oh, but you *can* and you *will*. I just need to show you *how*.'

He moved toward me with arms outstretched and pinned me against the door—but the door pushed back, gently at first, then with tremendous force, knocking us both across the room. The demon tripped over his artwork, slipped on a patch of congealed blood and fell on his backside; I stumbled into the bed, tried to stop myself falling, and failed miserably. We both looked toward the doorway, where a familiar figure stood, frowning at the scene before him.

'Mal!' said Alastor.

Kaleidoscopic light

'Al,' said Malache, bowing his head. 'I thought you'd be finished by now.'

'My creative impulses have been satisfied, but certain *carnal* needs remain unfulfilled. So I congratulate you on your sense of timing—assuming your intention was to ruin the romance of this moment.'

'It's past midnight. The deal was—'

Alastor waved him away. 'Forget it.'

Malache closed the door behind him and stared at the interlocking bodies on the floor. 'Subtle,' he said. 'Have you tagged them?'

'On the woman's spine. One long string of alternating digits. I'm sure the geniuses in your cadre of bureaucrats can work it out.'

'What about the gift for the overseer?'

'Stop fretting, you petty little pen-pusher. I gave them to my delightful companion here. They're no longer my responsibility.'

'Fine. You can go now.'

'Allow me to get dressed first, won't you?'

Alastor picked up his knife, wiped the blade on the bed, then pulled his clothes theatrically over his bloody frame. Malache ignored him and turned to me. 'You should get cleaned up. I'll deal with our friend here.'

I moved toward the bathroom but Alastor intercepted me and gave me a gentle peck on the cheek. 'I'm going to dream about you tonight,' he said. 'Fly away and wash that wounded, wonderful body of yours.'

I locked the door behind me, turned on the shower, removed my boxer shorts and stepped into the flow. The heat of the water calmed my troubled mind. For a moment, I watched the blood of two dead people coil around my feet and seep into the drain; then I closed my eyes and thought of nothing.

When I emerged, Alastor was gone and a cold breeze was blowing through a broken window. I noticed fragments of glass on the carpet.

'You're quite safe,' Malache said. 'I told him he couldn't leave via the entrance, so he tried to climb through the window; but it was stuck, so he got angry and punched his way out. There was a terrible racket… Anyway, we're running late. Put your clothes back on— I'll wait for you downstairs.' He opened the door, checked the corridor and left quietly, leaving me alone with Alastor's creation.

I approached the couple slowly, stepping between patches of thick blood until I was standing over them. I hunkered down beside their conjoined heads and stroked their entangled hair softly. 'I hope you find love again,' I said. 'Whoever it's with, wherever you are, whenever it happens.'

I retraced my steps, washed the blood from my hands and got dressed; but when I put on my trainers I felt something soft and knobbly beneath my feet. I removed my shoes and found the two souls Alastor had given me. They were squashed flat: round and thick, with edges that fanned out like sunflower petals. I examined the larger one more closely, and saw colour beneath the dull brown surface: a rainbow of shimmering kaleidoscopic light. I watched the colours flicker awhile, then put the souls in my pocket and made my way down to the lounge.

Malache was waiting for me at the bar. He paid the bill and we headed for the exit.

120

I collected my coat on the way, and quickly patted the inside pocket—the box was still there. Reunion was such sweet relief! Sometimes, in rare moments of optimism, I had the feeling that the box would always find its way back to me, whatever happened... But the world wasn't a fairy tale. It was a Grand Guignol nightmare, in which devils made us believe that evil was good and good was for the weak.

I clung to Malache more tightly than ever as the Vespa skidded and ploughed its way through the snow toward The Chimera.

He unlocked the door to the pub with his skeleton key.

'Everything okay?'

I nodded. 'It's been a long day.'

'Indeed.' He took my withered stumps in his. 'Don't worry about the overseer. All he wants is your obedience: so long as you do as you're told everything will work out fine. He's all bark and no bite—'

'He took my hands from me.'

'Fine. He's *mostly* bark. Anyway, there were mitigating circumstances back then; he's more relaxed these days.' He released my stumps and patted me on the arm. 'Look on the bright side, friend: four souls down, six to go! You know what you're doing now. You feel the rhythm and the pulse. Everything will be a breeze hereafter!'

Tonal variety

The Bookbinders Arms.

I remembered it as soon as I walked in: the old name for this place. How could I have forgotten? The answer had been staring me in the face every day, when I walked into the workshop.

My zombie brain!

The creature was already waiting for me when I reached the alcove. I had grown accustomed to his odour now: rancid, fetid, faecal. It seemed trivial compared to everything else I had experienced in the last three days.

'You're late. Did Alastor detain you for his pleasure?'

'Somewhat.'

'Everywhere he goes, that libidinous beast lingers like a foul stench.' His voice quivered with anticipation. 'Do you at least have a soul for me?'

'I have two.'

'Give them to me now.'

I stood up, placed the souls in front of the lattice and turned around. The instructions were now ingrained: I was an automaton, programmed to do whatever he required. Behind me the grille squeaked open, and I felt the heat and heaviness of the creature beyond. If those clawed hands wanted to tear me apart or drag me into the foul abyss he inhabited, there was nothing I could do to prevent it.

'You may sit.'

I did so. A moment later the sucking, chewing and swallowing began. The demon talked through them.

'Where are your angels now, Half-life? Who defends these little souls?' *Suck*. 'No matter; business is business... And I begin our meeting with another apology. Yesterday, I underplayed your role in my success. I don't wish to overplay it now, but the facts are clear: in exchange for your soul you gave me Hades' lost key, which allowed me to unlock the great gate of hell. It made the transition from the Agency to the Bureau easier than otherwise; without it, our procession to the overworld would have been a slow, sombre slog.' *Chew*. 'It was a timely gift, too. Eternity can be terribly boring, and the Underworld frightfully dull. The same tortures and torments, year on year; the same heat and suffering and endless cries of agony. There's no... tonal variety.' *Swallow*. 'So, if my brain ever became so diseased that it felt the need to thank anyone, you would feature somewhere on the list.'

He continued to chomp, gnaw and slurp, but his mini-speech appeared to be over. I was wondering how he managed to produce so much noise from two small souls, when he started up again.

'Now, tell me your sin.'

'I don't have a sin worth relating.'

'Nonsense. You were human, once. You have a belly full of shame. Every time you open your mouth something vile pops out. Get on with it.'

I searched my mind for something to please him.

'When I was a child I threw one of my father's watches against a wall because I was angry at him—'

'No, no, no!' He slammed his fist and spat something wet through the grille which spattered against my shaven head. 'I want *death*. If you have any hope of reuniting with your soul, you must accept your darkness. The gods and saints have all committed murder! What have you killed?'

'Fine. I'll tell you the reason why I was angry, and that will answer your question.'

'I don't think there was any doubt that my mother loved me when I was growing up,' I began. 'If anything, she loved me too much: there were times when I felt less like a son and more like one of her possessions. My father's feelings toward me were less obvious, however. I believe he was kind, and he loved me in his own way, but he was emotionally distant—so much so that I treasure the only two occasions I recall connecting with him: once, when we rowed a boat up the river, another time when we tried to catch butterflies in a meadow. I don't remember anything else, and the only reasonable explanation is that he was absent.'

'Death does strange things to the mind,' the demon said. 'Perhaps you have simply forgotten those other moments.'

'In any case, it was difficult to get his attention. However, I learned very early that when I was upset my mother would become even more affectionate than normal; so I reasoned, in my childish way, that I could attract my father's love through some misfortune, that he would see how distressed I was and comfort me, physically.' I paused, trying to order the sequence of events in my mind. 'When I was nine years old we bought a puppy. I was the one who took it for walks because my father was always at work and my mother was always busy. I loved that dog, and my father loved it, too. One day I walked it down to the river. There was a stretch of water just below the weir, deep and calm, almost like a pond... And I had the story planned in my mind: I would throw the puppy into the water, it would swim to the bank, I would go home and tell everyone how it had fallen in and nearly died; I would be upset, and my father would feel so grateful he would put his arms around me and hold me. So I stood on the bank, lifted the dog into my arms and threw it in... It tried to swim, but I could see it struggling, and it wasn't getting closer to me; then it started to panic, and it thrashed about and yelped—and then it disappeared beneath the water. I was too afraid to run in and rescue it, because I couldn't swim either and I knew I might drown, just as the dog was drowning as I watched.'

'You psychopath!' the demon interrupted. 'I bet you enjoyed seeing it die, didn't you?'

'No. I went straight home to my parents. I was crying—genuinely, because of the loss of my pet and the fear and guilt writhing in my stomach—and I told my mother the fantasy version of the story, with its tragic ending. She was upset but sympathetic. Then I told my father—'

'And he hugged you, a choir of angels sang, rainbows filled the sky and you all lived happily ever after.'

'No. He said: "What the hell were you doing walking by the river?" Then he didn't speak to me for a whole week... But later that day I went into his study, and I saw one of the watches he used to repair on his desk, and I was so angry with him I picked it up and threw it hard against the wall. It smashed into tiny pieces; I felt terrified and elated all at once. But the weird thing is, I don't remember him reacting to it. I don't remember if he even said anything, then or afterward. It was like the incident never happened.'

A long silence followed. Finally, the demon said:

'This was an improvement. But I've heard enough about your infancy now. Next time, I want to hear about your adulthood—a better tale, a deeper sin, a conscious choice untainted by innocence.'

'Okay,' I said.

I returned to the canal. The snow had melted into a vile, muddy slush that seeped into my shoes and froze my manicured feet. I didn't care. The confession had depressed me. I hadn't thought about that dog for years. Or my anger toward my father.

I found the railway bridge. The air was bitingly cold. I sat down on the grass beneath the arch and gazed at the dark water, and saw stars reflected in the darkness.

The stars shimmered as something disturbed the surface. I saw the dog thrashing in panic as it struggled to swim to the bank. But it didn't get out, it couldn't get out.

It never gets out.

PART FOUR

Orobas the Mad

A dark mirror

That night, I dreamed of the Seven-Eyed Lamb.

It's a bright spring morning. I am standing by Carfax Tower, looking south down the slope of St Aldates. The streets are deserted, but I see a figure running up the hill toward me. At first I think it's a man wearing a mask, but the closer it comes the smaller it seems, and its shape—so ambiguous in the distance—is soon manifest. It is a pure white lamb with seven eyes.

'Hello,' it says. 'Are you my friend?'

'I think so. Why are you wearing that mask?'

'This isn't a mask,' it laughs.

I don't believe it, so I tug gently at its face. Sure enough, the flesh peels away like rubber and the mask hangs loose in my hand.

But there is another face beneath, exactly the same as the one I removed but for a single detail: one of the eyes is blind. I tear off this new face, but there's another beneath it—and another, and another; and every time I remove a mask, another eye is blinded, or gouged out, or burned black.

And all the while the lamb chuckles to itself, as if this is some wonderful game, and it's the only one that knows the rules.

After the sixth mask, a single, glittering eye remains in the centre of its forehead. 'This is as close to my true face as you will ever come,' it says.

'Why did you lie to me?'

'Because evil is a lie and evil is your friend.'

'I don't understand.'

'Show me your soul, then you will see.'

I remove the small wooden box from my coat and place it on the ground. The lid springs open to reveal a shrivelled, black stump within. The lamb lowers its head and bites off a small piece, which it chews indifferently awhile, then swallows.

It looks at me with that solitary eye and says: 'At first I thought it was sweet, then I thought it was bitter, and then I realised it tasted of nothing at all. This is not good.'

'I'm sorry.'

'Your apology is worthless. Atone for your sin.'

It whispers something more, but it's inaudible, so I bend down and put my ear to its lips, but I hear only a senseless bleating. Then the lamb turns around and begins to kick my head and chest with its rear legs, and it doesn't stop kicking—

I opened my eyes. It was not spring. A man was prodding me in the ribs with his finger.

'That's a relief,' he said. 'Sorry for poking you.'

'It's okay,' I mumbled.

'For a minute there I thought you'd left us.'

'I'm still here, I think.'

'Yes, of course.' He rubbed his gloved hands together and looked down the towpath. Then he took out his wallet, removed a note and pressed it into my hand. 'It's too cold a day to be sitting outside.'

'Thank you,' I said.

'You're welcome, friend.'

He walked away. But there was something wrong with me, an abnormal fragility, because his use of the word *friend* made my eyes well with tears.

I couldn't remember what time I had to be at the office, but it didn't seem to matter anymore. The details changed but the pattern remained the same. Sleep, wake, kill. A pattern within a pattern. Work for people, work for Death, work for devils. Another. Obey, resist, break free. And all part of this frantic, futile struggle to exist.

I needed to shake off the morning gloom.

130

I stood up stiffly and walked over to the canal bank. Calm black water, like a dark mirror. I looked down and saw a zombie staring back at me. He looked much like everyone else—a little thinner perhaps, a little paler, more haggard; his eyes were lifeless and his face didn't age. But these variations were superficial, even trivial: beneath his mask, he was fundamentally *different*.

I removed my coat, sweatshirt and tee-shirt, then knelt down and splashed icy water onto my face and chest until I felt awake and alive.

As I waited for my skin to dry, I noticed something on my torso had changed. My tattoo had been augmented: Caym's blood-coloured heart had sprouted a pair of white wings, raised aloft as if about to take flight. They were sewn into my flesh with cooking twine, like cross-stitch; soft, raised dashes of thread. For reasons I couldn't explain, it made me feel good to touch them, to have this new mark on my body. A reward for service. Recognition for a job well done.

I put my clothes back on. I checked the wooden box. Then I pulled my hat over my ears and followed the path into town.

I walked to The Jericho Café on Walton Street, a place I had often visited when I was alive. It was small and private and you didn't need a bank loan to eat there. It hadn't changed much in the last twenty years, either: the same painted walls framed by dark wooden edging, a brightly lit counter serving hot and cold food, two large windows overlooking the street. I ordered a black coffee and a flapjack and sat at a round table in the corner.

Zoë joined me.

'I'm glad we're not stuck in a food bin today.'

'I made a promise to Resh.'

'You said you'd *try*. That doesn't mean you won't.'

I shrugged and sipped at the coffee.

'Do you like her?' she said.

'I think so.'

'She isn't human.'

'I'm not sure I know the difference anymore.'

'*And* she's married.'

'Yeah... Do you want some flapjack?'

'No, thanks.'

I took a piece for myself; it was warm and buttery, soft oats mingling with slices of apple and a hint of cinnamon.

'I'm not in love with her or anything. I don't even know her. But she's kind and she's not afraid to touch me... Anyway, you can't help the way you feel.'

'True. I was beginning to like you too, before you came back that night—'

'Let's talk about it another time.'

I looked through the window, glumly. I saw people who would always be strangers to me, a procession of impenetrable surfaces. I might guess at their feelings from an expression, or the way they held themselves, but I would never know their innermost thoughts. I couldn't see into their hearts.

And they couldn't see the Zoë in my heart.

I knew that she wasn't real. The real Zoë had moved away a long time ago. Maybe she was married with children now, or had decided to travel the world and never stopped; I didn't know and never would. But my heart had transformed her from that flesh-and-blood person into my own private ghost. She would never tell me about her day, or what was bothering her, or who she liked or didn't. She had become nothing more than a phantom sounding board.

And what about me? What was I becoming? If I pulled off the mask, what would I find underneath? Perhaps a thing more devil than human. Or just a husk within a husk within a husk.

132

Sex by description

I checked the clock on the wall behind the bar. It was a quarter to ten. I finished my coffee and cake and persuaded my aching limbs to move. As I was leaving, the barista gave me a cheery wave.

'Happy Christmas,' he said.

'Happy Christmas,' I replied.

The outside world was grey. Dirt had tainted the white snow; nothing pure remained. Snow had melted from the rooves; snow had been trampled to slush and filth on the pavement; the road was a dark river of oil, grime and ice. But I picked my way back to the workshop without a trip, slip or stumble.

No one paid much attention when I walked in. Resh was standing by Nergal's workbench, Dumuzid was nowhere to be seen. Everything else was the same as yesterday, and the day before, and the day before that... Apart from a trail of blood leading from Malache's office to the entrance. And a powerful smell of offal. And the bloody handprints on the back of the door.

'Don't worry about the mess,' said Nergal. 'We had a delivery, but one of them tried to escape. Almost made it, too.' He beckoned me to join him. 'Take a look at this.'

I stepped gingerly over the blood trail and crossed to his table. He and Resh were watching a pornographic movie on a laptop. The screen showed a man in a gimp mask and two scantily-dressed milkmaids sitting together on a bale of straw inside a haybarn. Three people in tight-fitting bird costumes entered the scene: their names were Chicken Lickin', Cocky Blocky and Ducky Fucky. They all seemed pleased to see each other; but the scenario struck me as implausible.

I turned away and approached Dumuzid's workbench, where I saw the Bible he was rebinding for his client. It was open at the Song of Songs—a passage I had never bothered to read in my twenty-eight years of life, or any time thereafter.

I read it now.

Its words and rhythms mesmerised me: it was an earthly hymn to the divine, a poem of love and sex and holy union, a voyage through language itself—a work so breathtakingly beautiful that it choked my heart.

Dumuzid appeared beside me. 'I'm going to change "Rose of Sharon" to "Nipplewort of Slough",' he said. 'And "your eyes are like doves" would sound better as "your thighs are like slugs—"'

'Leave it alone!' I snapped.

He sat down quietly and ran his fingers over the page. 'Something the matter, zombie?'

'Spare us a few scraps of civilisation, at least.'

'Us?'

'Humanity. The living.'

'Ah.'

His rheumy eyes studied me but he didn't say anything. I turned aside and watched the other two watching their movie, my eyes still warm with tears.

'Is that fennel?' said Nergal.

'It's a leek, you twit. Fennel is fat at the bottom.'

'Birds don't eat leeks! Why is he shoving it in the cock's mouth?'

'That's not his mouth.'

'Oh.'

'So you identify more with the living than the dead?'

'Most of the time,' I said.

'And yet every night you watch them die.'

'I can't fight a demon.'

'Few can. But—what is the Lifer phrase?—*there is more than one way to skin a cat*. Personally, I find the most efficient technique is to decapitate the animal then

134

strip its hide from the neck down; but I admit that other methods are possible. You should bear that in mind.'

I had no idea what he was talking about.

He gripped my hands weakly. 'I like you, zombie. You would make a fine devil. And because you have performed satisfactorily and kept the demons off the streets, I will make an exception on this occasion: I will leave this trivial little passage as it is... But I would ask you, respectfully, not to tell me what I can or cannot do again.'

I nodded, and turned away.

'I'm bored now. I think we've seen all the positions and combinations. Who posted this anyway?'

'Dripcrack.'

'The one with the Gila monster?'

'That's Snotbush. Dripcrack has a Komodo dragon.'

'Right. Called Garga.'

'Gargon.'

'How do you remember all this shit, Resh?'

'I pay attention, you thick aurochs.'

I wondered where Malache was. For all their talk of efficiency, it seemed odd that I should come here every morning when I could just as easily collect the envelope in the evening. Perhaps it was a test of loyalty, or an ingrained habit; or it was simply convenient, because it coincided with breakfast, a haircut, a pedicure—and whatever else they had planned for me.

'You might want to see this, Rabbit.'

Resh's voice woke me from my reverie. I gambolled toward her like an eager little white lamb.

'Are we still on Darknet?' Nergal said.

'Uh-huh. Alastor posted these himself.'

The haybarn was gone from the laptop. In its place I saw a dozen thumbnails of the hotel bedroom and the two victims from last night. As Resh clicked through them, I read the captions beneath: the room itself ('the arena where

I fought my prey'), the conjoined couple ('my chef-d'œuvre'), and a voyeuristic image of a blurry, naked figure in the bathroom ('my delightfully coy assistant'), which turned out to be me.

'We should tell him to delete that one,' said Resh.

'But you can't *really* see who it is,' Nergal countered.

'It's the principle, you lout.'

Dumuzid looked over my shoulder. 'His buttocks are getting plenty of likes, though.'

'Which merely proves that the internet is awash with asinine commentary and cheap titillation.'

Nergal shrugged. 'I'll email him. See if I can change his mind.'

I walked away again. I didn't really have anywhere to go, but Malache still hadn't arrived.

I found myself standing outside his office. The metallic blinds were down but not closed. I looked inside and was surprised to see Malache sitting at his desk. Sensing my presence, he looked up and gave me a cheery wave. I opened the door and walked in.

'I was expecting you an hour ago,' he said.

'I've been here since ten o'clock.'

'And no one told you I was waiting?'

'They were busy doing... other things.'

He raised a silencing finger as he briefly examined his phone. I sat down and looked around. There was a trail of blood on the floor here, too. *One of them tried to escape.*

'Alastor *adores* you,' he said at last. 'He's given you a glowing report; says he'd love to work with you again. I'd be surprised if the feeling is mutual, though.'

I shook my head.

'Anyway, listen. I have another proposition for you... I know you're only here to get your fingers back in some kind of working order, but have you thought about your options in the longer term? What are you going to do next week, next month, next year? I put it to you that you could

136

do much worse than stay with us. Everyone here likes you, the demons are satisfied with your contribution, the overseer has spoken about you in encouraging terms... Don't make the decision now, obviously; but assuming the feedback remains positive and everything turns out as it should, I think there could be a place in the Bureau for someone like you.' He studied me for a response, but I remained expressionless. 'Look—everything has changed. This isn't the town you grew up in or the world you knew before your death. People live in their own private bubbles now, insulated against one another; and rather than fighting that trend, we actively encourage it. Once you remove the old criteria that defined humanity—kindness, empathy, courage, honesty—it makes this place so much easier to control; which, in turn, makes life simpler for us all. It has advantages for you too, of course: in some ways, everyone is a zombie now, but you're one of the lucky few who realise it. That's a useful skill in the current climate.'

'Not everyone lives in a bubble. Only this morning I met someone who was concerned about me. I didn't ask him for help; he gave it freely.'

'A statistical blip, that's all; a black sheep... In any case, do you believe he got nothing in return for his concern? All relationships are transactional. His heart would have swelled with pride for his noble deed; he would have felt the smug satisfaction of the superior to the inferior; he would gain kudos from sharing your story with his friends and colleagues. Altruism is a fantasy: actions are motivated by self-interest.'

'Even if what you say is true, it doesn't matter. His kindness made me feel better. It was a good thing.'

'We tend not to frame the world in those terms anymore; the concepts of good and evil are outdated. We speak of success and failure, what works and what doesn't, who wins and who loses. The end is what counts: the means is just a debating point for fools.' He leaned back in his chair. 'But even if you were to take the moral view, I believe we *are* a force for good in this world. We're making it more efficient. We're excising the complexity and the artifice. We're removing the nuance from discussion by degrees, so that everyone can participate. The Bureau isn't a dictatorship, it's a democracy—and in a democracy a small number of people suffer so that the majority prosper.'

'I think you fundamentally misunderstand people.'

'And I believe we understand them all too well.' He leaned across the table and placed his hands on mine. 'But your objection is precisely why I value your contribution so highly. You have a genuine connection to the living that has been, and will continue to be, very useful to us. You are a necessary corrective to our vanity and pride— and I would urge you to seriously consider my offer of further employment... In the meantime, how about a drink? Or a cigarette? Or perhaps something a little more... *illicit*.'

'I'm fine, thanks.'

'I hope you're not feeling sorry for yourself. You and I might have different views about this world, but I think we can both agree that—apart from the terrible cold— there's nowhere else we would rather be right now.'

I nodded reluctantly.

'Excellent! Friendships grow in common ground. I hope ours will be a long and lasting one.'

'Do you have the note?' I said.

Less like an outsider

I left Malache's office with a white envelope in my pocket and questions buzzing around my head like bluebottles. The bluebottles were arguing among themselves. They couldn't decide whether I should live or die.

138

Dumuzid was waiting for me. He looked like a dishevelled shop dummy. 'I drew the short straw,' he said dolefully. 'It's my job to chaperone you today.'

I said nothing, hoping the buzzing would stop.

'Actually, that was a joke. I don't mind escorting you. It's a change from dealing with the living.'

'Where are we going?'

'To smarten you up.'

He returned to his workbench and rummaged through a dozen cardboard boxes beneath the table. After a few mild curses he found a pair of furry snow boots and something that resembled the pelt of a brown bear, with hat and gloves to match. He put them on solemnly, devoting special care and attention to the fit and fastenings. Finally, he checked his appearance in a small mirror on the shelf behind his desk, patted himself on the belly and joined me at the door.

'Let's go,' he said.

I followed him out. From behind he looked even more ursine. His bear feet crunched on the hard snow, his furry body clambered onto the green Vespa at the kerb, his hairy paws grasped the handlebars and started the engine. When I climbed onto the seat behind him I put my arms around him and buried my face in his warm pelt.

He was a cautious driver. He kept to the speed limit and stopped at every junction; he indicated his direction of travel and was polite to his fellow road users; he even apologised to a pedestrian who lurched into his path. The whole journey was a quiet, soothing experience which lulled me into a pleasant torpor. I was on the edge of falling asleep when it ended.

We parked down a side street off The High. I dismounted, the bear engaged the kickstand and we walked back to the main road. We arrived at a gentleman's outfitters called Goatherd and Forrester, whose refined wood-and-glass shopfront occupied the whole block. The name, like The Chimera, had changed since my death, and I couldn't recall the original now; but I remembered that the man who had killed me had once bought a suit here. He might even have been wearing it when he threw me into the alligator pen.

We walked inside. We were immediately and aggressively attended to by a young, impeccably attired shop assistant. 'Good morning, gentlemen,' he said obsequiously. 'How can I help you today?'

'My friend requires a little enhancement,' Dumuzid replied. 'Jacket, trousers, shirt, maybe a pair of socks.' He turned to me. 'How about a coat?'

'My coat's fine,' I said, patting the box in my pocket.

'No coat. And no tie, either. I'm thinking smart-casual, but not cocaine-snorting-city-trader smart, and not dress-down-for-work-day casual.'

'I'm sure we have what you're looking for,' the assistant said blandly. 'What are your measurements, sir?'

I shrugged.

'I think you'll need to start from scratch,' Dumuzid said.

The assistant produced a soft tape measure from his waistcoat, unrolled it, and began a graceful dance, orbiting me, extending his arms, positioning the tape against various parts of my body and making notes in a ring-bound notepad.

I looked around while he worked. The interior hadn't changed from my last visit, when I was alive, though the styles were a little more flamboyant. All manner of clothing was on display: suits, jackets and trousers, shirts, ties and waistcoats, socks, shoes and gloves, belts, scarves and handkerchiefs. The material came in lambswool and merino, cotton and corduroy, moleskin and tweed; the patterns ranged from striped through all kinds of tartan to all manner of checks; from Paisley to Argyle to houndstooth; from floral to plain. I could have my clothes bespoke or take them off the peg—

'Could you lift your arms for me, sir...? A little higher, perhaps? Many thanks. And if you'll just turn around, I can get the measure of your—exactly so. That's the last one. Thank you for your patience.' He tore off the notepaper, folded it in two and placed it in the hollow where my palm used to be. 'The jackets are over there to your left, shirts can be found at the rear, trousers are on the right. If there is anything else I can do for you, please don't hesitate to ask.'

He glided away as if he was on wheels.

I glanced at the note. I had a twenty-six inch waist and a thirty-two inch chest; a series of numbers were also applied to leg, inside leg, neck girth, shoulder span, arm length, sleeves, and so on. I handed the paper to Dumuzid.

'Let's just see what fits me,' I said.

We headed to the back of the shop first, where I found some Argyle socks and a long-sleeved Black Watch tartan flannel shirt. Next we went to the trouser section, where I picked up a pair of blue jeans and a belt; then to the shoes, where I selected some tan leather brogues. Finally, we trawled the jackets until I discovered a single-breasted navy blazer, which proved the perfect complement to the rest of my outfit.

'You might as well put everything on now,' Dumuzid said. 'We'll dump those rags you're wearing when we leave.'

I nodded. I felt no great attachment to my clothes, even though I'd worn them for the past two decades. They were a mask for my stitches, a dressing for my wounds; they kept the rain off in winter, they stopped my skin burning in summer. A zombie chooses what he wears on the basis of availability and need, and is generally indifferent to the ever-changing demands of fashion; and yet it felt good to choose clothes that I liked—clothes that made me appear less like an outsider.

Dumuzid explained our decision to the assistant and paid the bill; then he followed me to the changing room and waited outside. I slipped off my trainers and asked him to swap the elastic laces into the brogues; I could have done it myself, but not speedily. Finally, I stripped down to my boxer shorts and leaned against the wall; I left my new identity on the hangars for now.

'May I ask a personal question?' I said.

'Of course.'

'Are you a shapeshifter?'

'I prefer the term metamorph, since the transformation involves more than mere shape; but yes... As a matter of fact, in the Underworld I am a rather handsome creature with a killer stare and youthful skin.'

'And Malache is a metamorph, too?'

'Naturally. Devils could not walk the earth safely or effectively if they inhabited their innate forms.'

'Do you know his alternate shape?'

He took a while to answer, which made me wonder if I had contravened his sense of etiquette; but his tone was calm. 'Now that you ask, I don't believe I've ever seen it. I had few interactions with him before we came here; and as I explained, he is somewhat secretive. In any case, some devils consider their transformation a private matter... Why do you ask?'

I wasn't entirely sure, because it involved connections I was only just beginning to make, but my answer wasn't untruthful: 'He mentioned a long-term position at the Bureau. If we're going to work together, I'd like to know as much about him as possible.'

'What can I say? He's a nice guy.' He passed the brogues, now with lock laces, under the door. 'As for you—I'm sure you'll fit right in, once we've rounded off those rough edges.'

I dressed slowly, savouring the freshness of new clothes against my skin: the soft warmth of the shirt, the solid roughness of the jeans, the smart lightness of the jacket on my shoulders. The diamond pattern of the socks appealed to my eye; the shoes were easily the most comfortable I had ever worn. And when I finally looked in the mirror, I felt like a different person. I felt like a Lifer.

I opened the door. Dumuzid seemed genuinely delighted. 'The clothes make the man! A magnificent metamorphosis!'

The assistant wheeled into view. 'I couldn't agree more, sir. An excellent choice: simple but stylish. Could I interest you in a replacement for—I hesitate to be critical, but the stunning clarity of your outfit rather emphasises the contrast—that dishevelled beanie?'

'No,' I said.

'And who am I to argue? It's been a pleasure to serve you gentlemen. Would you like me to dispose of your former attire?'

'We'll do it later,' said Dumuzid.

The assistant bowed his head, then slipped silently away.

At no point during this exchange had I felt under threat. If anything, I was in control of the situation; my transformation had given me confidence. As I left the changing room my stride was purposeful, my back straight and my head high—

'Don't forget your coat,' Dumuzid said.

The blood turned to ice in my veins. How could I have been so wrapped up in my appearance that I had forgotten what was most important to me? I cursed my stupidity, then returned for the coat—and its wooden box—and headed for the exit. My companion followed, carrying my old rags.

There was a waste bin outside. Dumuzid stuffed my tracksuit bottoms into it, and was about to dump the rest when I stopped him. 'I've changed my mind,' I said.

He looked at me wearily. 'Can't let go of the past?'

'Something like that.'

'Wait here. I'll get you a bag.'

He dropped the remaining clothes on the pavement and went back into the shop, returning a couple of minutes later with a blue canvas rucksack. I extracted my tracksuit trousers, folded my other clothes neatly and packed everything away. Then I fastened the leather straps and slung the rucksack over my shoulder.

'Unless you need something else, I'll get back to work,' he said. 'Do you mind if I leave you here?'

'Not at all. Thanks for everything.'

He smiled. 'You have a devil's politeness.'

I accompanied him to the Vespa. He lowered the kickstand then climbed stiffly onto the seat; but he didn't leave immediately.

'That box in your coat... Why do you want to open it?'

'I need to know if my soul is still there.'

'And if it isn't?'

'I won't stop looking until I find it.'

After a pause, he said: 'You should keep it closed. Once you open it there's no predicting what will happen. Perhaps you'll absorb your soul, or perhaps it will fly away on the breeze and you'll never see it again. Even if you do manage to hold onto it, there's no guarantee you will like what you become.'

'I'll take my chances.'

He grunted. 'To be dead is to feel safe, because nothing happens. To be alive is to feel unsafe, because everything happens. Why not remain a zombie? Limit what will happen to you. Choose how safe you want to feel.'

'No,' I said. 'I want to live again.'

And in that moment, in that place, I felt like I believed it.

A brown bear puttered off on a green scooter. I watched him turn onto the main road, then I headed in the opposite direction. Eventually I came to Christ Church Meadow, a wedge of land between the Isis and the Cherwell rivers. A few well-trodden paths criss-crossed the field, and there were dog tracks here and there, but the snow was largely untouched. If the demon had burned my hands in this place, I might have soothed the pain much sooner. And when I returned to Zoë's flat I would not have seemed so strange.

144

'I didn't think you *would* come back,' she said.

'I wasn't sure, either. I knew we had no future, but I wanted to show you what I had become.'

'You freaked me out.'

'I know. I'm sorry... The demon abandoned me by the river and the Agency was in flames, but the thought of you made me stand up and walk. I carried myself to your flat. There was a light in your window—'

'I was reading in bed.'

'—and I staggered to your front door, and even then I couldn't decide whether I should ring your bell or not. I just stood there, my hands burning in agony, clutching a box I believed contained some supernatural essence. And I convinced myself, I thought: maybe it will be okay, maybe she'll understand, I can tell her everything and she'll see who I really am, and it will be fine, because love will make it fine. So I knocked on your door—'

'Shh,' she whispered. 'Not yet.'

'But I need to tell you.'

'No. Let's do something fun instead.'

'What should we do?'

'Use your imagination.'

Without thinking, I left the footpath and ran into the snow, which lay deep and soft on the meadow. I lay down on my back and spread my limbs wide. I flapped my arms like a bird to make a pair of wings; I moved my legs to make a long, white dress. I sat up in the imprint of the snow angel I had made, and smiled.

'Not bad,' she said. 'Now make a snow demon.'

'I wouldn't know how.'

'It's much the same as the angel.'

'I don't think that's true.'

'You know it is.'

She was a voice on the wind, a feeling in the air. A half-remembered ghost.

'Are you going away now?'

'Yes—but listen. You're always telling me you want to feel alive, and how that thing in the box will make you whole. But maybe it's not so much that you want to live again... Maybe you just want to love again.'

Abandoned places

The sun broke through the clouds and filled the meadow with light. I took the envelope from my pocket, tore at the wax seal and shook the contents onto the snow. Two photographs this time, both showing a young woman with blonde hair in a pony tail, and a curious smile.

The note said: *Female thing 0772244661188. Female thing 0772244661189. Ignore the evocation. Clip-clop, trick-track, time is ticking to six of the clock—Master of Disguise.*

I crushed the paper and photos into a ball. I was about to put them in my pocket when I saw a black dog bounding across the snow toward me, pursued at a slower pace by its owner, a man in a blue tracksuit. The hound arrived quickly, leapt at my body, fell away, rolled in the snow, slavered, jumped up, twisted in mid-air, landed heavily, sat down and looked at me expectantly.

'Hello, boy,' I said.

It nuzzled me with its snout, licked the skin, sniffed at my hooked palm, found the ball of rubbish and wolfed it down in one gulp.

'Good dog,' I said.

The man joined us, gasping for breath. He reached for the animal but it eluded his grasp and scampered away through the drifts. 'Sorry,' he panted. 'I untied the lead and he just took off.'

'It's no problem.'

'He didn't attack you, did he?'

'No,' I said. 'He's a very good boy.'

I spent the afternoon in the Westgate shopping mall. I didn't shuffle into glass doors like the zombies in *Dawn of the Dead*, but I did wander around the shops gazing vacantly at a variety of consumer goods. I also spent too long staring at the twinkling lights of the artificial Christmas tree in the square—until I realised that my mouth was hanging open and I had started to drool.

I still had plenty of money left from this morning, so I bought a coffee and a blueberry muffin from one of the snack bars and sat on a rotating stool, rotating awhile. I didn't know if it was the Christmas spirit, my new clothes or the prospect of a new job, but the world seemed less terrifying than of late. I almost felt like I belonged here.

Time passed. I thought of nothing much. Whenever an uncomfortable idea entered my head, I simply looked at nearest storefront and the discomfort went away. This wasn't a bad way to live, I thought. It was preferable to suicide.

When the sun went down I left for the office. On my way out of the mall I noticed a machine that resembled a large eyeball on a stalk. The stalk acted as a slender support, the eyeball was transparent and contained dozens of small plastic capsules. A colourful sticker on the front proclaimed, 'Gotta Gacha? Getta Gacha!', and featured images of devils with tridents, comical cross-eyed demons, severed heads in Santa hats and green-faced zombies with their arms outstretched. There was a mechanism to exchange money for one of these toys, so I put a coin in the slot and turned the handle. A yellow capsule dropped into a metal container beneath; I picked it up but couldn't see what was inside. However, in tiny print around the circumference I read the words: Green Devil Recycling.

I wanted the zombie figurine, but didn't want the disappointment of it *not* being the zombie, so I put the unopened gacha in my rucksack and walked the short distance back to Babylon Bookbinders.

'Right on time,' said Malache, emerging from his office. He straightened his tie and ushered me out to the waiting Vespa. 'Great outfit, by the way. Smart but not intimidating; perfect for the job.'

I climbed aboard the scooter and held onto his waist; he accelerated away in a spray of ice and slush. Everything felt natural thereafter: the ill-tempered hum of the engine, the skidded turns and uneven jolts, the warmth of his back against my cheek. His jacket wasn't as soft as Dumuzid's bear coat, but its familiarity was comforting.

It was a long journey. Beneath a clear cold sky and the light of a full moon, we left the outskirts of Oxford and drove deep into the countryside, first along a main highway, then via a series of winding roads and twisting lanes to an isolated hamlet. We passed a pub and a row of cottages before arriving at a small repair shop; Malache steered the Vespa onto a gravel forecourt and the engine choked to a stop.

'The prey is next door. Walk down the track and open the gate; there's an abandoned house at the end. Orobas will meet you there.'

'Is there anything I need to know?'

'His style is a little unusual, but if you keep your distance you'll be fine... I'll see you in a couple of hours; the demon will be long gone by then.'

I dismounted. He sped away with a wave. When he was gone there was only silence and moonlight.

I followed the track for a hundred yards. It was rutted and wet with melted snow, so I hopped over the holes and walked along the edge to keep my shoes clean. At the end I found a wooden five-barred gate with a rope latch. I lifted the rope, passed through a clump of trees and arrived at the meeting place.

It was an old, two-storey derelict house. Every aspect was overgrown: bushes and creepers had invaded the driveway, trees pushed at the brickwork and slate, grass

148

grew tall in front of the windows and a climbing ivy had taken hold of one gable end. The building itself was no better maintained: all the windows were broken, the frames had splintered or come loose, and the roof had suffered a partial collapse. The whole house was possessed by an air of neglect; I couldn't fathom why anyone should be here.

The front door was hanging off its hinges, so I eased my way inside. The interior was even more dilapidated than the exterior: the ground and first floor ceilings had been destroyed, leaving an unbroken view to a hole in the roof, through which moonlight entered and illuminated the scene. The ground floor partitions were still standing, but the walls were damp and covered in strips of peeling wallpaper, and the bare wooden floors were black with mould and beset by ruin: fallen timber, chunks of plaster, discarded mattresses, smashed porcelain.

I stepped over the shattered remains of a bathroom sink and opened the door to what had once been the lounge. I saw an old sofa, a couple of broken chairs, two fallen roof beams and all kinds of household litter piled against the walls—but the centre of the room had been cleared of debris. Within this hollow, surrounded by the ramparts of decay, two women in matching jeans and hoodies stood with their heads bowed.

Behind them I saw a makeshift altar: a small table covered with a red cloth, into which the design of a black pentagram had been sewn. On top of the cloth they had placed a sheep's skull, which appeared to have retained some fleshy remains of the sheep; around the skull, in a rough circle, were arranged five candles, a couple of twisted figurines and a silver goblet. The women were standing barefoot on the wooden floor inside a pattern of chalked circles and triangles; their hands were folded, as if in prayer, and they were muttering something I couldn't hear. One of them held a sheet of paper inscribed with a complex sigil consisting of triangles, circles, crosses and curls.

All of this I absorbed in a moment, because almost as soon as I entered they turned around. I saw that they were twins, in their late teens or early twenties. I had no idea why they had come to this place, and they clearly felt the same way about me.

'Who are you?'

'What are you doing here?'

'Perhaps he's the demon.'

'Don't be stupid. He's too skinny.'

'And ancient. What is he—like, thirty?'

'Older. Wait, are you the police?'

'Or do you own this place?'

'Neither,' I said. 'I'm just looking for somewhere to sleep.'

'In those clothes? I don't think so.'

'No one believes that, loser.'

'Anyway, you can't sleep here.'

'It's already occupied.'

'So why don't you get lost?'

'What's your name, weirdo?'

'I don't have a name,' I said.

'What the fuck?'

'What a freak.'

'We should throw him out.'

'Let's ask him nicely first.'

'Okay. Would you kindly fuck off, anonymous loser guy?'

'You should run,' I said. 'It's going to kill you.'

'What?'

'Who?'

'The demon,' I said. 'It's coming.'

'Well, *duh*. What do you think we're doing here?'

'We're summoning it right now.'

'We want it to come.'

'It's going to help us.'

'And you're going to leave.'

'So, as I think we already said, *fuck off*.'

I looked at the ground despondently; then I turned and left. A zombie can't convince anyone to do anything—he

150

barely has power over himself—and I realised I couldn't save them. For a moment I considered walking away altogether, but I couldn't do that either, so I waited by the front door. And listened:

'Do you think he's gone?'

'Honestly, I don't give a fuck.'

'We'll kick the shit out of him if he comes back.'

'That'll be fun.'

'Have you got the grimoire?'

'It's in my bag.'

'Good. How do we start?'

'We command it to appear in the name of god.'

'Which god?'

'I don't think it matters.'

'Hold up the sigil, then. Let's get started.'

After a pause, one of them began to read something in Latin, and though I didn't understand what she was saying, I felt a certain energy in her words, which translated to the world around me: a vibration in the air, a rumble in the earth.

'Do you think that's enough?'

'Let's wait and see.'

'I sensed something, though.'

'Me, too. I think it's going to work.'

'What should we ask for first?'

'I want her house.'

'And her three cars.'

'I want her horse.'

'And the stables.'

'And the stable boy.'

'Then I want her to suffer.'

'Smash her mobile phone.'

'Break her legs.'

'Give her a disease.'

'Make her really ugly.'

'After that we'll kill her.'

'A long, slow death.'

'Excruciatingly painful.'

'It'll last for years.'

'Shh! Did you hear something?'

'Do you think it's coming?'

'I don't know. Listen!'

I heard heavy footfalls and the laborious panting of a large animal; then I felt warm breath on the back of my neck and sensed something hot and sweaty that smelled of fields and farmyards. The hair on my flesh prickled as an aristocratic masculine voice whispered softly in my right ear.

'I am Orobas from the Bubble of Internal Bananas,' he said. 'Don't take this personally, but I'm going to stamp and trample you to deadly death.'

I turned around.

I saw a pantomime horse.

Crazy Horses

'Wait,' I said.

It wasn't clear at first if what I was looking at was a costume or the true form of the demon. The piebald pattern was unvarying but not unnatural, the proportions were unusual but not grotesque; the teeth were large and prominent but not beyond the range of equine possibility. But as soon as it moved, I saw the seam down the middle and the second body beneath the skin; and when it spoke, the voice came from another head within that goggle-eyed, buck-toothed face.

'Why wait until later when I've waited until now?'

'Because I'm not your prey.'

'How can you be certain, two-legs?'

'I'm not female and there's only one of me.'

The creature whinnied impatiently. 'But the tracker led me here!'

'My scent is only a guide—'

152

'Scent?' he neighed. 'You mean that weak little odour wafting from your skinny little body? No, no, that's not it. My sensor tells me you're the one—'

'They're inside,' I interrupted.

'Inside this building?'

'Yes.'

'Both of them?'

'Yes.'

'Then why are we standing here? Lead on, whatever you are, with your inadequate limbs, onward, forward!'

I had to wedge the broken door against the wall and clear away the rubble and wood before he deigned to walk inside. 'I'm a prince of the Underworld,' he explained. 'I command twenty legions. You can't expect me to do it myself!' He whickered softly and pushed his cloth snout close to my face. 'One more thing before we begin: are you now, or have you ever been, a hippophobe?'

'I don't think so.'

'And you have no problem with how I look?'

I shrugged. 'You are what you are.'

'Exactly. Live and let live. Apart from my prey, who should be killed. Now, where are they?'

I opened the door to the lounge.

'Who's this?'

'What are you?'

'I am Orobas, from the Boutique of Eternal Delights—'

'Are you kidding me?'

'This is bullshit.'

'You're not Orobas. You're some guy in a costume.'

'The same guy as before. Putting on a different voice.'

'Fucking joker.'

'Let's teach him a lesson.'

'Grab that stick.'

'Pick up that rock.'

I watched from the doorway as the twins launched a two-pronged assault on the horse with whatever weapons

153

they could find. It began with sticks and rocks but soon progressed to lengths of timber and pieces of furniture, and their attack could hardly have been less violent had they been demons themselves. Blow upon blow struck Orobas on the head, neck, legs, back, belly and rump; and all I heard from the beast were moans of pain, yelps of indignation, cries for help.

'Quickly, undead! Free me from this confounded skin!'

I didn't move, but his words alerted the women to my presence. They looked several times from me to the horse and back again, all the while continuing to clobber the creature, but less frequently, and with longer pauses between blows.

'Wait, if he's there...'

'Then who's this?'

'I don't know.'

'Let's find out.'

'Tear off the mask.'

'You grab the head.'

'You grab the tail.'

They tugged at his front and rear, straining their sinews as they vainly tried to rip the costume from the demon's body; Orobas responded with kicks and bites, but his attempts to connect were equally unsuccessful. An impasse ensued.

I entered the room and approached warily. The twins turned toward me; I raised my stumps in a gesture of peace. 'It's joined in the middle,' I said.

They looked at each other, smiled, then quickly found a fold of cloth concealing a zip; shortly thereafter, with a few moans of protest at his rough handling, Orobas was freed from his prison.

The demon who emerged was not what I had expected. He had a long head and a golden mane, powerful hindquarters and an unruly tail; but his chest and arms were human, and he stood upright on two legs. He stared at his

154

attackers, eyes black with wrath. Realising their error, the women quickly prostrated themselves before him.

'Mighty Orobas, forgive us.'

'We intended no offence.'

'We summoned you for a purpose.'

'To wreak vengeance on our enemy.'

'To give to us that which is hers.'

'Which she doesn't deserve.'

'And we so richly do.'

'Powerful prince, we ask that you serve us—'

'I am not your servant!' the demon said ferociously. 'I am Orobas from the Bureau of Infernal Affairs, and you will die beneath my hooves!'

'Well, that didn't go as planned,' one twin said.

'Did we do something wrong?' the other replied.

Orobas leapt toward them, a wild stallion, choleric and unrestrained, kicking and whinnying, rearing over them and bearing down, knocking them to the ground, stamping hard on their soft flesh and fragile bones. They resisted for a while, but at last merely clung to each other, trying to protect themselves—and for a few more seconds they whimpered and cried, until those giant hooves came down upon their skulls, and the only sounds that followed were pounding, cracking, squelching.

And the demon didn't stop.

I watched numbly as he stamped on a rib that lay in a mass of blood and torn clothing.

'Why didn't you help me?' he panted.

'I don't know.'

'I should kill you for your disobedience.'

'You should. Will you?'

'I will not. A prince's wrath is tempered by mercy. I pardon your weakness.'

'If I put my head beneath your hoof, would you crush it?'

'Is that what you want, two-legs?'

'Maybe.'

Stamp, trot, stamp. Like a mad dressage. Pulped flesh, splintered bone. Nothing remotely human.

'Why did you wear that silly costume? They were summoning you. You could have appeared as you are.'

'Yes, but how does one get here? One cannot walk this world as a horse demon; it would frighten the children and old ladies. The Boss eschews such behaviour, so I called on the help of my friends in low places, and they fashioned this disguise. All I needed was a clip-clop, trip-trap verbal routine to go with the choppers and swivel eyes, and my cover was complete. I passed through this world unhindered.'

'You're strange,' I said.

'On the contrary, I am no different from you. The undead put on a mask to prevent others from seeing who they really are. They fake conversations with people they would rather avoid. They hide in plain sight.'

'I don't kill people for pleasure.'

'But you watch them die for your profit. You lead hunters to their prey, then you stand aside and wash your hands of the whole business.' He whinnied with delight. 'Come and join me, insignificant thing. Get those deformed hands dirty; revel in this flesh and blood!'

'No, thanks.'

My refusal had no effect: he continued to reduce the bodies to a thin, red mash beneath his hooves. For a while I watched him trample back and forth, felt the splashes of blood and sprays of gore; until my mind couldn't take anymore and sought a distraction.

It found my parents in the darkness and dragged them to this place of death.

'Why did you bring us here?' my mother said. 'This is horrible.'

'It's shameful,' my father added.

'I wanted you to see what I've become.'

'This isn't how we raised you,' they said in unison.

156

'No. But it's who I am.'

'You could be arrested.'

'It's a bit late for that, dad.'

'You're not blaming us, are you?' my mother asked.

'No. You were perfect in every way. The fucking perfect parents of a fucking perfect child in a perfectly fucking happy home.'

'So why did you bring us here?' they repeated.

I lay against a pile of rubble and thought about the answer for some time.

'Because I wanted you to be proud of me,' I said.

They disappeared. All the people I have ever known have disappeared. One minute they're here, the next they're gone. Like an existential game of hide-and-seek: the hiders are never found, but you keep looking because you can't accept that they've left the game.

'This is cool!' a small voice said.

A boy was sitting beside me; the boy was me. I remembered his wild brown hair, and the life in those dark eyes. Eyes that saw worlds in a grain of sand, oceans in a drop of water.

'Is it real?' he said.

'Yeah, it's real.'

'Ugh. What did they do to deserve it?'

'Nothing. They were just in the wrong place at the wrong time.'

'So why were they killed? What's the point?'

'There's no point to death. It just is.'

'I don't understand,' he said.

'Me neither,' I replied.

I was alone again, watching a mad horse demon trample flesh and blood beneath his hooves. After a time he lay down and rolled in the gore, covering himself from mane to tail, lapping up the blood, whinnying. At last he raised himself upright and stood on his hind legs once more, nodding his equine head with joy.

'A pity you wouldn't join me, undead. You should not deny yourself the sensual pleasures.'

'I see no pleasure here.'

'Then you need better eyes. Violence is no less gratifying than any other amusement; killing is the ultimate indulgence.'

'Not for your victims.'

'A parochial view, but I forgive you.' He crossed the floor toward me, dripping bloody pulp from his torso. 'Life and death are inevitable, and they are engaged in perpetual conflict. But that conflict doesn't have to be tragic. It can be a thing of beauty: a shadow play in which the protagonists are first illuminated by light, then fall prey to the dark. A painting in which the dazzling chiaroscuro of being—well, you wouldn't understand, would you?' He turned away in disgust. 'Perhaps you could make yourself useful instead. I have one more task before I leave; your assistance would be appreciated.'

He trotted over to the discarded pantomime horse and dragged it toward the slaughter. Immediately he began to scoop the remains into the empty costume.

I stared at the ground.

'I am asking for your aid, undead.'

'I know.'

'Do you refuse to give it?'

'Yes.'

'Your disobedience is noted.'

He shovelled the crushed flesh, blood, organs, muscle, skeleton, eyes, nails, hair and clothing into the costume. It took some time, and he was careful to gather as much material as possible, scouring the boards for anything he might have missed. In the end, the loose matter barely filled half of the disguise, and when he zipped the two parts together the result was little more than a crumpled, bloodstained mess.

'Now for the ID tags,' he said.

'I don't have the numbers. A dog swallowed them.'

'Be quiet, you semi-conscious idiot! I don't need your help; my friends also prepared this wonderful set of horseshoes.' He lifted one hoof, revealing a shoe with the number 0772244661188 printed in reverse along the crescent. He didn't bother to show me the other; he simply clopped through the remaining blood for a few seconds, then stamped one hoof on the neck and the other on the rump, branding both.

'Our time together draws to a close,' he said, standing back and admiring his work. 'I will return to hell with a feeling of immense satisfaction and discuss my evening with colleagues in front of a roaring fire. You will bed down in some hole or hovel like an animal, feeling empty, because there's a black hole inside you that you can never fill, no matter what or how much you pour into it. Does that sound accurate?'

'Pretty much.'

'Your self-awareness does you credit.'

'I'd still rather be me than you, though.'

'I will overlook your insult. Your desire is limited by morality, your judgement clouded by ignorance—'

'Don't you ever get tired of your own voice?'

'Of course not. And who would dare tell me otherwise? Anyway, I really must be getting along. Perhaps we will meet again someday.'

'What about your trophy?' I said. 'Xael bit off an ear, Caym took a photograph, Alastor stole a hand—'

'I will take the memory of your resistance. It will keep me amused at night when I think of the suffering that awaits you.'

'And the souls?'

'Those little things?' He looked around, bent down to sniff the stuffed pantomime horse, then stood up again. 'I believe they may have fallen through a crack in the floorboards; you'll have to retrieve them yourself... Now, goodbye. You have entertained and provoked me, undead, but you will no longer detain me.'

He clopped past me on heavy hooves, and was gone. When I looked through the broken window, I saw an ordinary horse trot down the track, leap over a hedge and gallop into the moonlit fields beyond.

I hung my coat and jacket on the back of the door and poked around in the pools of blood for some trace of the souls. I found a narrow hole in the floorboards, but it seemed unlikely anything larger than a pebble could pass through, and the boards were firmly nailed down.

Malache arrived a short while later, solemn in his black suit and tie. After surveying the scene and kicking the pantomime horse with his shoe, he said, 'Orobas has returned to the circus, then?'

I grunted.

'You should go and see his act if you get the chance. They call him Brocco the Bone Breaker; he takes great pleasure in throwing his riders. There's not a trainer can tame him.'

'I'll add it to my bucket list.'

He smiled weakly. 'Do you have the souls?'

I shook my head. 'They're in here somewhere. Orobas thinks they're under the floor, but I can't lift the boards.'

'I'll get the tyre iron,' he said.

You've just been lucky, I guess

'You didn't know me, so you didn't believe me. You didn't trust me, because we didn't have time. And when I asked you to run, you did not run. I could have led the demon away from you, but I led him toward you; and for this, I am sorry.'

'Noble words,' said Malache. 'But you're talking to a pantomime horse stuffed with offal. That's going to be a dull conversation.'

'I don't want to leave them without an explanation.'

'Why? They can't hear you.'

'It just doesn't feel right, that's all.'

'Fine. If you want to sweet-talk a belly full of tenderised body parts, be my guest. In the meantime, I'll rip up this floor.'

He took the tyre iron, wedged it into the hole between the boards, then stamped down on the exposed end with his heel. The wood splintered but didn't yield immediately; it took several more attempts before he could pull the broken pieces free with his hands.

He shone his mobile phone torch into the gap. 'There's definitely something here,' he said. 'Come and see. I'm not sure I trust myself to handle them.'

I skirted the bloodstains, crouched on the edge of the hole and examined the patch of earth revealed by his light. I saw two objects, lying side by side. One looked like a glass cube covered in glitter glue; the second was more nebulous, a fluctuating rod of quicksilver wrapped in wisps of gossamer. I felt a mysterious energy and power radiating from these twin souls. I reached through the gap and gently lifted them free.

'Job done,' said Malache. 'Time to head home.'

It was a long, slow ride to The Chimera. I rested my head against his back and clasped his waist tightly, like a lover.

I felt safe in his company; he had accepted me without judgement. A zombie is an abandoned house in the city of men, but he hadn't seen in my ruin a place to be shunned or destroyed. He had nurtured me, rebuilt me from within, given me the confidence to exist alongside the living— and I was grateful.

161

At some point during the journey I fell asleep, and was jolted awake when we arrived. It had been a brief sleep without dreams. A counterfeit death.

Malache kept the Vespa's engine running. 'You know the routine by now, so I won't labour the point,' he said. 'However, I must insist that you spend the night at the office. Your appearance has greatly improved over the past few days; sleeping outdoors would reverse those gains. Go to the workshop when you're finished here. I'll leave the door on the latch.'

I dismounted sluggishly, took his skeleton key and unlocked the entrance to the pub. As I was returning the key, I said: 'Something is bothering me.'

He turned off the engine. 'What is it?'

'You told me that my odour acted as a lure for demons. Nergal said it was so powerful it sometimes drove them to a frenzy. And for the past four nights, it seems to have worked: those creatures have met me without fail. But there's one thing I don't understand: if my scent is so attractive, why haven't I encountered a single demon in the past twenty years? Why is it only happening now?'

He restarted the engine and smiled pleasantly. 'You've just been lucky, I guess.'

I paused before entering the courtyard, and sat instead on one of the wooden stools in the bar. I looked around, trying to remember. I had visited this place when I was alive, but almost everything had changed since then: the name, the layout of the room, the chairs, the bottles and signs. Even the clock looked unfamiliar.

But I remembered Amy.

We had come here toward the end of our three-year marriage, when the embers of our love had already turned black. We sat at a table like this, in a crowd of chattering people; but we didn't talk much because there wasn't much left to say. This was just somewhere to be, and someone to be with, until we found better.

162

What words did we say to each other when we finally opened our mouths? *You are heat and light and air and hope. You are darkness and hatred and blood.* Or did we say nothing, like two beached fish comically, tragically gasping for air? I don't recall: the memory is gone.

I haven't thought about Amy in years. She was the world to me, once; now she is a scattering of atoms in a corner of my mind. I used to believe I could never live without her; then I realised I could never live with her; then I forgot both feelings, as if they had never meant anything to me. I forgot the raven's wing hair that I saw again in Resh. I forgot those words she had given me: *It just doesn't feel right.* And in forgetting her, I forgot part of myself.

Is she alive or dead? Is her ghost sitting here with me now, in this ghost of a place I once knew? If I turn my head to the right, slowly, carefully, will I see the light reflected in her eyes once more?

I turned my head.

I saw nothing.

Meaningful relationships with others

'Have you never wondered who I am, Half-life?'

'Not really.'

'Don't you even want to know my name?'

'If I say no you'll tell me anyway, won't you?'

The demon laughed: a foul and foetid booming guffaw that rattled the grille behind my head. 'We are beginning to understand each other. The sweet tendrils of connection intertwine to form an emergent bond; now let me strengthen that bond, so that you may know me better.' He coughed noisily, and the words that followed had evidently been rehearsed a thousand times. 'Some call me the Angel of Death. Some, Apollyon. I am the Spear of the Nameless

One, the King of Locusts, Ruler of the Abyss. I am the Inevitable. I am the Thing Most Feared—'

'I only have one name,' I interrupted, 'and I've forgotten it.'

'Is that insolence, sir?' said a sycophantic voice. 'Perhaps you should punish him.'

'I administer punishment at my discretion!' the demon replied sharply. After a pause, he continued in his self-satisfied tone. 'I go by many names, all of which are accurate, some even noteworthy, but none is particularly relevant. All you need to understand me is the knowledge that I am evil incarnate.'

The sycophant clapped his hands. 'Very good, sir. But what *is* evil? Does it even exist anymore?'

'Worm, I have *literally* just told you that I'm evil incarnate. Are you deaf, or are you suggesting that I don't exist?'

'Of course not, sir. I was merely facilitating the next part of your speech, and hoping against dear hope that you will tell us what evil is.'

'Well, ordinarily I would not condescend to something so tawdry as a definition—but since you asked, I have one or two opinions.' He coughed again, perhaps choking on his own pomposity. 'Listen well, Half-life... Evil is not merely the absence of good, though it requires its absence in order to thrive; nor is it, in isolation, the qualities of complacency, negligence or blindness to the acts of others. Evil can make use of an enabler, but it does not need one; evil can mask itself as good, but the mask is unnecessary. It bears only a tangential connection to morality—that sweet little comfort blanket for fools—because the moral commit evil acts just as easily as the immoral... At its heart, evil is something much simpler, perhaps the simplest and most ancient of all weaknesses: *evil is the lie*. It is the lie that hides in the heart of men but directs their every move. It is the lie that betrays a confidence, cheats on a lover, stabs a rival in the back. It is the lie that steals and defrauds, then

164

crawls inside the small print; that murders, rapes and conquers for its own pleasure; that hovers over the buttons that could annihilate everything on this planet. It is the lie in all of you, just waiting to be heard; and all I have to do is offer a sympathetic ear.'

I was too busy considering the internal contradictions of his speech to notice that he had stopped: he had claimed to be evil incarnate, but if evil was the lie, then everything he had said was untrue, including the statement that evil was the lie, and all that followed thereafter... But I let my objections slide.

'Excellent definitions, sir!' hissed the sycophant. 'Your clarity and brevity continue to astound me.'

'Thank you, worm.'

'Malache told me that the concepts of good and evil were outdated and you no longer see the world that way,' I said.

'Malache is a liar,' the demon said.

'A *shameless* liar,' his companion added.

'He lies in ways you can't even begin to grasp.'

'He lies at breakfast, lunch and dinner, and all points in between.'

'I know him as I know myself,' the demon concluded. 'And for that reason alone, I have never trusted him... But enough about him; I am hungry for souls. I heard whispers from a friend of mine that you were not as compliant as he would have liked this evening. I hope that your defiance did not extend to breaking our agreement?'

'I brought two souls. Which makes six in total.'

'You continue to surprise me—both pleasantly and otherwise. I believe I am going to miss you when your work is done. Perhaps you will consider serving me even after you have reclaimed your humanity; your skills would be moderately useful, and I could provide you with certain protections against—and advantages over—your fellow men.'

'I'll put them on the ledge,' I said.

One of the souls made a loud crack when he bit into it; the other sounded like an eel thrashing in a muddy pool. I hoped he would break a tooth and choke on them. I hoped they would poison him.

'May I have a nibble, sir?'

'You may not.'

'Not even the tiniest morsel?'

'Not so much as a sniff. Now shut up or fuck off.'

'Of course, sir.'

'Your scent has changed, Half-life. I detect an unpleasant *freshness* about you.'

'I have new clothes,' I said.

'I didn't ask for an explanation; I was merely observing. Now, tell me your shame before I finish these delightful young things. Then you may leave.'

'I was a private detective when I was alive—'

'How does one become a private detective?' he said.

'It's a long story. Would you like to hear it?'

'No, don't bother.'

'So, my work involved investigating those who had somehow wronged the people who hired me; and the cases usually focused on one of two things: money or sex. There was no GPS back then, so I had to rely on legwork and crude methodology to succeed—film cameras, simple tracking devices, paper trails, and so on. Generally, a photograph or video footage was enough: it was the easiest way to expose an affair, or reveal an association between two people who denied a public connection. But the images I took weren't always the kind you could process on the High Street, so I developed the film myself in a makeshift dark room in the office.'

'All very fascinating,' the demon said sardonically. 'But lacking the important element of sin. Do you think you could move things along?'

'I had a file on every case, going back to the beginning; but I also kept duplicates of the photos and movies for my own use. Many of the sexual acts I recorded are regarded as normal now, but were seen as depraved at the time: I collected them all in my own private catalogue, without regard for the integrity of my profession or the feelings of those involved. Every night I would select one from the collection and—recalling what it had felt like to be present at the scene, and imagining my own involvement in the corruption I had witnessed—I would use them to achieve a climax. And my fantasies weren't limited to sex; I often took pleasure in the violence, too. Graphic beatings, sadistic torture, broken bones and burned flesh—I discovered that nothing was a better stimulant to sexual arousal than the darker side of human nature. I was ashamed, of course, but the guilt only made the experience more exhilarating. However, I reaped that shame in the real world, when I tried to form meaningful relationships with others—'

'I'm sure it was all terribly depressing. But in a nutshell, what you're saying is your sin was sexual in nature?'

'More than that. I used people's wretchedness for my own satisfaction; people who had trusted me with their deepest secrets.'

'But it was the sexual element that bothered you. Otherwise we are simply discussing a breach of your professional ethics.'

'I suppose so.'

'Then it doesn't count. Sexual desire is not a sin; it's not even a misdemeanour. It's a perfectly natural response to mortality, and as broad a church—if you'll forgive that word—as you'll find in the vast range of human experience... No, I can't accept it. Those acts aren't sinful, and they don't make you evil. You're nothing more than a delivery boy careless of the packages he delivers; a drone who doesn't question his role. And your stories continue to dissatisfy me: next time I want a better tale, a deeper sin. I insist on it!'

I left The Chimera confused about his demands and apathetic about satisfying them. What counted as sin for a demon? Everything that shamed me was within the normal range of his experience; he simply absorbed it, like a giant, bat-winged sheet of blotting paper. But I was relieved that another meeting was over, and I was closer to the end than the beginning. Four more days at most, then this wearying cycle of patterns-within-patterns would finish.

The air felt warmer outside. I half-wanted to return to the canal, or the coal cellar, or the park; but I could find no reasonable objection to Malache's offer of a night in the workshop. So I trudged slowly back to Babylon Bookbinders, where I found the door unlatched, as he had promised.

Malache the Liar? I refused to believe it.

I looked around the room for somewhere quiet to rest; but the whole place was quiet, so it didn't matter where I chose. With that burden lifted from my mind, I crossed the floor to Resh's workbench, crawled silently underneath, and curled into a blissful ball of sleep.

PART FIVE

Astaroth the Fragrant

I am made of death

I am made of death, not stone. I have feelings. There are times in the night when I mourn the life I once had. There are times when I weep for the dreams I have lost. I am troubled when the living turn away in disgust. I am haunted by memories.

And when these feelings stir, I escape the thick glass cylinder that imprisons me, I connect with something other than myself. I feel alive.

Because I am made of death, not stone.

When I woke I was staring at the underside of Resh's workbench. A yellow sticky note was pinned to the wood. *Hello, stranger*, it said.

'Hello,' I replied.

I crawled out into the morning light, a milky whiteness that cast angular shadows on the floor. There was no one else around, and I saw only a couple of passers-by on the street outside. The workshop was quiet and restful, and I was grateful to Malache, once again, for insisting I sleep here. I yawned, stretched my stiff limbs, bemoaned my aching back, and smoothed the creases in my jacket; then, for want of anything better, I decided to look around.

I checked Resh's table first. A large mock-up for a poster covered most of the surface. The mock-up showed a handsome man in a black jacket, white shirt and black tie. He was grinning and giving a double thumbs up to the viewer; he appeared amiable, trustworthy and professional. Unusually, his skin had a green tint, but it wasn't sickly like a corpse's skin, it was more of an apple shade, a soothing green. At the bottom of the poster a simple slogan was printed in bold type: I WISH I HAD A FRIEND LIKE DEVIL JOE.

It was a striking image, and entirely reassuring, but there was something odd about it that I didn't notice immediately—a subliminal element, some holographic trick that only registered in my peripheral vision. I had to focus to make sense of it, but when I did I realised that it was a message that had been in my mind all along: LIKE THIS ADVERT? EARN CA$H BY SPREADING THE WORD. FOR YOUR FREE POSTER PACK, CONTACT YOUR NEAREST GREEN DEVIL RECYCLING DEPOT. The words looped in my mind like images in a zoetrope, making me nauseous; however, as soon as I looked away, the nausea passed and the message faded.

Nergal's space was cluttered and chaotic: scraps and screwed-up balls of paper littered the area around his battered laptop; tools and pencils lay scattered everywhere. But amongst the crisp packets, plastic bottles and chocolate bar wrappers I saw a hand-written note, entitled 'Encyclopaedia Suggestions':

The abacus was invented by Euclid in 289 BC.
The last victim of the Black Death was Leonardo da Vinci.
In the nineteenth century, Charles Babbage created a viable schematic for the internet but couldn't persuade his backers to fund large scale trials. He committed hara-kiri shortly afterward.
Videotape is a by-product of the oil refining process.
As experiments in alchemy ultimately led to the study of chemistry, so medieval torture methods—the rack, knee-splitter, Catherine wheel, and so on—eventually spawned the multi-billion dollar chiropractic industry.
The first selfie was taken by Richard Nixon in Beijing in 1972. Only one copy remains: it is stored in the archives of the Hollywood Horror Museum.

There were many, many more, but I walked away before I fell down the rabbit hole.

Two large books were placed side-by-side on Dumuzid's workbench: the Bible brought in for repair two days ago, and the *Dictionnaire Infernal* I had seen in the window display.

The work on the Bible appeared to be finished: Dumuzid had replaced the broken cover with an ornate leather binding, sewn and glued the pages, and neatly trimmed the edges. I opened it, searched for the Song of Songs and was pleased to find it unaltered; I found changes in several other sections, however. Most were minor misspellings of Jesus and misattributions of his good deeds and miracles, but there were grosser emendations, too. For example, all mention of the serpent in the Garden of Eden had been replaced by the word 'marmoset'; and Jesus' forty day fast in the Judaean desert had been curtailed to nine days. As far as I could tell, the name of Satan had been replaced by 'a friend' throughout.

The *Dictionnaire* was a catalogue of demons, combining hand-drawn sketches alongside short, descriptive paragraphs. I briefly skimmed the entries for Alastor, Caym and Haborym, but the drawings exaggerated their strangeness and the text bore little relation to the creatures I had encountered. Dumuzid had placed a bookmark at Orobas' entry too, which showed a horse walking upright with his arms spread wide.

I waited for the others to arrive, but they didn't come, and I was hungry and needed to clean yesterday's blood from my shoes, so I put on my coat and left the workshop.

I still had a couple of coins left, so I returned to the café in the passage. Rain had fallen overnight and washed away the last traces of snow, but the air was thick with mist, which gave the lights of the shop an alluring, ethereal quality.

I ordered a mochachoccachino and a chocolate chip cookie and sat in the corner by the bookshelf. I selected Kierkegaard's *Either/Or*, which seemed like the ideal book for a zombie, but the opening pages gave me a headache, so I abandoned it. Then I found *Doomsday*

Book by Connie Willis, a story about time travel and the Black Death, and it gripped from the first paragraph. Before I knew it I had read a hundred pages and I was late for my appointment with Malache.

I still hadn't cleaned my shoes, however. I went to the bathroom at the back of the café, slipped off my brogues and dabbed away the last traces of the twins' blood. I decided to wash my hands and face too, so I removed my coat and jacket and scrubbed myself until I gleamed. Then I remembered that every demon so far had marked my body with a memento, so I took off my shirt and checked my torso. Caym's heart was still held aloft by Alastor's wings, but I saw nothing new.

I turned away, and was beginning to dress myself when I caught a glimpse of my back in the mirror. Looking over my shoulder, I saw what appeared to be a fresh tattoo: the life-size imprint of a horseshoe. It lay black and blue against my pale flesh, the open end reaching toward my neck, the toe crossing my thoracic vertebrae. Examining it more closely, I noticed my ID—7218911121349—imprinted along the length of the arc. It was a neat touch; but I wondered once again how and when the demon had managed to brand me.

I shrugged, got dressed and left the café. I was made of death, but I still had work to do.

A little kindness

I felt no fear walking along the crowded passage to the main road. Everyone wanted to be somewhere else. They had no interest in the drifter, the vagrant, the half-alive—particularly one so smartly dressed.

But as I exited the alleyway, I stopped short. I caught a glimpse of someone I recognised. A woman with pale skin and black hair, leaning against the fence that

174

surrounded the graveyard of St Mary Magdalen. I watched her for a moment, and even considered approaching her, but a voice in the mist whispered a warning in my ear:

'It's not me. It's not me.'

'It looks like you.'

'Lots of people look like me.'

There were days when I saw Zoë everywhere. Hair colour, skin colour, the shape of an ear, the curl of a mouth, certain mannerisms, a way of walking. Everything fools those who want to believe.

'Maybe you *will* see me one day,' the voice said. 'And it'll be too late for me to turn aside. I'll have my children with me, but I'll usher them behind me so they won't be afraid of you. I might pretend that I don't know you; I might not even need to pretend, it's been such a long time. That will be a shock, don't you think?'

'I wouldn't mind,' I said to the mist. 'As long as you're happy.'

When I arrived at the workshop, I saw the client who had brought in the Bible for repair. She was standing beside Dumuzid's workbench in a warm winter coat. She looked apprehensive; but when he gave her the book she broke into a tearful smile. She leafed through the pages slowly, skipping the words in favour of a tactile assessment, gently lifting the sheets of tissue paper that protected the colour plates, carefully appraising the quality of the leather binding.

'I found a couple of items during the restoration,' Dumuzid said. He handed her a photograph and a hand-written note.

The woman read the message, then looked at the photograph. She showed it to Dumuzid. 'That's my great-grandmother. She would have been in her twenties then. She ended up raising my mother all by herself; her mother wasn't around much and no one knew who my grandfather was.'

Dumuzid grunted noncommittally.

'Anyway, thank you. You've done a wonderful job. How would you like me to pay?'

'Cash. Please.'

He handed her an invoice. The woman took out her purse, removed a quantity of bank notes that, when I was alive, would have paid for a week's holiday on a Greek island, then placed them carefully on the workbench. She thanked him again, slipped the Bible into a carrier bag, and left.

Nergal was typing on his laptop. The poster mock-up had disappeared from Resh's desk. There was no sign of Malache and there were no lights in the office. I walked over to Dumuzid in the vague hope that he had an envelope for me so I could spend the rest of the day alone.

'Hello,' he said.

'Hello,' I said.

'Zombie!' called Nergal. 'I didn't see you come in.'

'I guess not,' I said.

'Good morning, Rabbit,' said Resh.

'Good morning,' I said.

'Resh, give me your matches,' Nergal said.

Without looking up, she took a box from her desk and tossed it to him; he caught it nimbly in one hand, then ambled over to Dumuzid.

'Good work, well rewarded,' he said, picking up one of the bank notes. 'Did you really find those things inside the Bible?'

'I found the photograph. I wrote the message myself.'

'What did it say?'

'Nothing much. A few words.'

'Don't be coy, old man. It doesn't suit you.'

'Fine. I wrote: "A little kindness goes a long way".'

Nergal struck a match. 'Courtesy is one thing—I can see the utility in it—but I'm not sure the Boss wants us to be *nice* to the living.'

176

'What harm can it do? If they like us, their resistance weakens and we have more chance of success.'

Nergal didn't reply. Instead, he touched the lighted match to the money in his hand. The note quickly caught fire. He clung onto it until the flames licked his fingers; then he dropped it onto the carpet and extinguished it with his foot. He picked up another note from the desk and repeated the process. I looked at him in disgust. He saw my expression and grinned.

'Burn it, spend it—what's the difference?' he said.

'There are people who could use that money.'

'Well, I'm using it now. For my own pleasure.'

'Why not give it to someone who needs it?'

'Because I prefer to burn it... Anyway, what's the problem? I'm not destroying it in front of their noses—although that would be fun, too.'

'You're missing the point.'

He shrugged, picked up a third note and set light to it. 'I'll tell you what... If you do something for me—whatever I ask—I'll give you half the money in this pile and you can spend it as you wish. Blow it on whores, whisky or the poor. Your choice.'

'What do you want me to do?'

He took another bank note, but left it hanging in the air. 'Something to amuse me... How about a little jig?'

I felt no shame. I stood in front of him, let my arms hang limp at my side, and began to dance. First I kicked out my left foot, then my right. Left, then right, then left once more, moving slowly at first but gradually picking up speed until I was hopping from one foot to the other in a steady rhythm. Nergal put down the money and smirked, Dumuzid stared blankly. I continued to hop; but I moderated the pace to a quick shuffle, a regular beat that allowed me to improvise with my arms. First, I raised them upward until they were parallel to the ground, then higher until they formed an arch above my head. At the same time

I began to spin around on the spot, still leaping from left foot to right; and I performed a dozen turns in this fashion before dizziness got the better of me, and I had to stop.

Nergal clapped his hands with childlike joy; Dumuzid's expression hadn't changed. I looked toward Resh. She was shaking her head.

'An excellent dance, zombie!' said Nergal. 'If you performed it every day for a year I wouldn't grow tired of it.' He picked up half the notes from the pile and stuffed them into the side pocket of my coat; he crammed the rest into his jeans.

The world was spinning, and I struggled to focus, but I watched Resh stand up and walk toward him. 'You'll have to forgive my husband, Rabbit; he was suckled by morons. We could shove him into the grinder and what came out the other end would still be more intelligent.'

Nergal kissed her on the cheek. 'Didn't you enjoy his little caper, my iron maiden?'

'Not as much as you did, you dumb dodo.'

'You have no eye for culture.'

'And you have no heart.'

They returned to his table, still arguing.

I was drawn back to Dumuzid, who had remained silent and dignified throughout. He smiled wanly and regarded me with the eyes of a dead cod. I saw a variety of tools on his workbench. They reminded me of the strange instruments my father had used for repairing watches.

'What's that?' I asked.

A metal compass with two fine points, pivoted on a roller.

'A pair of spring dividers,' he said.

I pointed to some of the other tools. The arcane terminology of his answers felt like a shared intimacy: *Lumbeck press, vertical plough, gauge pricker.*

I picked up a long wooden block with a sliding top.

'What does this do?'

178

'It's an awl gauge and bodkin.' He took it gently from my hands. 'I use it to mark sewing holes when I'm threading sections together.'

I indicated a short-handled blade with a triangular tip.

'And this one?'

'A shoe knife. It silences zombies who ask too many questions.'

'Okay,' I said.

Remembering the mistake I had made yesterday, I walked to the back of the shop and peered through the blinds into the office; but Malache wasn't there. However, I heard once again that weird mechanical whirr, and pressed my ear to the glass for some clue to its origin; but all I sensed was an increase in volume and a few weak vibrations. Then I heard a door opening, and looked up to see Malache emerging from the machine room. A moment later he unlocked the door to the workshop and addressed me from the threshold.

'Either I'm late or you're early,' he said. 'I just don't know anymore. Anyway, come in. We need to talk.'

I sat in the mesh chair and waited for him to begin. He offered me a glass of Southern Comfort, which I accepted, and a cigarette, which I refused. He asked about the smell of burning in the workshop, so I told him the story of Nergal's profligacy. The destruction of company profits didn't seem to faze him; he remained expressionless throughout.

When I had finished, he said: 'I received your performance report from Orobas this morning. He claims you were obstinate and uncooperative. Now, as far as I'm concerned, results are what count, and from that perspective everything is rosy: the prey was found and no one else was killed. But perhaps you should consider upping your game a little—particularly if you'd like to remain in our employ.'

'The agreement only said that I should help. It didn't say what level of help I should provide, or whether I could refuse tasks I found intolerable.'

'As far as the literal interpretation of the wording goes, you're absolutely correct... However, in a working relationship it benefits you to put in a good shift—go the extra mile, as the living say.'

'I'll bear it in mind.'

'That's all I ask.' He smiled pleasantly. 'And I repeat: from my perspective, everything is fine. You're doing precisely what is required of you—'

'Tell me about the tracker.'

He paused. 'What do you mean?'

'When he arrived, Orobas said, "the tracker led me here".'

'Clearly he was referring to your scent.'

'No. He made a point of differentiating between them.'

'Look, Orobas' brain isn't all it should be. He's riding half-saddle, as it were; he's never been fully in control of his words. I suspect it was a simple misunderstanding—'

'Your superior said you were a liar.'

He studied me coolly; a moment passed before he spoke again. 'This has been a refreshingly frank conversation; however, before you make any further discourteous remarks, please consider the following questions. Have I ever been anything but sympathetic to you? Have I given you a reason not to trust me? Have I gone back on my word or betrayed you in any way?'

'No,' I said reluctantly.

'Of course not. My sincerest wish is that everyone who works here is happy in their role. A dissatisfied employee is an inefficient one, and that's bad for business. So, with that in mind, is there anything else you'd like to get off your chest before I hand you the envelope?'

'Yes. You say I should trust you, but I've been here five days and you still haven't told me about the machine you keep behind that door.'

For a moment he appeared genuinely nonplussed. 'The grinder, you mean? It's nothing special; a simple recycling apparatus, that's all. Waste is delivered to a depot at the back, we load it into the machine—the

180

official name is quite a mouthful, I won't burden you with it now—and it transforms that waste into a variety of useful products. Those products are then delivered to factories and farms all over the country. For example, a lot of the yield ends up as dog and cat food, or as fertiliser for crops and flowers—think fish, blood and bone, but without the fish... Well, I'll spare you the details; suffice to say it's pivotal to our work here. However, I do recall promising you a tour a couple of days ago, and I fully intend to keep that pledge. I don't have time today—there are one or two precautions we need to take first, anyway—but tomorrow morning I'll unlock that door and you can see for yourself.'

'Okay,' I said.

He leaned across and laid his hand on my shoulder. 'Friend, I hope I have renewed your trust in me; you have certainly repaid my faith in you. Don't be afraid of success! If it comes, embrace it with open arms... And if you can, put in a little more effort with Astaroth this evening: he's labouring under certain physical disadvantages and needs more help than most. Do as he asks and everything should work out beautifully.'

'I'll try.'

'Good man. Now, here's the envelope. You might find when you open it that you recognise the face in the photograph. Pay no attention; it's merely an unfortunate coincidence.'

Tentacled Martian overlords

I sat behind Nergal on his flame red Vespa and listened to him cursing under his breath. Malache had asked him to escort me, Nergal had expressed a desire to remain in the workshop, Malache had insisted, and here we were.

I held on tight as he ploughed through the mist, skidded into Cornmarket and accelerated toward Carfax. He careered down St Aldates, rasped past the police station and barrelled along Thames Street toward the shopping mall. Cutting between traffic, he sped down a ramp into the car park, took a wild turn around the first sub-level, pulled three consecutive wheelies, then came to a screeching halt in a disabled parking space.

Nergal leapt off the seat. I trailed him shakily to the lifts and we ascended to the ground floor. The doors opened onto a square filled with people.

This mall hadn't existed when I was alive, and I hadn't walked through it more than a couple of times since. It was a world of boutiques, department stores, expensive restaurants and high-end jewellers. Zombies were not their target market: to my eyes, the shops we passed might as well have contained goods from Mars, created exclusively for Martians, and bought by tentacled Martian overlords.

My companion led me up the escalator to the second tier, where we followed a magical trail of glittering brands to a brightly-lit storefront. The store was called '6': its simple black logo featured heavily within and without. The window display contained hundreds of mobile phones, all of which looked alike.

'This is just one of our outlets,' said Nergal, proudly. 'We have three branches in every town and city across the country. It's not the most popular name on the High Street, but we're making progress.'

We walked inside. There were a dozen people browsing and half as many again being served by assistants at the rear. The assistants were young, beautiful, expertly coiffured and dressed in the same lime green outfit. When they smiled, their teeth gleamed like tiny stars.

'Why have we come here?'

'We're going to buy you a mobile, you pale buffoon.'

Nergal told me to look around and choose a model I liked; then he left me for two tall women who were inspecting a rack of novelty phone cases. He tried to engage them in conversation, but they just laughed, patted him on the head and turned away.

I looked at the mobile phones in front of me. I saw names and designs I recognised from adverts and billboards across the city. I chose one at random, rested it in the hollow of my stump, couldn't make much sense of it, and put it back. Then I took another; but it was no less perplexing. The last phone I had owned had featured just five physical buttons with pictures on them; these had touchscreens with icons whose purpose bewildered me. Why did I need to Find My Phone when the phone was in my hand? Why would the undead want a Health app? An image with an envelope on it looked promising, but it told me I had to set up an account before I could use it. It all seemed unnecessarily complicated.

Nergal appeared beside me. 'How are you getting on?'

'They're all the same. And they're all so confusing.'

'You get used to them. Then you grow to like them. Then you realise you can't live without them. And if you want to work with us, you're going to need one.'

'Which would you recommend?'

'Naturally, I'm going to suggest something from the Green Devil range. Gorilla Glass as standard, a shock-resistant anodised aluminium alloy casing, waterproofing to a depth of ten metres, four 12-megapixel cameras, three-day battery life, dual SIM slots and the classic devil logo on the rear.' He picked a model from the shelf. 'This is the one I have. Bluetooth, blockchain, NFC: everything you need to connect to the modern world. It's a good size for your hands—the ones you'll get at the end of the week, anyway—and in the meantime I can tweak the settings to help with your deformity.'

I barely understood a word he said, but I agreed.

Having decided on the model, we waited in line for an assistant. The women to whom Nergal had failed to introduce himself were the only ones ahead of us. They were discussing something they had seen on the internet. I wasn't really listening, but I overheard the words 'horrific', 'gang-related' and 'hoofprints everywhere', before I tuned out altogether.

I looked at Nergal. He looked at me—from behind a mass of curly red locks, bushy red eyebrows and a thick red beard and moustache. It struck me for the first time that three-quarters of his face was hair.

'Dumuzid tells me all devils are metamorphs,' I said.

'Metamorph is a pretentious way of putting it. I prefer the term shapeshifter.'

'So you have an alternate form?'

He nodded. 'In the Underworld I am considered a giant among men. It's one of the reasons I'm not fond of this place: it diminishes my stature.'

'Do you know anything about Malache's other form?'

'Haven't a clue. Why don't you ask him?'

I didn't pursue it. I heard the women in front mention a bloodstained pantomime horse, then they were beckoned forward.

'I should add,' Nergal continued wistfully, 'that the taller, more handsome and—dare I say—more *virile* version of me is the one Resh fell in love with. A lot has happened since then, of course; and you may wonder how we've managed to stay together so long. So I'll let you into a little secret. The key to a long-term relationship is: *keeping yourself in shape.* Pumping iron, doing the circuits, racking up the miles— that's what keeps the ladies interested.'

After a couple of minutes we were summoned by an adonis in lime-coloured trousers. He took us to a waist-high podium embossed with the Green Devil logo, where he asked all kinds of personal questions which Nergal answered on my behalf. The assistant then offered me a sheet of potential telephone numbers, so I told him my ID

184

tag and asked if he had that one instead, but he said that wasn't a real phone number and I had to select one from his list, so I acquiesced, but I knew I would forget it as soon as he took the list away, and I did. Then I had difficulty signing the contract because they had to find an ink pad for me to press my stump into. Then the assistant slid a SIM card into the phone and handed me something called a 'care package'. Finally, my companion paid with the money he had taken from Dumuzid's desk, and we left the store.

As soon as we were outside, Nergal asked to borrow the phone. I waited in silence as he entered the contact details for everyone at Babylon Bookbinders and changed the settings to make the icons larger and more responsive. Then he handed it back to me.

'How do I use it?'

'You press things,' he said huffily. 'If you don't know what the things do, press them anyway. If something goes wrong, press something else.' My bewilderment must have been obvious, because he sighed and took me through the basics of making a call, sending a text and downloading apps. 'You have a corporate account, so don't worry about payment,' he added.

'Thanks.'

'You're welcome, zombie. Now here's the plan. I'm going to leave you, and in a couple of minutes I'll call you on my phone. You'll answer on your phone, we'll have a conversation, then I'll say goodbye. Got that?'

I nodded. He walked away.

I pushed the mobile into my jeans pocket and ambled around the mall. My clothes and haircut lay upon me like a suit of armour; I brushed against people and it was bearable. It felt so natural to be among Lifers that for a short while, as I leaned against a barrier and watched them walking below, I forgot that I was undead.

My phone rang. I squeezed it from my jeans, swiped to answer, dropped it on the ground like a drunk, almost kicked it from the mezzanine, carefully scooped it up again and said, 'Hello.'

'Let's test the signal,' said Nergal. 'Walk and talk.'

I walked, but it took all my powers of concentration to navigate the crowd, descend an escalator and talk at the same time.

'Are you still there?'

'Yes,' I said.

'Tell me something about yourself.'

'Like what?'

'I don't know... How do you see your future?'

'A dark river stretching out to eternity.'

'That's a bit of a downer, if I'm honest.'

'When I get my soul back things will be different.'

'Right. The thing in the box. Are you sure you want to open it?'

'Why? Are you saying my soul isn't in there?'

'How should I know? I'm just suggesting you leave things as they are. If it's not there, you'll be disappointed. If it *is* there, it could be even worse: once you open that box you expose your soul to all the world's shit. It could be crushed, burned, mortified, petrified, shredded, pulped—and it will make you mortal again. And at the end of your mortal life, in a few short years, it'll be extracted and traded once more. My advice is: forget it... Where are you now, by the way?'

'Near the car park.'

'You should turn around, then. I've already taken the Vespa; I'm almost at the workshop. Speak to you later, zombie. Ciao.'

I thought: I am nameless, and I will open the box, because when I free my soul I free my name, too. My soul is who I am: I can't keep it in a prison. It would be like living in a cage for the rest of my life.

186

I took the escalator to the roof level: a flat space colonised by restaurants and cafés. I bought a cinnamon pretzel and a takeaway coffee and sat on a long wooden bench amid a clump of potted plants. The mist had cleared now. The sky was cool and blue. High white clouds scudded like skeletal fingers chasing unattainable riches.

I decided not to open Malache's envelope just yet. Instead, I eased the phone out of my pocket and clicked on the app store. I found a game that looked promising: *Plants vs Zombies*. It was based on the premise that vegetation and the undead were mortal enemies—a concept which was new to me—so I downloaded it and began to play. I quickly discovered that I could only control the Plants in their quest to defend a house from waves of Zombies; but the undead were so stupid and stereotypical, I didn't take it personally. In any case, it was an enjoyable way to pass the time.

'You'll turn into a ghost,' said Zoë.

'Leave me alone. I'm busy.'

'You know what a ghost is, don't you? A stain on the air. A shadow of something that once lived. That's what you'll become if you stare at that thing all day.'

'Be quiet. I'm winning!'

But the zombies crushed my last line of defence and defeated my valiant sunflowers, and when I looked up, Zoë was gone.

In truth, I was afraid to open the envelope. The last time I had witnessed the death of someone I knew, it had been a friend. She was buried alive in a coffin; I heard her fingers clawing at the wood. I didn't want to go through that again.

But I had to find out. It was my job.

I bit through the wax seal; I tipped out the note and photograph; I looked at the picture—and felt a wave of relief. It was not someone I recognised after all. Perhaps Malache had been stung by my questions and had lied to me out of spite... But he was not a liar.

I looked at the photo again.

Maybe there *was* something familiar about that face. I couldn't recall where or when I'd seen it, but it was almost certainly in the past few days. I struggled to remember—a smashed plate, a stream of abuse—but there was no clarity. I felt shame for not knowing.

I picked up the note reluctantly. Parts of it were smeared with a stinking grey slime, but I didn't care. I read the words quickly then tossed the paper aside. *Living thing. All the sevens. I'll bring the recipe. Assistant required for dinner—Master Chef.*

Temper, tempura

I sat beneath the cool blue sky and played with my new toy. It was a device of seemingly infinite possibility, and a welcome distraction from my responsibilities. I decided to see what else it could do. I remembered the movie Nergal had been watching on his laptop yesterday, and quickly discovered that similar content could be found on my phone.

When I was alive, pornography had been restricted to top-shelf magazines, brown paper bags and 18-rated videos; and the people who craved it were conventionally regarded as emotionally deficient or morally flawed. But something had changed during my time in the coffin: the broad spectrum of human desire was no longer a guilty pleasure, and sexual gratification was available to anyone with a search engine. You had to be literal with the search terms—as if you were speaking to a corpse—but the results were instantaneous.

It was a revelation both liberating and poignant. It removed the shame and censure, but took away the effort and mystery; it democratised and expanded the range of what was acceptable, but turned sex into just another banal consumer product... And though it interested me at

188

first, after an hour of watching minor variations on several themes, I felt jaded.

This boredom persisted into the afternoon. I wasn't hungry or thirsty, so I continued to explore the mall. All the stores were the same: big windows, bright lights, special offers, bland music, polite assistants, pleasant interiors. After a while, I sat down again and watched Lifers flowing around me. I envied their graceful movements and their apparent contentment. I knew that inside they suffered just as much as any zombie; but it was hard, on the surface, to imagine their unhappiness.

Blue turned to black; the mall emptied out. I headed back to the workshop, passing a Lebanese café on the way. I saw a display filled with plates and pyramids of sweets and pastries. I walked inside and bought a box of baklavas.

I sat on a metal bench in Bonn Square and opened the box. The baklavas were small enough to eat whole, so I removed one with my teeth. It was sugary and delicate, with an irresistible blend of tastes and textures: light, flaky pastry, sweet, sticky honey, finely chopped walnuts and pistachios, fragrant traces of cinnamon, cloves and jasmine.

A woman sat down beside me. I had seen her a few times over the years. Much like me, she carried her home on her back and slept wherever she found shelter. I offered her a baklava; she took it without comment. When she had finished, I offered another and took a second for myself; and in this way, over the space of a quarter hour, we shared what was left. The time passed in silence, but at the end she stood up and said: 'Thank you.'

Then I made my way to the office.

There were no lights on when I arrived and I saw no sign of Malache within. I tried the door, but it was locked; so I leaned against the window and waited. After a few minutes I checked my phone. It was six o'clock: earlier than the first three days but later than yesterday. The note hadn't specified what time *dinner* was.

Half an hour passed. I did nothing.

Another half hour. I tried every app on the phone. I tried calling Malache, but he didn't answer. I tried texting; again, no reply. I left a post on the Green Devil message board, but no one knew where he was. Maybe he was busy. Or had left his phone somewhere. Or he just didn't want to talk to me.

At the end of the third half hour, I heard the gravelly rasp of a small engine. I looked up, expecting to see a suited man on a black scooter. Instead I saw a red Vespa driven by Nergal, with Resh riding pillion. Her arms were wrapped tightly around his waist, her face peered over the top of his head. He accelerated as he approached, but pulled up at the last moment in a squeal of wheels.

He handed me a folded slip of paper. 'This is from Mal. He told me to tell you he was sorry he couldn't be here, but he'll pick you up as usual later. He said the demon will meet you at The Noodle Bar.'

'Okay,' I said.

'Have you been waiting long?' said Resh.

'Not really.'

'You look cold.'

'I always look cold.'

She smiled sympathetically.

'Anyway, job done,' said Nergal brusquely. 'Let's party!'

He revved the engine, spun the scooter around and pulled away with another squeal.

'See you tomorrow, Rabbit!' said Resh.

I waved goodbye to her winter-coated back.

When they were gone, I unfolded the note. *Sorry I can't be there*, it said, *but I'll pick you up as usual later. The demon will meet you at The Noodle Bar—Mal.*

I knew the face in the photograph now. It was the chef who had argued with Ignazio in the café. A loud, angry man with no hair. I had forgotten the cause of their argument, but I remembered it had been defused with a smile and an arm around the shoulder.

I trudged slowly down the street. I wanted to be somewhere else. I would have happily traded places with Nergal, even if that meant finding myself in a crowd. How did a devil party anyway? Were he and Resh going to a roller disco that served nibbles and alcohol, or some weird costume event where everyone dressed up as angels and faked an interest in each others' holiday plans?

The door to the café arrived at me. There was no sign of the demon, so I walked inside.

'I'm sorry, sir. We're closing in ten minutes. We open again at nine tomorrow.'

'I won't stay long. May I have a glass of water?'

The place was empty and the owner appeared to be absent. Only the chef remained, cleaning and polishing the kitchen surfaces.

'One glass? Very well.'

I removed my coat and folded it into the rucksack, then pushed the rucksack under the table by the window. I sat down. The chef filled a glass with tap water and placed it in front of me. I clasped it between my stumps, raised it to my lips, and sipped.

'Is Ignazio around?'

He shook his head. 'He goes home at five-thirty on the dot. Never comes in before ten. And all day long it's bark, bark, bark like a dog. Seven wants more rice, five thinks the squid is too chewy, nine says the green tea is tepid...'

'Sounds like a tough job.'

'I've had worse.' He spotted a Swiss cheese plant in the corner and set about polishing its leaves vigorously. 'I stay because I enjoy the craft. I like seeing people eat and appreciate what I make. For me, every meal is like a tiny work of art: the order is the spark that lights the fire of my creativity!' He found a spray bottle and turned his attention to a maidenhair fern by the counter. 'There are certain things the art must not do, of course. First and foremost, it must not give the audience food poisoning. And it cannot stray too far from its purpose: a light, crispy batter must be light and crispy, not thick and flaccid; a prawn must be a prawn, not a fat, deformed shrimp. But after the outline is sketched, I am free to interpret as I please. Even a simple dish can be composed in such a way that it makes the customer feel good about themselves and the world around them.'

I remembered the steaming, salty noodles he had cooked for me, and recalled how they were arranged: a beautiful raised spiral, like a miniature white galaxy.

'I was here a few days ago. I enjoyed your work.'

'Thank you, sir.' He smiled briefly—then the door opened behind me and his expression soured. 'Who the hell is this now?'

I felt a draught on my neck and turned around. Someone had entered the café—a stranger who was struggling to keep himself under control. He was a tall, dark-haired man with a waxy moustache and a damp sheen to his skin; a man in a cheap suit, shiny shoes and a pink shirt. When he moved, his limbs appeared stiff and unnatural. When he spoke, it was with forced calmness.

'I'm hungry. I need something to eat.'

'Sir, that is impossible. The kitchen is closed. I am about to go home; I suggest you do the same.'

'I can't hold it in for much longer.'

'What are you talking about? I must insist that you leave immediately. This is intolerable!'

'Just need to know which one of you—that wonderful smell—' He glanced at me with bloodshot eyes. 'You're the undead, aren't you?'

I nodded.

'So he's—but I can't—I have to—let go.'

And with those words, he exploded.

Something's Cooking in the Kitchen

It was as if someone had lanced a gigantic abscess: the stranger's body erupted in a shower of blood, mucus and pus, spattering all four corners of the café. It splattered the walls, floors and windows, sprayed the Swiss cheese plant and the maidenhair fern, covered the newly-polished surfaces in the kitchen, burst over the tables and chairs—and spurted all over the chef, and all over me.

I wiped my face and hands. I looked at the chef. He stood motionless, staring blankly ahead, thick grey slime dripping from him like candlewax. His eyes only flickered into life when the newborn demon spoke.

'My name is Astaroth. Please accept my apologies. This malady is a curse; its bitter rhythms afflict the innocent and corrupt alike. But you have nothing to fear for the next few hours.' He looked glumly at my paralysed companion. 'Well, not from the disease, at any rate—'

'What *are* you?' the chef interrupted.

The demon was a grotesque hybrid. Wiry hands and feet ended in bird-like talons; a moon-faced head was topped with a golden crown. A pair of angelic wings sprouted from his back, the feathers stained grey by this creature's dominant characteristic: a putrid mass of ever-moving, ever-changing slime. It appeared to be both a part of his body and a discrete entity, like some fetid parasite that had swelled and run rampant; it clung thickly to his torso and drooped, dripping, from his arms and legs; it nuzzled at his neck and circled his wrists and ankles—and all the while it shifted, undulated, pulsed like some diabolical organ. The stench was nauseating: a sickly, bitter poison that brought to mind all the dead things you had ever smelled and all the rancid food you had ever tasted—and it proved too much for the chef, who collapsed to the floor and vomited.

'I hope this doesn't ruin flavour,' the demon said.

'What flavour?' I asked.

'The flavour of the *meat*. The key ingredient. Here—take a look.'

He reached into that mound of foulness, produced a recipe card covered in plastic and wiped off the excess mucus. With a short bow, he placed it on the table in front of me.

MAN TEMPURA

Introduction

There is some debate in the demonic community about the best way to serve the inhabitants of our newly-acquired territories. Should they be eaten raw or cooked? With or without herbs and spices? Freshly killed or left to mature? It's not the job of this cookery club to resolve those thorny issues, but we can *recommend this timeless classic: a simple dish that is sure to please anyone looking for a quick and nourishing snack.*

Ingredients

The batter
150g plain flour
150g cornflour
2 eggs, lightly beaten
350ml sparkling mineral water
A pinch of salt

The man
A deep fryer
100g plain flour
Salt and pepper to taste
3kg or less of uncooked select man parts

Instructions

1. Sift the flour and cornflour together into a large bowl or hollow elephant skull.

2. Make a hole in the centre of the flour and add the eggs and mineral water. Whisk until it forms a batter that's slightly thicker than fresh blood.

3. While you're waiting for the batter to settle, heat the oil in a deep fat fryer. Test the temperature with your fingers—when it's painful, it's ready!

4. Choose your man parts. You'll have your own favourites, but this club recommends the extremities: ears and lips are a particular delicacy, but anything small will do.

5. Roll the parts in flour until completely covered. Don't worry if a little man juice contaminates your cutlets—as far as we're concerned, it just adds spice to the experience!

6. Dip your flour-dredged delicacies in the batter then drop them into the fryer. Cook for three minutes, until the outside is crisp and golden and the inside is pink and tender.

7. Don't be a baby—pick out those crunchy little devils with your fingers and dab them dry with kitchen roll.

8. Serve on plates with a salad garnish, in bowls with a little sauce on the side, or just take them hot and fresh from the fat. However you choose to eat them, these bad boys are a guaranteed flavour sensation!

As I read the instructions, I was aware of Astaroth oozing toward the chef. A brief conversation followed: I didn't hear all of it, but I caught the words 'inspection', 'hygiene issues' and 'they'll close us down for good'. Shortly afterward the discussion was replaced by muffled cries and an unpleasant slurping sound. When I finally looked up, I saw the chef lying face down on the ground. He was covered in slime and no longer alive.

'Now for the unpleasantness,' said the demon. He slithered into the kitchen, surrounded by that gurgling grey mass, and tipped out one drawer after another until he found a carving knife of the right shape and length. Then he returned to the seating area and half-knelt, half-spread on the floor beside the chef's body. 'I'll whittle away at this corpse. You heat up the oil and prepare the batter.'

I took the recipe card and headed for the kitchen, careful not to slip in the spreading pool of slime he had shed along the way. The demon lowered his head as I passed and spoke a few words in a strange, quiet voice: 'I am Astaroth from the Bureau of Infernal Affairs. I thank you for the gift of your flesh. May your corpse find peace.'

Then he started to cut.

I made the batter, as instructed. It reminded me of making pancakes as a child with my mother. I tried to ignore the background sounds of carving, chopping and trimming, and the peripheral sight of a demon slicing strips of flesh from a corpse.

After a while, he said: 'I have fallen so very far, undead. What you see now is not what I once was. Would you like to hear my story?'

'Okay,' I said.

'Thank you for your indulgence... I'll begin at the beginning. In the old days, many of us were creatures of great power and beauty, worshipped, loved and feared in equal measure; but when the new religions arrived, it was obvious to all but the most stupid and vain that we must yield our power and leave the stage. So we left—and in our absence, quite naturally, new myths flourished. We were rebranded as outcasts and demons; it was said that we had been thrown from paradise into the pit of hell. All lies, of course. We simply found another place to live. Somewhere a little less holier-than-thou.'

I let the batter rest and heated the oil in the fryer.

'But how, you may ask, did I change from that beautiful young thing revered at the dawn of the world into this foul and fetid form that disgusts all who encounter it? That's a more recent tale, and it can be summed up in one word: Pestilence.'

196

I looked up in time to see him slice off the chef's top lip. 'Pestilence from the Agency?'

He nodded. 'We seized control two decades ago, but the transition was far from smooth. Confusion reigned; wild ideas emerged; demons and devils jostled for power and influence. I was no different: I believed it would benefit our cause in general and mine in particular if I came up with a plan for a dramatic reduction in the human population. A plague seemed the most efficient route; to that end, I contacted Pestilence, who introduced me to his private collection of infections, diseases and disorders. The economy of death was a black market back then, and I paid a handsome price for his most recent formula— something he called *Batch 08/99*. Unfortunately, I forgot to ask him how I might propagate the disease, and when I returned to his laboratory I found he had disappeared without leaving a forwarding address. I was desperate to prove my worth in this new world, and it would have been humiliating to waste something so expensive, so in the end I simply swallowed the phial he had given me—with the unfortunate result that you now see before you.'

I looked up again. He cut off an ear. I looked away.

'I'm sorry,' I said.

'There's nothing to be done—until I find that pockmarked worm and force him to give me the antidote... Forgive my irritation, undead. I have lived with this condition for two decades; it has proved somewhat inconvenient.' He sighed, and I heard the knife clatter to the floor. 'Do you know what they call me behind my back? Astaroth the Fragrant. Does that seem fair to you?'

'I think the oil is ready,' I said.

He gathered together the toes, fingers, lips, nose, ears and eyeballs, along with various other strips and scraps of flesh, then placed them carefully in the sink and turned on the cold tap. He washed and dried them, rolled them in flour, dipped each one in batter, and dropped them

197

individually into the deep fryer. They sizzled and spat as they landed, but soon settled into mild bubbling.

'Would you mind watching them for me?' he said, shuffling toward the window seat. 'If I do it, I'll leak this filthy slime into the oil.'

I nodded. I felt nothing, because I wasn't here. I was a corpse who dreamed he had left the coffin.

The room filled with the sounds and smells of frying food. I watched the lumps of battered flesh bounce and sizzle until they turned golden brown, then lifted them out with bamboo tongs onto a sheet of kitchen paper. When the last was done, I dabbed the tops with a second sheet to soak up the excess oil. Remembering the chef's words, I arranged the pieces artfully in a shallow bowl, in a radiating pattern, so that the sight of them might bring as much pleasure to my guest as the taste. To this display I added a small white plate on which I placed three sauces—soy, chilli and spicy mayonnaise—along with some shredded carrot and ginger. I carried both dishes to the demon's table, mindful of the mutilated corpse and pools of slime in my path.

'Magnificent!' said Astaroth, as I set the food before him. 'This is a feast, undead. Will you join me?'

I shook my head.

He bit into a crispy round tempura that might have contained an eyeball or a big toe. 'I understand your reluctance—personally, I wouldn't care to eat a fellow demon—but you may never have the opportunity to sample such delights again.'

'I'm not hungry.'

'As you wish... It's delicious, by the way. Thank you.'

I couldn't watch him eat. The thought of it made me afraid. I wasn't a corpse after all, I was a living, breathing creature—and the thing that frightened me was that I was *tempted*. Tempted to say yes, I'll eat it, I want to experience everything, even this, because when I feel my soul I will feel the taboo against consuming human flesh.

198

'You work at the bookbinder, don't you?'

'Yes.'

'How is Dumuzid?'

'He's fine. Dedicated to his work.'

'Always was, right back to his shepherd days.'

I said nothing.

'And Resh? Is she still married to that stunted hairball?'

'If you mean Nergal, then yes... Do you know them?'

'I used to, a long time ago. We grew apart, as families do.'

He grumbled to himself and looked regretfully through the window. He seemed to withdraw; the undulations on his infected flesh slowed to a crawl. I watched him reach absent-mindedly into the bowl and pick out something broad and flat; he dipped it in the chilli sauce then nibbled at it distractedly, lost in a private dreamworld.

I left him alone and moved to another table, where I stared at the desecrated body on the floor.

'Thanks for the water,' I told it.

When I was alive one of my favourite books was an encyclopaedia of trivia. I memorised its strange stories and amazing facts because I thought they would help me talk to people, which was something I found difficult even then. To that end it was useless, but the things I learned eventually served a purpose after my resurrection: whenever I couldn't bear to think about something, a related piece of information would occupy my mind instead. I hadn't considered this book for a very long time; but my brain, seeking a distraction from the present horror, retrieved a few half-remembered trivia from its section on cannibalism:

The pharaohs of Ancient Egypt believed ritual cannibalism was the gateway to an eternal afterlife.

Gabriele D'Annunzio, an Italian author and soldier, once claimed to have eaten a roasted baby.

Some insects, spiders, shrimps and chimps are cannibals.

Endocannibalism means eating a family member. Exocannibalism means eating a stranger.

A consensus of opinion asserts that human flesh tastes like pork, but Jeffrey Dahmer, a serial killer who ate some of his victims, stated that it tasted more like filet mignon.

'My apologies, undead. I suffer from a rather maudlin form of nostalgia which possesses me without warning. It shows me a past that never really existed and contrasts it rather cruelly with my current affliction. But I am almost done with this most excellent meal; I won't detain you much longer.'

I heard the crunch of another tempura. I tried to blank my mind but the sound of his eating broke through, accompanied now and then by the flop and slap of that rippling infection. It felt like a long time before he stopped, and when he did he indicated the corpse at my feet.

'Do you have an opinion on this situation?'

'I just want to be made whole,' I said. 'I try not to think about what I need to do to achieve it.'

'A sensible response. Some of the newer religions will tell you that my prey committed the sin of anger and therefore deserved punishment. They may question whether being smothered and consumed is an appropriate penalty, but their desire to balance sin with retribution is unshakeable. My own viewpoint is much simpler: I was hungry and I needed to eat.' He paused briefly to suck sauce from his fingers. 'I mention this because I see some of my own attitude reflected in you. You don't overcomplicate your decisions by applying moral judgements: you do things because they have to be done in order to get what you want. It's a pragmatic approach that I find rather refreshing.'

There was only one tempura left in the bowl. But he didn't eat it: he just stared into space again. I couldn't stand the tension. I had to hurry him along.

'Will you take a trophy with you?'

'Naturally. It's a perk of the job.' He stood up, shuffled over to the chef's body and rummaged through his clothing.

A look of puzzlement crossed his moon-like face; he looked around until he saw a coat hanging on a door at the back of the kitchen. He glided toward it, rifled through the pockets, pulled out a set of car keys and examined them carefully. 'A Mazda GTS. Five thousand on the forecourt. By the way, if you're ever in need of a used car—'

'What about the ID tag?'

He shambled to the till and found a notepad and pen. Droplets of slime dripped from his arms as he wrote a message on the top sheet. He tore off the note, then returned to the body and placed it on the forehead. It was a bill, on which he had written the words: *Tempura and dipping sauces—excellent food and service.* Below that, where the total would have been, he had scribbled thirteen numbers: *7777777777777.*

I looked up. He was already standing by the door.

'And the soul?'

He pointed to the last remaining tempura—a crispy nugget of meat in the shape of a lozenge—then smiled and bowed his head.

'Thank you for a lovely evening,' he said.

Filthy business

When he was gone I scooped up the deep fried soul and dropped it in my jacket pocket. It was still warm, and no lighter or heavier than its size suggested. I tried to match its rhombic form to the lumps of flesh he had carved, but my mind was firing blanks. All I saw were random shapes dredged in flour, covered in batter, dipped in oil. The greasy odour of that oil hung in the air around me. I could almost taste it.

I looked at the body on the floor again.

Then I threw up.

Malache arrived a few minutes later. He hovered on the threshold, then lightly stepped between the puddles of grey slime to where I was sitting.

'This is quite the mess, isn't it?' he said. 'Did Astaroth have one of his episodes?'

I nodded, still too nauseated to speak.

'Don't worry. We'll soon get you cleaned up, and tomorrow morning you'll be back to normal. Dum said you kept your old clothes...'

I nodded again and pointed to my bag.

'You have the gift of foresight, friend. I suggest you have a wash, hand me what you're wearing and change into your former attire. If my memory of this place serves, there's a bathroom at the rear.'

He pointed to where Astaroth had taken the keys from the chef's coat.

I threw up again.

I placed the soul beside the sink; then I undressed, opened the door and tossed the dirty clothes back into the café. I washed my face and hair in the mirror and removed all traces of that vile mucus from my hands. There wasn't much: my outfit had absorbed most of it. When I was sure that nothing remained, I opened my rucksack and retrieved my coat, trackpants, sweatshirt, tee-shirt, socks and trainers. I put them on, and immediately felt better. I checked my face one last time, put the soul in my coat pocket and left the bathroom.

Malache was standing by the entrance, holding a white plastic bag containing my clothes. He had mopped the worst of the stains from the floor but had left the body untouched. He looked impeccable, as usual.

'I'll have someone clean these overnight and drop them off at the workshop tomorrow,' he said.

I walked toward him, feeling unsteady and unwell. As I reached him he put down the bag and embraced me. I felt the warmth of his arms around me—the security of a parent, friend and mentor.

'It's okay,' he said. 'Three more souls and it will all be over.' He patted me on the back and pulled away. 'Unless you want to carry on working for us, of course. In which case, you can expect many more nights like this.'

We left the café and walked up the street to his Vespa; then we took the short trip to The Chimera. I wanted to lie down and sleep and forget everything, but I still had one more task to complete.

A man was waiting for us outside the pub. He was middle-aged and bristle-chinned and wore a hint of ham about his face.

'Just as I thought!' he said, by way of introduction.

'What exactly was it you thought?' asked Malache, dismounting from the scooter. I remained on the seat in case we needed to make a quick exit.

'The two of you, here again. I've seen you every night, breaking into the pub and getting up to whatever filthy business people like you are involved with.'

'First of all, I have no need to break in.' He pulled out his ring of keys and waved them in the stranger's direction. 'Secondly, you're correct about the filthy business—'

'I knew it! It smelled something awful last night.'

'It's *filthy* because my associate is attending to the storm drain in the courtyard. It's been years since it was last cleared out; some major repairs are needed. As for the *business*: we work for Green Devil Downspout and Drain Cleaning Services.' He handed the man a card. The man wrinkled his nose in disgust, then pocketed it.

'Where are his tools?'

'Inside, of course. Do I have to explain everything?'

'Listen, smart mouth, I've spoken to the landlord and he knows nothing about you or your friend and doesn't know why you're here.'

'Your intimacy with the landlord is neither here nor there; I am employed by the owner. It is she who pays my bills. If you have any complaints about our work, the smell, or the noise we make, please refer them to her.'

The man harrumphed, then harrumphed a second time for emphasis, and said, 'You don't fool me. I've got your number. I'll be keeping my eye on you two!' He walked away, grumbling to himself; but I didn't dismount until his front door had closed.

I looked questioningly at Malache, but he simply smiled in response. I smiled, too; but somewhere in my mind I registered that he had lied effortlessly, and without missing a beat.

I sat in the snug once more. After a while, Lucy joined me. She was the friend I had seen suffocating inside a coffin, buried alive by a jealous partner. But that was long after I knew her. When we came here, we were lovers.

We had declared our love for each other in words, and had reached the point in our relationship where, if we didn't see each other every day, we believed we might wither and die. She didn't really like pubs, but she had come because I was here, and I was here because she had come. Life was simpler then.

'What would you like to drink?' my ghost asked.

'I didn't come here to drink,' her ghost replied.

And we kissed so fervently, and with such hunger, that no one could have separated us then or now.

The only time I had to speak freely

I am not afraid. This realisation struck me as I sat by the grille and heard the demon approach. He was no longer the monster of fire and claw that had once haunted my dreams. He was smaller now: a creature of chittering insects and foul breath, of laboured lungs and idle threats. He was an arrogant bully, a beast of bluff and bluster. And I wasn't afraid.

'Why did you call Malache a liar?' I said.

'Because we are all liars. It is our purpose here.' There was no rebuke in his voice. 'But quell your feelings of superiority, Half-life. You are a liar, too.'

'You don't know me.'

'I don't need to; it is enough to know that you can talk. Language, by its very nature, is an instrument of deception. To speak is to sow confusion, to listen is to misunderstand. And it is so very easy for your kind to exploit that confusion and misunderstanding to force an advantage.'

'You have a cynical view of the living.'

'Based on observation. The human narrative has been shaped not by objective truths but by your ability to convert others to your worldview.' He leaned closer to the grille. 'However, those times are gone. We control the narrative now. We decided who wins and who loses—and there's nothing you can do, it's already too late. While you were sleeping, we stripped the nuance and subtlety from your tiresome debates and replaced them with slogans, dog whistles, trigger words. We can change reality with a single lie. We can tell people how to think and feel. We determine who they are and what they say. We can even convince them that they're free. Do you think you are free, Half-life?'

'Not yet.'

'You're wrong. You are the master of your own fate. You can leave here whenever you like. All you have to do is accept responsibility for your actions and suffer the consequences of your mistakes. You have the magic word at your disposal but you're too afraid to utter it.'

I didn't contradict him. Whatever I said, he would deny it, or reinterpret it to mean something different. I was here merely to feed his ego.

'I have a soul for you.'

'Only one? I expected more, but it seems the last two days were an aberration. Well, place it before me.'

I put the tempura on the ledge and turned around. The grille opened and closed. He began to eat.

'Yet again I appear to have misjudged you—this is a most excellent soul. It is brittle without but tender within, and what it lacks in size it makes up for in flavour. Did you cook it yourself?'

'Yes.'

'Splendid. I am tempted to offer you a role immediately—you would make a fine personal chef—but decisions made in haste are soon regretted. I will wait until your work is complete.'

'I didn't say I would accept anyway.'

'Well, you would be stupid to refuse; but the point is moot. I haven't offered, you haven't finished, the world spins regardless. Now, tell me your tale. I have no need of spice for this delicious treat, but however insignificant it might be, your shame is always diverting.'

I could leave whenever I liked, but I chose to unburden myself. I had no friends among the living or the undead, and my parents' grave was empty. This was the only time I had to speak freely.

So I sat with my back to the wall and said:

'Twenty years ago, when I left the Agency, I was promised help with a job, some corrective surgery and a supply of cosmetics to disguise my pallor. The surgery never happened, and the job and cosmetics took a long time—'

'Bureaucracy,' the demon said complacently. 'Your former employers were obsessed with it. I'm surprised they managed to kill anyone at all.'

'Anyway, for a couple of years afterward I wandered the streets. I spoke to the living only as a matter of survival. I didn't have the emotional capacity to make friends; even people who shared my situation were little better than strangers to me. So I don't know the name of the man whose coat I took—'

'That's your sin? Petty theft?'

'There's more to it. It was my first winter on the street, and a week when the snow fell in blinding storms. It was hard to find shelter, and one night I was looking for somewhere to sleep when I came across a man lying in a doorway—a man who looked like me. I was tired, I'd spent hours wandering around, and I had no coat; I only had a thin blue jacket from my time at the Agency. This man had two: he was using one as a blanket and the other as a pillow. I was angry that he had an excess of something I needed, and I told myself that he wouldn't miss it, so I eased the coat from beneath his head and walked away. I found another doorway nearby, drew the garment over me and slept until morning.'

'Like I said: theft.'

'No. The next day I went back to where I'd left him, looking to return the coat but not really expecting to find him; it was an attempt to assuage my guilt. But he was still there, lying in exactly the same position. I tapped him on the shoulder to wake him, but he didn't move. He was already stiff by then, and his skin was white, but I remember most of all how blue his lips were. I felt for a pulse and put my cheek to his mouth, but he had neither heartbeat nor breath.'

'So what? He was likely dead the first time you met him.'

'But I don't know for certain. And either way it damns me: either my theft tipped him over the edge, or I stole from a corpse... But what shames me even more is that I should have returned his coat as a gesture of respect; yet I didn't even consider it. I kept it, I wore it that whole winter, and I've worn it ever since. It's the same coat I'm wearing now.'

I expected him to finally acknowledge my monstrous character and condemn my tale in the strongest terms— but, to my surprise, he laughed out loud. 'I didn't realise you could be so amusing, Half-life! That's a terrific punchline: *It's the same coat*!'

He continued to laugh for some time.

I waited for him to stop.

At last he said: 'Naturally, I find no sin in this. What you did was a matter of survival; you simply took what you needed... But that's not what I find so funny. I look upon your story with different eyes: I believe you continue to wear the coat because you relish the guilt. You literally carry your shame on your back! It's a constant reminder that you don't deserve anything good because you're such a terrible sinner. A modern day hair shirt! Of course, if you threw away the coat, you would have to acknowledge that you were finally free—but the shame is so delicious, isn't it?' He laughed again. 'Well, that's not the way I see the world; but whatever. Thanks for the joke. And next time, you know—better and deeper. Something that really hurts!'

PART SIX

Xaphan the Dissatisfied

The world was good

Tapephobia: the fear of being buried alive. I understood it before I died; not so much now. I have been inside a coffin. It's quiet and comfortable and no one bothers you.

When I was a child I used to sink to the bottom of the swimming pool and hold my breath and look upwards; and for a few moments, before I needed to breathe again, the world seemed small, secure and timeless. That's how the coffin felt after my death.

So I knew that if I opened my box and found nothing inside, and I was offered the chance to return to the grave, I would take it.

I woke in the workshop and crawled out into a new day.

My dry-cleaned jacket and jeans were hanging from a hook on the door. Everything looked neat and sharp, without a hint of the slime from Astaroth's infected skin. I quickly changed into my fresh clothes and packed the rags into my rucksack.

I felt different this morning: I saw my life more clearly now. I knew that I was capable of good and evil; I knew that I was able to make choices. I might choose unwisely, but I was no longer afraid of the mistakes I would make. I had made them before, when I was alive, and only one had killed me. The rest had helped me to live.

I put on my coat and walked out into the world.

The day was cold and eerily still. Yesterday's mist was gone, but the air felt thick and heavy.

I saw a crowd of people further down the street, and two cars parked sideways, forming a barrier to traffic. Curiosity drew me toward them. As I came closer I saw that The

Noodle Bar had been sealed off and police were guarding the entrance. Nearby, an officer was interviewing a bystander.

I didn't know how to respond. I could take responsibility and explain what had happened, but the consequences would be disastrous: the end of my agreement, the loss of my soul, my exposure as an infiltrator among the living. The self-protective option was to keep quiet, so I stood at the back of the crowd and listened. I discovered that everyone knew the facts of the murder but no one could explain the foul stench, the trails of slime or the missing body parts.

'Do you live locally, sir?'

I turned around. The officer was talking to me. I wasn't afraid of the police. I had always trusted them. We had collaborated when I was alive. My father had been a detective. I knew how to act—

'Yes,' I said.

'Do you know this café?'

'I was here a few days ago. I pass this way every day.'

'Did you see anything unusual last night?'

'No.'

'Do you know of any reason why someone would harbour a grudge against the business or its owners?'

I shook my head. 'The noodles are excellent.'

Was that normal? Should I have said it?

'Where do you work, sir?'

'The bookbinder, at the end of the road.'

'And what do you do there?'

'I'm an intern.'

She handed me a card: it displayed her name and contact number. 'Thank you, sir. If you remember any other details, however insignificant, please get in touch.'

She went to interview someone else. I waited a moment, then walked slowly away. I headed along Cornmarket toward the café in the passage, thinking about what had just happened. I saw my life more clearly now, and I knew that the demon was right: I was a liar.

I have always been a liar.

The café was almost full, but I found my usual seat at the table in the corner. *Doomsday Book* was still on the shelf, so I ordered a cappuccino and a pack of chocolate wafers and picked up where I had left off yesterday. I thought I might read a hundred pages a day for the next five days; but this would take me beyond the period of my agreement, and I had already pledged myself to the coffin if things didn't work out.

For now it was a relief to escape myself and enter a world created by someone else's mind. And this was just one story: there were racks of other tales waiting to be told; and there were libraries and bookshops packed with tens of thousands more. Reading every book I could find wouldn't be the worst way to spend eternity.

Perhaps I didn't want the coffin after all.

I settled into the narrative. It dragged me away from this table, out of this café, beyond this time, and into the plague-ridden hell of fourteenth century England... Two hours later I returned. I could have lingered much longer, but duty compelled me to follow my routine.

I didn't need to wash, but I was curious to know what mark had been seared, sewn or inked into my flesh. I went to the bathroom and stripped to the waist. I looked in the mirror: nothing had been added to my chest, so I turned around and examined my back. There, in the centre of the horseshoe—almost invisible against my pale skin—someone had tattooed in white a memento of my time with Astaroth: a stylised representation of a chef's hat.

I immediately felt sick. I sprinkled my face with water, ran my hands under the tap and waited for the nausea to subside. Then I got dressed and headed for the workshop.

Outside, the Christmas theme had been cranked up to max. I didn't see the fake Saint Nick telling people to Embrace Their Happy, but there were plenty of other Santas about. Like a rapidly mutating virus, they were all variations on a theme: this one was slightly fatter than the next, that one's beard was shorter than the others, this didn't have a bell, that didn't have a hat. All delivered a different message: some sold trinkets, others advertised shops, a few wished a Happy Christmas to passers-by. How could I ever have believed this lie as a child? Yet I had trusted it implicitly, along with all the other falsehoods that had softened the blows of life and lessened the fear of death.

I checked my phone. It was the twenty-third of December. The date didn't mean much to me, the season even less, but the faces all around told a different story. I recognised joy, impatience, anger, stoicism, excitement, boredom; each Lifer rushing here or there, alone, with partners or dragging children behind them, walking into stores empty-handed, walking out burdened with presents and wrapping paper. And I realised, as powerfully as if I had been struck with a hammer, that all this activity, all this emotion, all this diversity didn't frighten me anymore. I felt at ease with life.

And the world was good.

The grinder

The crowd outside The Noodle Bar had swelled with onlookers. I saw television and radio vans parked along the street. A barrier had been placed in front of the café, and a police officer was making a statement to the media. I passed them all without stopping.

I entered the workshop. Nergal and Resh didn't notice my arrival; Dumuzid was staring into space and tapping his teeth with a pencil. He smiled when he saw me.

'Good morning, zombie. Quite a disturbance outside! Still, it shouldn't be a problem, as long as they don't go poking their noses in here... Anyway, take a look at this. Tell me if it's accurate.'

The *Dictionnaire Infernal* was open on his desk. The double page entry was dedicated to Astaroth: illustration on the left, text on the right. Neither bore much relation to the creature I had encountered, but Dumuzid was altering the drawing to reflect the demon's infected state. He was scratching out an amiable dragon and replacing it with a mound of diseased flesh; but the flesh was too gross and failed to replicate the chaotic undulations of the original. Astaroth's face was blander and rounder than I remembered, too; and there was an exaggerated hook to his toes and fingers; and the crown was completely different—

'Yeah. Pretty accurate,' I said.

'I should have asked you to take a photograph; all I have to go on is a bunch of rumours on Darknet.' He tapped his teeth again. 'Do you want to see Xaphan?'

'Who's that?'

'Your next demon.'

He began to flick through the book, but I stopped him.

'I'll take what comes.'

He nodded and returned to the page he had been working on, but his expression was peculiarly coy. 'By the way, did Astaroth ask after me?'

I nodded. 'Resh and Nergal, too.'

'What did he say?'

'Not much. Just that you'd grown apart.'

He sighed. 'I suppose that's all I could have hoped for.'

'How do you two know each other?'

'It's a long story, but he's my ex-wife. He was known as Inanna back then, although later generations called him Ishtar; and Ishtar the goddess eventually became Astaroth the demon... I guess you could say he went with the flow.'

'He's had more names than the Boss,' Nergal said. 'I'm just grateful we're not blood relatives.'

'He's Resh's younger brother,' said Dumuzid. 'The tale of how we all became entangled is another long one. Look it up on your phone sometime, if you're interested.'

I said that I would, but I didn't know if I meant it. I wasn't sure I could trust anything that came out of my mouth anymore.

I didn't notice Malache until he was standing beside me. 'Good morning,' he said. 'I have great news.'

He led me to his office and closed the door behind us. We sat down at his desk. I waited for him to offer me a drink or a cigarette, but neither was forthcoming, which made me wonder if the news wasn't so great after all.

'I've just received feedback from Astaroth, and I'm pleased to say he's given you a glowing report. He describes you as "extremely helpful", "very polite" and "an excellent cook". He's awarded you nine-point-five horns out of ten! For reference, Orobas only gave you four—'

'Nine-point-five *what*?' I said.

'Horns—it's the grading system on RMI.' I looked at him blankly. 'Rate My Intern—a website for Green Devil employees. We leave reviews and scores for anyone who works for us. You have five reviews so far, with an average of...' He scrolled up the screen. 'Seven-point-three. That's very good; many of our trainees struggle to get above five. As I said, you have a knack for this kind of work. You should seriously consider my offer of employment.'

'Before I commit myself to anything—'

'You want to know what's behind the door. I get it. And I have the answer right here.' He brandished a brass key between thumb and forefinger. 'However, since you're not a full-time employee, there are certain protocols we need to observe first. The Bureau has nothing to hide, but there are certain sights you're not yet ready to see—corporate secrets, and so on.' He opened his desk drawer and removed a small bottle of pills. 'You'll need to take one of these. We'll wait for the effect to take hold, then go inside.'

'What does it contain?'

'An hallucinogenic drug. It will modify your perception of the grinder without concealing its essential nature.' He tapped one of the pills onto the table. 'Since you're a zombie, half a tablet should suffice. We don't want you bouncing off the walls, do we?'

I had the sensation of floating. Then the room began to spin slowly, like the first revolution of a Waltzer ride. I focused on Malache; he stayed still and silent, smiling. The room spun a little faster. The table reared up on two legs and walked through the door in disgust; the office window melted, rolled down the wall and leached into the ground; the chair beneath me ignited its rocket engines and broke through the ceiling. Like the Cheshire Cat, Malache became a grinning face, then a smile with twin rows of tiny teeth—but he was the only stable point in the world, and I thought if I could just focus on that smile I would get through whatever I was going through. Then the Waltzer accelerated to full speed and pushed me against the wall, and the room twisted violently on its axis, and I lost the sense of where I was, who I was, what any of this meant, but those teeth kept smiling, and a darkness grew around them, a thick darkness as thick as the morning air, and it spread outward and upward until the whole room turned black—and the last thing I saw before I passed out was Malache's wide, self-satisfied, feline smile.

'Hello, friend.'

I opened my eyes. The air was a soothing shade of green. Malache was holding my hand.

The office had changed. The framed certificates were replaced by posters I had pinned on my bedroom wall as a child: the fantasy worlds of Roger Dean, some sentimental Athena prints, the Beatles on the crossing at Abbey Road. The table was now my bed, with its faded Star Wars duvet cover. One chair had transformed into an Atari VCS and a portable television, the other had become a cheap wardrobe.

I looked through the window into the workshop. All of the desks were now the desk in my father's study, and the walls were lined with his books. Resh was older and bore a resemblance to my mother, Dumuzid was younger and similar in appearance to my father. Nergal's transformation was even more dramatic: he had become a stunted, red-haired homunculus with exaggerated facial and bodily features.

'Rumpelstiltskin,' I said.

'Take your time,' said Malache. 'The worst is over with.'

I took a couple of unsteady steps toward the door, but I wasn't sure which door it was, or why I was moving. Malache grabbed my right arm to make sure I didn't fall, then carefully steered me to the right door, which was the right door. He unlocked the right door, put his right hand on the right handle—then opened the right door and guided me right through.

The air was clearer here; but there were dimensions, sounds and shapes which took a while to resolve. The room itself was larger than the workshop in all aspects: twice as high, twice as long and half as wide again. At the far end I saw a pair of sliding metal doors, which were closed. I heard fairground music, too: a combination of pipe organs and pop rhythms. Overhead strip lights glowed greenly, but they weren't really necessary to illuminate the machine that dominated this place.

It looked like a funhouse. It *was* a funhouse: a riot of colour, motion and noise two storeys high, running the entire length of the room. The entrance, at the near end, was a huge, gaping clown's mouth which fed into a dark corridor. Beyond that, I saw slopes and stairs, walkways and railings, moving pavements and wobbly bridges, poles and stepping stones, tube slides, helter-skelters, a wall of distorting mirrors, and dozens of small, oddly-shaped windows. The skin of this machine was equally

218

anarchic: a psychedelic mixture of Day-Glo patterns and neon lights, stripes blending into stars, spots erupting into animal prints, clashing colours and forms covering every surface in haphazard fashion. And all the while the organ music and disco beats played on in an endless cycle, sometimes in harmony with the moving parts, but more often asynchronously, jarringly.

Then I noticed the people. They were queuing in a broad line from the metal doors to the entrance, stewarded by two creatures in devil costumes. All had happy smiles and sparkling eyes, and most went willingly; although a few needed encouragement from the devils' tridents. As they approached the mouth they narrowed into single file and vanished within. I saw some reappear on the first or second storey, screaming with excitement and smiling still; but they had changed in the meantime—an arm or leg looked shorter, a hand was missing, there was only one eye, or a nose was split down the middle. Yet still they walked on, until they disappeared altogether—and as much as I strained to look, I saw no one emerge.

'This is the grinder,' said Malache, proudly. 'A model of economy, simplicity and control. It's official title is the Green Devil Reprocessing And Conversion Engine, and I'm proud to say we own GDR-ACE-1. Back in the day, it was the first of its kind in the country, though there are many more—'

'Can I have a look inside?'

I lurched toward the entrance but he pulled me back. 'That's not a good idea right now. But if our agreement doesn't work out, we can have a chat about your options... In the meantime, just for my own curiosity, tell me what you see.'

'A fairground funhouse.'

He nodded and indicated the people in the queue. 'Everyone here has taken the same drug as you, so the collective experience is invariably pleasant. That promotes an atmosphere of conformity, which allows us to maximise capacity, reduce handling time and mitigate stress. But every Lifer interprets the machine in a unique way: one might see a fairy-tale castle, another a pirate ship, a playground, or a toy shop. All are cherished memories from childhood: we discovered, over time, that such illusions minimise the fear of termination.'

'Where's the exit?'

'This way,' he said.

He took my arm again, and we passed through the ghostly lines of the living. On the way, I collided with one of the devils, and his costume looked so lifelike I had to pinch it to discover what it was made of; but the devil gave an indignant squeal and swung at me with his trident. My companion offered an apology and ushered me away.

'Of course, the problem is getting people to come here voluntarily,' he said, gently easing aside an old woman who was blocking our path. 'But we realised early on that the tried and tested methods work best—temptation, in particular. Some of these people will have been lured by the offer of cheap consumer goods, some by the promise of an illicit sexual relationship; there are many other routes. For a few, the drug itself is enough: you'd be surprised how many Lifers just want to try something new. There's very little coercion involved... Ah—here we are.'

We had reached the sliding doors. There were more costumed devils here, packing what emerged from the machine into boxes and crates. These containers were then stacked into neat piles.

The doors opened. I saw two Green Devil Recycling lorries parked outside. Their rear gates were raised to allow the devils to load the goods onboard. It was a delightful scene: the lorries were decorated with flowers and smiling emojis; their engines chugged with a beguiling musical hum; their odour was perfumed and mouth-watering, like candy floss or Turkish delight—

At that point, the drug began to wear off.

Different is beautiful

The floor shone with polish; the floor gleamed with blood. Workers transformed from devils to men and back to devils once more. One moment the objects they packed into crates were glittering baubles and trinkets, toy capsules and delicious cakes, a cornucopia of wonderful objects the like of which had enthralled me all week; the next they were piles of hair and teeth, membranes and clumps of offal, chopped body parts and splintered bone. Sounds switched eerily between discordant fairground music and the low machine hum I had heard every morning—now augmented by the shredding of flesh, the grinding of skeletal remains and the terrified screams of the dying. From one breath to the next, odours changed from aromatic and sugary sweet to the cloying tangs of the butcher and slaughterhouse. And the grinder itself was no longer a haphazard structure of colour and light, but a stainless steel machine of gears and cogs, blades and giant hammers, conveyer belts and funnels, which swallowed people at one end, processed them pitilessly, and dumped their remains into rows of metal troughs by the doors.

Only Malache remained the same in this alternating reality: a short, immaculately dressed young man with an incongruous mop of blond curls.

'Have you seen enough?' he said.

I nodded, pretending not to see.

He led me back along the line. The faces no longer smiled and sparkled, but were glazed and slack-mouthed. As people shuffled vacantly toward the entrance, two men in green boiler suits poked and struck them with canes.

'It really is a thing of beauty,' said Malache. 'The perfect population control device: a machine that marries economy of effort with incredible productivity. And it's all just a question of logistics: what's the right level of soundproofing, how many people can you process, what's the most efficient maintenance schedule, do you have enough lorries to deal with the output, and so on... We aim to have it running twenty-four hours a day in the next few months—if we get the license. But we have a couple of employees on the city council, so it shouldn't be a problem.'

'I don't feel so good,' I said.

We returned to the office. The world continued to pulse between truth and illusion; until, at last, the periods of normality overcame the nostalgic junk in my mind. Malache waited patiently throughout, and eventually produced the bottle of Southern Comfort I hadn't known I needed.

He poured me a glass. I took a couple of large gulps. The burning eased the sickness in my throat.

'Thank you,' I said. 'And thanks for keeping your word.'

'Perhaps you will trust me a little more from now on.'

I grunted, and took another swig.

'Examine any organisation you like,' he continued. 'You won't find one hundred per cent honesty in any of them—and I genuinely believe we do better than most.' He poured himself a glass and sipped it pensively. 'Anyway, now that we've got the gruesome business out of the way, it's time for... some more gruesome business.' He smiled charmingly and removed a familiar white envelope from his pocket. 'Here's the note. If you're lucky, there'll be three photographs inside and this will be the last night of your internship.'

I returned to the workshop. I waited for someone to announce that they were going to drive me somewhere, but no one did. However, if patterns meant anything at all, I calculated it was Resh's turn to accompany me, so I sidled up to her desk and stood very still.

'How can I help you, Rabbit?' she said, without glancing up from the poster she was working on.

'I'm just waiting.'

'For anything in particular?'

'Not really. But in the last five days, I've been taken for a meal, a haircut, a pedicure, a new set of clothes and a mobile phone. I figured there might be something else on the list.'

'I don't think so. That's about all we give the new interns. You're pretty much on your own now.'

My brain turned into an embarrassed walnut. My beating heart punched itself in the aorta. I started to move away, hoping an oubliette might open in the floor and I could slip quietly down and be forgotten; but Resh looked up before I had retreated more than a foot. Her expression changed from concentration to sympathy.

'Poor Rabbit. You look even paler than normal. Maybe I should treat you after all... In fact, I know just the thing you need. Give me a couple of minutes, then I'll join you.'

'Can you two stop talking?' said Nergal. 'I'm writing a business proposal for transplanting infant buttock skin onto the faces of the aged rich but every time I try to define suitable criteria for the feasibility study *one of you speaks.*'

'Go lame and shoot yourself,' said Resh, and returned to her work.

I stood by the entrance and watched the street. The crowd outside The Noodle Bar had thinned and the media vans were gone, but the policewoman who had interviewed me was still pacing back and forth. I was distracted by the neck-bobbing habits of pigeons for a while, too. Nothing much else happened.

Five minutes later Resh appeared, wearing her coat, scarf, ear muffs and mittens. We left the workshop and climbed on her purple Vespa.

'Hold onto my waist,' she said.

I put my arms around her and rested my cheek against her back. She drove quickly and with a certain recklessness, but I never thought we might smash into a wall or roll over in a blaze of fire; though either would have been a romantic death. Eventually, we reached the northern outskirts of the city and parked outside an unremarkable block of flats: a grey, square tower with functional windows and token balconies.

'This is my bolthole when I want to escape that uncouth oaf I married. I've spent many happy evenings here, untroubled by his beer-drinking boorishness.'

'It's good to be alone,' I said.

'Sometimes. I'd miss work and friends, though. You need a bit of contrast in life, I think.'

We entered the building and ascended two flights of concrete stairs to a landing with four doors. She took out a key and opened the door to Flat Seven.

It was a basic apartment with a lounge, kitchen, bathroom and bedroom, but the rudimentary layout was offset by extraordinary decoration. The walls were papered with vibrant images of lush gardens, in which lions, bulls and dragons roamed; the furniture was ornate, with wooden scrolls and intricate carvings enhancing every chair, table and bookcase; a number of simple antique figurines were arranged on the shelves and side tables; a small stone fountain created a soothing focal point in the lounge. The whole effect was a practical demonstration of the contrast she had described: stimulation and calm, the elaborate and the plain.

'Do you like it?'

'Yes. Why have you brought me here?'

'There's something more I can give you—an experience that will make you feel truly alive... Come into the bedroom.'

I began to construct a list of excuses in my mind. I had no functioning sexual organ. My hands were like clubs. I was afraid. I was embarrassed by my wounds and the pallor of my skin. My heart was in chains. I was afraid (again). But a minute later I found myself standing in her bedroom, looking at a double bed covered with the skin of some fleecy animal, and removing my clothes.

'Leave your shorts on,' she said. It seemed a strange request, but I obeyed. 'Now, lie face down on the bed.'

I did so, feeling stupid and uneasy. Maybe this week had been nothing more than a devilish joke, and I was about to feel the cold blade of some cruel knife in my back...

In fact, she removed her mittens, sat down beside me and placed her hands on my shoulders. She rubbed them gently at first, then began to work her fingers into the knots and coils, untangling them with great skill. She moved slowly downward with a combination of tenderness and firmness, resolving the tightness in me, smoothing out the hard ridges and aching nodes. I bathed in her, I absorbed her, I felt her pressing against me and yielded to the pressure. Her hands against my skin were the perfumed oils of paradise.

'You're as stiff as a stone lintel, Rabbit. I'm surprised you haven't collapsed under the strain. When did you last have a massage?'

'I don't remember. It never seemed necessary before.'

'That's zombie talk. When you're reunited with your soul, you can ignore what's necessary and choose what you *want*. Every feeling, every desire, every human instinct will return to you as if you had never been apart.'

'I'd like to believe that. But I don't even know if my soul is still there. It might have withered through neglect.'

'I'm sure it hasn't. You can sense it, can't you?'

'Sometimes.'

'Sometimes is enough... Besides, you wouldn't have carried that box around with you all these years, if you thought it was empty.'

I closed my eyes and drifted on a tide of sensation. I was the unravelled knot, the finger riding my spine, the gentle fists pounding my shoulders. I was pleasure and exquisite pain. I was my skin. I moved down to my legs, and became the kneading of my thighs, the rubbing of my calves, the thumbs seeking resistance.

'I like your markings. The horseshoe is Orobas, isn't it?'

I nodded, and briefly told her the story of each design. 'My favourite is Alastor's wings. I think they're beautiful... But Malache said the grinder was beautiful, so I'm not sure what the word means anymore.'

'There's no beauty in that machine. The best you can say is that it's functional.' Her hands stopped, and I returned to a world of fleece blankets and luxuriant wall prints. 'Not that beauty has to be conventional—for me, different is beautiful. I see beauty in the withered and strange, in degradation and death; I find it in wounds and the wailing of lost souls. I have known countless dead, and all have their own beauty. Your body is beautiful too, because it is unlike any other I have seen.' She resumed her massage; I felt a shock of pleasure. 'And your dance yesterday: it was silly, and eccentric, and awkward, but all the more beautiful for that.'

'You're unusually kind for a devil.'

'Devil is just a word,' she said dismissively. 'A corporate label designed to promote a sense of cohesion; it means nothing. My Underworld isn't a moral nightmare of torture and punishment, it's a place to care for the dead, without judgement.'

Hands on my skin like velvet.

'What do you look like there?'

'My alternate, you mean?' She seemed surprised to be asked. 'I'm exactly the same as I am here. Apart from the winter clothing.'

'What about Malache?'

'He isn't one of us, so I can't say.'

I relaxed into somatic pleasure once more. Nothing else mattered. The choices fighting for control of my mind faded away. Who I could trust, what would happen to me, who I had once been—these questions were unimportant. I didn't even think about my soul. I was these fingers, this flesh. Bliss incarnate. And she was right: it made me feel truly alive.

226

'Are you crying?'

I nodded. 'It's been a long time since I felt this way.'

'Would you like me to hold you?'

'Yes.'

I felt warm tears trickling down my cheeks. Tears that released me from myself. Tears that brought a happiness I hadn't experienced since my death. Tears of melancholy for the life I missed.

She lay down beside me and wrapped her arms around me. 'It's okay, Rabbit,' she whispered. 'It'll be over soon. Then you'll know.'

The influencer

I wanted to clear my head, so I refused her offer of a ride back to the office. I waved goodbye at the flat, then walked down the Banbury Road into Summertown. Memories accompanied me: buying furniture in this arcade, a client who had lived in that house, a restaurant I had visited with my parents—and further along, a boat hire I had gone to with Amy. We had taken a punt down the river; I had spent the whole trip believing I would drown.

When I reached North Oxford I became aware of Zoë walking beside me. 'I'm going to my flat,' she said. 'Do you want to come?'

I nodded. I didn't mind passing time with a ghost.

'I'm not a ghost,' she said.

'But you're not real either.'

'That's harsh.'

I shrugged. I could still feel the real warmth of Resh's fingers against my skin, the strength of her real arms around me.

'She's a liar, just like the rest of them,' said Zoë.

'Then I won't make the mistake of getting too close.'

'You can't escape who you are.'

'No. But when I free my soul—'

'You will still be you, dragging around that heap of junk in shabby cloth.'

I walked more quickly to try and shake her off, but she anticipated my every move.

'I don't think she's good for you, that's all. She's toying with you. They all are.'

'I don't care.'

'That's your problem. You know what they're like but you can't help yourself. You suspect they're using you as bait but you still put yourself on the hook.'

We reached her old flat. There was no light in the window. She had left this place a month after our last meeting, but I had kept coming back in case she returned. At first I had visited every week, then every month, and now I couldn't remember the last time I was here. But it had been twenty years since I last saw her.

Time to give up.

'Can you help me with the note?' I said.

I unsealed the envelope and she placed the paper in my open hands. The message was longer than usual: *Revenge is sweet, hmm? We will see. But he won't get away with it this time. I know what he looks like, I know where he lives. I don't need the help of an undead. What do you mean you're writing down everything I say? I didn't tell you to start, you idiot! Yes, you might as well just carry on. ID: 0981352837111. Lazy little thieving fucker. Forget what you just heard, undead. Come along at six. That's just before he starts his broadcast, so it'll irritate the hell out of him. Why are you telling me I only have fifty-three characters lef*

There was one photograph. It showed a young man with a bland expression on a nondescript face. He looked entirely plain, insipid and uninteresting. Or maybe I couldn't tell the difference anymore.

'Are you leaving now?'

She nodded. 'I'll be back tomorrow. Wait for me here. Then we can say goodbye properly.'

I checked the time on my phone: already three in the afternoon. It was cold, so I put my stumps in the pockets of my coat—and found the money Nergal had given me yesterday. The grinder and the massage had driven it from my mind; now it weighed heavily upon me. But there were people who could relieve me of this burden.

I followed the road until I reached Little Clarendon Street. Here was a man by the cashpoints, standing with his head bowed, his body wrapped in an old duvet; I fumbled a note into his cup. On the steps of the Admissions office I saw a woman sitting cross-legged on a threadbare rug, with coins at her feet; I added to the collection. I continued onto St Giles and headed for the city centre—I found a man outside the delicatessen, another beside the charity shop, a woman huddled against the wall of St Cross. I turned right, past the playhouse to the bus station square. Three more: a grey-haired man on the bench beneath a tree, a woman with pale skin outside the Old Fire Station, a young man who talked to himself beneath the arch. I moved up to Cornmarket: a man on the harmonica who danced like a zombie; a teenage boy with holes in his arms, who seemed to be asleep; a woman with a gap-toothed smile who sat beneath a poster of a woman with shining teeth. And down to Bonn Square—a woman selling a magazine to earn money; a woman telling jokes; a woman who said nothing...

This was how I passed the afternoon, divesting myself until only a single bank note remained. I didn't question my motives at the time, but afterward I wondered if the burden I had been carrying all along was not the money, but the weight of those seven souls I had delivered to the demon.

I had acted with compassion, altruistically; I had tried to salve my conscience, selfishly. But life had never been a series of neutral choices leading to neutral outcomes. Motives might be complex and results unpredictable, but there were still some acts that were more good than bad, and others that were more bad than good.

This felt like a revelation, and it struck me with tremendous force. Then I remembered: when I was alive, I had known it instinctively.

I checked the time again: almost six. I had a message notification too, so I opened the app and found a text from Malache: *You're running late. Stay where you are and don't move. I'll come and pick you up.*

I interpreted his instructions literally: I stood very still on the pavement until I heard the growl of a scooter racing down the road toward me. Malache skidded to a halt by the kerb, waited for me to get on, then accelerated away through a pedestrian zone. His driving was more reckless than ever: he ignored traffic lights and stop signs, hurtled over a couple of roundabouts, careered between lanes under the railway bridge, and dashed into Osney—where he took a sharp left into a street of redbrick terraced houses.

Each house had a recessed porch and a bay window on the ground floor and two plain, rectangular windows on the first; they differed only in maintenance and decorative detail. The terrace we stopped at had a terracotta path leading to a red front door. The garden had been filled with concrete. There were brand new slates on the roof.

'My apologies for the wild ride,' said Malache. 'I wanted to ensure we arrived before Xaphan. His sense of timing is impeccable and he's somewhat impatient; without your guidance I fear he may have chosen alternative outlets for his vengeful impulses. However, it seems we are in luck. If you wait outside, he will be along presently.'

I dismounted; Malache left. As soon as I saw his scooter turn onto the main road, I knocked three times on the front door, as loudly as I could.

It was opened by the young man in the photograph. His face had more character than the image suggested: his eyes were bright with anger, his lips pursed with irritation,

230

his round cheeks flushed with whatever else was bothering him. He stood on the threshold with an attitude of condescension, as if I were a lowly servant.

'What do you want? I've already told you people I'm not giving away any more autographs. Contact my agent and pay the fee like everyone else... Why are you still standing there? Are you deaf?'

'May I come in?' I said.

'No, you may bloody well not. Is there something wrong with you? The vlog starts in five minutes. Half a million followers waiting on my every word, and you expect—'

'Someone is coming to kill you.'

'Right... I get it now.' He smiled contemptuously. 'Look, subscribe to the channel, send me a message when I'm streaming, and I'll give you a reply you can share with all your weird fanboy chums... Until then, fuck off, you pasty-faced fuck.'

He slammed the door: as choices go, it was more bad than good. I didn't bother to knock again, but sat down on the concrete garden and waited for the demon to arrive.

I didn't have to wait long.

First, I heard a tuneless whistle; then I saw a young man who looked almost exactly like the one I had just spoken to: tall, round-faced and ordinary, but with an edge of barely-concealed rage. He was dressed casually in a grey hoodie, blue jeans and sneakers. He slouched toward me with his hands in his pockets.

'I see you got the note, undead. Shall we go inside?'

Transmission

'Don't bother knocking. He won't answer.'

'I don't need to knock,' he said.

He pressed his fingers against the door and twisted his hand as if turning a key. A hole appeared in the wood; but it wasn't like any hole I had ever seen. It should have revealed the interior; instead it led to nothing and nowhere—an airless, inky blackness. The demon was unfazed: he plunged his arm into it, reached around to the catch, and opened the door.

We entered the hallway. There were exits to the rear and left, and a staircase on the right. The demon raised a finger to his lips and began to sneak up the stairs, his feet as light as dust, his body limber as an otter. I thumped after him on clumping feet, tripped on the third step and crashed to the floor. He glared at me, then continued upward; I followed and reached the landing without further mishap. There were three more doors here; he pointed to the nearest and waited. After a moment we heard a loud voice.

'Okay guys, the countdown has begun. It's only five minutes until I unbox my brand new MaxAudio Carbon Fibre Ear Pods—they're not even out in the shops yet, but the super-nerds at MaxAudio have kindly given me an exclusive preview, which I'm going to share with you today. Until then, click on Like, click on Subscribe, and if you love what I do, consider donating via—wait—who are you? Big news, folks. I have a guest here in the studio. Don't be shy, come in... There's another one! Two fans have paid me an impromptu visit, how they got my address I'll never know—stay safe out there, people, never give anyone your personal details—but here they are. Join me, both of you—four minutes to go, everybody—what can I do for you?'

'I am Xaphan, from the Bureau of Infernal Affairs.'

'What? Oh, this is perfect. Stand in front of the camera... Okay, whatever. Guys, there's no need for alarm, I know this face. Whoever put him up to it—great joke! Maybe you've come to open the package with me? No? Anyway, you can't see him, folks but I'd like to introduce to you the Mysterious Mr X, creator of The X-Man Podcast.'

'And you're the thieving fuck who's stolen content from my channel for the last five years.'

'Strong words from our guest! But I'll gladly pick up the gauntlet, Mr X. First of all, every bit of content on this vlog belongs to me, and it's all original. Second, even if I did take inspiration from your—how many subscribers do you have, by the way?'

'Eighty-two.'

'Even if I did *borrow* some of your content, you should be thanking me for the exposure. The reality is, you can't match my numbers, and you don't have the lawyers I'm going to call if you repeat any of the accusations you just made. Face it: you've taken the dirt path of the struggling artist, while I'm racing at full throttle down the monetisation highway.'

Xaphan's demeanour changed abruptly. His whole body shuddered, he seemed to grow a little, and his skin turned a very dark red. He began puffing and blowing, like a pair of bellows, and with every breath his body became more wiry and angular. At last he shed his human form altogether and revealed his alternate—which resembled nothing more than a child's image of a devil: horns, curly hair, pointed ears and clawed hands.

One of those hands held a silver 9mm pistol.

'What the fuck?' the young man said.

The demon fired.

Xaphan crossed the floor and stamped on the computer until its insides cracked. Then he did the same to the young man with a bullet hole in his forehead.

I turned away and looked around the room. The walls were a neutral cream, unadorned by posters, paintings or photographs. The lighting was bright and evenly spread: a ring light, an overhead bulb, an octagonal softbox. I saw a desk and chair, a green screen behind the chair, and dozens of cardboard boxes marked *Not For Resale* behind the screen.

'No, no, no!' said Xaphan impatiently, as he stood over the crushed remains. 'That was far too quick. He didn't suffer enough. I want him to suffer!'

He sighed and moved his hands in a peculiar way, as if clawing at an invisible rope. Then he muttered a few words and the world

echoed
shifted

around me and I felt violently seasick and staggered forward and collapsed into darkness.

When I woke the nausea had passed. But I was back in the doorway, where I had been standing when Xaphan had fired the pistol.

And his victim had come back to life.

Now the demon was brandishing a machete. He swung wildly and sliced through the camera cable, disconnecting the live feed—then he swung again and cut clean through his rival's left arm. The young man's face turned white with shock; he managed only three words before the demon set about him once more:

'What the fuck?'

Xaphan chopped off the right arm, slashed wildly at his victim's torso, then hacked at his legs—

I left the room.

I couldn't see what was happening, but I heard the screams. It would have been better not to have ears. I rushed downstairs, but his cries penetrated the walls and floor. How much further could I go before I broke my agreement? Could I leave this house, the street, this city? But I would still hear those frenzied shrieks inside my head. I just had to wait for them to finish.

It took some time.

At last I heard Xaphan calling me. I moved to the bottom of the stairs and saw his devilish face peering over the railings at the top.

'Come here, undead. I need your assistance. I like to leave a place more or less as I found it, but I'm afraid I got carried away.'

I trudged reluctantly back up the staircase, wondering with each step whether I should comply with his request. As I reached the landing, I decided that I would refuse, grab the soul and leave. I took a deep breath and walked into the room, where Xaphan was frowning at a pile of dismembered limbs.

'Actually, never mind,' he said irritably. 'This is no good, either. It doesn't reflect who he *is*. Stay where you are. And close your eyes. The loop can be rather unsettling.'

I did as he suggested—but still felt the nauseating *echo*, the brutal sideways *shift*—

—and I was standing in the doorway again, and the victim was sitting in his chair.

The demon blinked three times, mumbled a short incantation and clicked his fingers.

'—the fuck?'

The young man disappeared.

Xaphan scanned the room, then peered at the floor. 'Watch your step. You never know what form their self-image will adopt. Sometimes it's a slug or a fly, sometimes—ah, there it is!'

I followed his gaze and saw a large insect on the carpet. Six hairy legs and a glossy green carapace. It was waving its antennae at the demon in what appeared to be a provocative manner. He crept toward it, raised his foot and stamped down hard; but the bug had already scuttled under the desk.

Xaphan cursed, knelt down and lashed out with his fists—but the insect eluded his blows. It darted beneath a drawer, scurried behind a radiator, then dashed over the carpet by the skirting boards. After a particularly frustrating sequence of near misses, Xaphan leapt up and down and shrieked like a toddler. Then he resumed his search.

I felt no desire to help, so I took out my phone and clicked on the Weather app. It showed me the weather right now, which was useless because I could see it through the window. I skipped to the forecast for tomorrow. Low temperatures, high winds and heavy rain: a storm was coming.

I looked up again. Xaphan was crawling on his belly by the boxes, easing one aside, lifting another, ready to strike. 'Come out, you ugly little bug. The Mysterious Mr X has a present for you.'

'Not so mysterious now, are you?' a tiny voice chittered.

The fact that the insect could talk disturbed me in all manner of ways, but didn't trouble Xaphan one jot. He smiled and edged closer to one of the packages, resting his hand gently on top. 'What did you say? You're so quiet, I can barely hear you.'

'I said: you're not so mysterious—*oh shit*.'

The demon had moved the box aside, exposing the bug's hiding place. It was trapped. A wall of cardboard surrounded it on three sides, and its only escape led directly into Xaphan's hands.

It made a last desperate dash for freedom, but two clawed fingers plucked it quickly from the carpet. The demon raised it to eye level; his mouth opened in a broad grin. The insect waved its legs furiously, but its antennae had drooped in defeat. Then—though I may have imagined it because it didn't seem possible—the bug looked in my direction.

'Help me! Help me!' it squeaked.

Xaphan dropped it into his open mouth, and swallowed.

'Ugh! That was so frustrating!' he said. 'Now I'm going to have to do it all again... Don't look at me like that—'

Echo, shift, and I was back in the doorway.

'Let me remove your mask,' said the demon.

'What—?' said the young man.

'I want to show the world who you really are.'

236

He cut his rival's throat with his claws, waited for him to bleed out, then slowly peeled the skin from his face.

Echo, shift, doorway.

'The—?'

Xaphan transformed his victim into an ice sculpture then shattered him with a hammer. The ice melted slowly on the carpet. The demon wasn't happy.

Echo, shift.

'Fuck—?'

He brutally beat him to death with a spiked club.

Time rewound. Space reset. The killing continued.

I wondered if there was a word for the feeling of dying at the moment of death. Probably not—what would be the point? In any case, Xaphan's victim experienced that feeling many more times before the end.

I retreated to the safety of my mobile phone. The perfect device for the undead: a walled garden of information. I browsed the internet and conquered the last level in *Plants vs Zombies* many times. But I was detached from the experience. I wasn't the same person I had been six days ago: there was something inside me now that hadn't been present since my death. Green shoots rising from the soil.

'What the fuck?' said the young man.

Xaphan shot him through the forehead.

'That's enough,' he said, disconnecting the camera from the computer. 'Funny, isn't it? You change something a hundred times, but the first idea is often the best.'

'I wouldn't know.'

'Of course not. Want to say a few words?'

I shook my head.

'As you wish... Nice perfume, by the way. *Eau de Styx*. Très chic.'

He folded his arms and studied the corpse with pride.

His smug expression irritated me.

'Every demon seems to be a master of something,' I said. 'So what's your specialty? Decisiveness? Pest Control? Not Falling Over?'

'I wish you had shown as much enthusiasm for your work as you do for insults. But I take no offence: you are you, and I am me, and one will never understand the other. Nonetheless, I am prepared to indulge you: in certain circles, I am known as the Master of Time.'

'Great. I'll think about you every time I pass a clock.'

He smiled impishly. 'When did you die, exactly?'

'I'm not sure. Why?'

'Because I could, with very little effort, send you back to the moment before your death and force you to experience your time again. Would you like that?'

Get it over with. Countless years. A knock on the coffin lid. Suicide, poisoning, drowning, dismembering, consumption, asphyxiation. A game of chess. A lowly job. No desire, no determination, no reason to live. Then Zoë and her pendant, and the treasures of the dead: money, power, love, achievement, optimism, beauty, duty and memory. My parents' graves, emptied of their bodies. A demon and a wooden box. Twenty years of wandering the streets alone, never connecting, always afraid. Frozen in time, trapped in space. Then Malache's smile, and six nights of horror, and the promise at last of an end to it all.

'No, thanks. I'm good.'

He chuckled. 'You are a strange one. Most people would surrender an arm for such a generous offer. Perhaps I should do it anyway, as a parting gift—'

'Your superior is expecting a soul tonight.'

'I see. I drive the hunt but he takes the fox. Well, so it is... But where might one find this delicious little essence?'

He knelt beside the corpse and sniffed its face, belly and thighs. Then he glanced at the computer. He turned it off and removed the side panel: a motherboard, a hard drive, RAM, a graphics card and a fan.

'It's always been on the body before,' I said.

'That shows how little you know, undead. Sometimes a Lifer neglects his soul and it slips out unawares. However, they rarely stray far from home, so it should be somewhere in this room.'

He rubbed his hands, tugged his ears and stroked his horns—until the answer finally came. He returned to the place where he had caught the insect and began to rummage among the packages. Eventually, he found an unmarked black box. He removed the lid slowly, then smiled and brought the box over to me.

I looked inside. I saw a cockroach lying on its back with its legs in the air. 'That's just an ordinary bug,' I said.

'Can't you smell it?' he said in astonishment. 'But what am I thinking? You're a sad little fellow with no particular skills. So you'll have to take my word for it: this thing is that miserable creature's eternal soul. He was trying to find it when—so that's how I—but never mind, you wouldn't understand... Here—take it before I eat it.'

He tipped the box toward my cupped palms. The dead insect was as light as sycamore seed. I placed it carefully in my coat pocket.

'Now for my trophy... An entire body to choose from... I could make a leather bag of his skin—but perhaps...' He returned to the desk, reached into the computer and took the hard drive. 'Yes. Much more appropriate. There's five years' worth of content on here. I'm simply taking back what's rightfully mine.'

'Don't forget the ID tag.'

He considered it for a moment, then shrugged.

'Fuck it,' he said. 'I don't have time.'

It's all in the text

The police arrived shortly after I left: two cars with flashing lights, travelling at high speed. They screeched to a halt outside the house; three officers rushed inside. I was standing at the end of the road by then, trying to look like I had no knowledge of anything.

I waited for Malache, but he didn't show up. After a while, I took out my wooden box and examined it beneath the street lamp. No hinge, no seam—but perhaps an indentation there, on one of the longer sides? More likely a trick of the light.

I felt suddenly desperate. All this effort, all these deaths might be for nothing. An empty box—or worse: a soul so withered by evil and indifference it would scatter in a gust of wind.

I closed my eyes and imagined running across the green meadow to the dark river. At the river's edge I threw the box into the water. I watched it sink, and jumped in after it—not so that I might rescue it, but to make sure that we both drowned.

I had felt nothing for the man we had killed. I had simply looked away. But even feelings weren't enough, if all they did was turn inward and examine themselves in isolation. To have any meaning at all, feelings had to project outward. They had to connect with others.

I had to help people.

For now, I was the obedient servant of a demon, and I had a gift to deliver. There was still no sign of Malache, so I followed the main road to the city centre, then headed north toward The Chimera. I had almost passed the bus station when I saw a familiar black Vespa coming in the opposite direction. I waited for him to pull into the kerb.

'Didn't you get my message?' he said.

'I haven't checked my phone.'

'Never mind. You're here now; though you look rather glum. How was your evening?'

'My head is still reeling from the timeshifts.'

'I should have warned you beforehand. I'm sorry—I sometimes forget that what is common knowledge to me might not be so for others. You'll be fine in the morning. Are you fit to face the overseer?'

'Do I have a choice?'

'Not really. But I like to be polite.'

I climbed on the seat and put my arms around his waist, but not as tightly as before, half in the hope that a sudden jolt might throw me off. Perhaps sensing this, Malache drove with great care, waiting for traffic and even slowing down for speed bumps. We arrived at the pub a couple of minutes later.

As I dismounted, I glanced across the street and saw the man we met yesterday spying on us from his window. I attempted to reach out to him by smiling and raising my stump in greeting; but, misunderstanding my intention, he shook his fist at me.

Malache revved the engine three times, then let it idle. 'The door is already unlocked, so I'll say goodbye. Perhaps I'll see you at the party tomorrow?'

'What party?'

'It's all in the text I sent you.'

He drove away quickly. The hum of his scooter faded into the distance, like a bee returning to the hive after a long day in the fields.

I had no other memories of The Bookbinders Arms. I had probably been here many more times than the two occasions I recalled, but those events were buried so deep that not even Death could have resurrected them.

I tried to invite Zoë into the snug with me. I thought we might pass the evening with a few drinks, get to know each other better, confess our sins, share our triumphs—and leave arm-in-arm, our bodies touching as we walked out into the moonlit night. She didn't appear, but I heard her whisper in the darkness. 'I'll see you tomorrow,' she said. 'Don't let me down.'

Amy, Lucy, Zoë... Love, light and life. Sometimes fate is invisible, sometimes it walks in shadow—and sometimes it leaps into the light and assaults you with a sledgehammer.

I checked my phone before I entered the courtyard. I saw the message from Malache.

My turn to be late. Got caught up in preparations for the office party. Same every week! Anyway, if I don't catch you tonight I'll see you at the pub tomorrow. The Puckered Sphincter. You're welcome to join us.

The most important question in the world

'What's this?'

'It's the soul of a man who died in multiple ways,' I said.

'It doesn't look like a soul. Nor does it smell like one. What's your opinion, worm?'

'Looks like a cockroach to me, sir.'

'Did you just bring me a dead bug, Half-life?'

'I brought what Xaphan gave me. He told me it was a soul.'

'And you believed him?'

'I have no way of telling a soul from an insect. You said there were as many varieties of souls as there were people. This seemed no more unusual than any of the others.'

'If I may interject, sir...'

'Go ahead, worm.'

'I don't wish to defend this creature, but I myself have come across a variety of essences on my travels, and several of the more influential Lifers do indeed have souls which take the form of insects. In fact, I once had the pleasure of extracting such a pest—it was a rather insignificant dung beetle, as I recall—from the President of—'

242

'That's all very well. But is this a soul, or is it a bug?'

'As I was about to say, sir: if you will allow me the merest sniff of the insect in question, I have a nose attuned to even the weakest essence, and I should be able to give you a definitive view one way or the other.'

The demon passed my gift to his subordinate; no one spoke for a while. I couldn't remember the last time I had sat at this table in silence. I allowed myself to imagine I was sitting here on a summer's day, warmed by the sunlight in the courtyard, a plate of hot food and a glass of cold beer set before me.

'To begin with, sir, the odour is extremely weak—so you must in no way blame yourself for a lack of refinement. There are few noses in hell that could pick up these faint traces; fortunately, I possess one such. That said, it is by no means subtle: there's a clodhopping dullness to this scent which I can only ascribe to a certain degeneracy on the part of its owner. However, I am pleased to confirm that it is indeed a soul. You may consume it at your pleasure.'

'I am grateful to you, worm, but not in any meaningful sense. I will eat it immediately.'

'If I might take just one more sniff—'

'You would do better to return it.'

'Of course. I meant no insult. However, if you would lend me your ear a moment, I have a suggestion that I am sure will interest you.'

They exchanged whispers. I was still thinking about hot food and cold beer, and summer sunlight in this winter darkness.

'An excellent idea!' said the demon. 'Half-life, my servant has indicated that a fair recompense for this miserable, flavourless and rather chitinous specimen would be a piece of your own soul. Hand me that cheap wooden trinket you carry in your pocket.'

'No,' I said.

'What was that word he used, worm?'

'I think it was *no*, sir.'

'I don't recognise it. What does it mean?'

'He is refusing to obey you.'

'I can't open the box and neither can you,' I explained.

'Don't tell me what I can and can't do! If I so wished, I could turn your feet into stumps to match your hands! I could make a seahorse of your head and a jellyfish of your liver! I could boil you alive—half-alive in your case—and have you for breakfast!'

'But you can't open my box. Only I can do it, and only when I have my hands.'

'In that case, I command you *not* to open it!'

'Fine,' I said.

He snorted noisily for a while, but eventually calmed down; and when he spoke again his customary pomposity had returned.

'Do you know what the most important question in the world is, Half-life? It is none of the trivial concerns that are doubtless infesting your brain at this moment—Where can I find food? How can I earn more money? Will I ever find love? It is simply this: *Who is the master and who the servant?* Consider its implications before you refuse me again. The servant must not disobey his master. Disobedience is the only sin worthy of the name. Do you understand?'

'Yes,' I said, thinking of cold beer.

'Then we have no quarrel. In the meantime, though I am dissatisfied with your effort, I consider you to have complied—minimally—with your agreement this evening. That leaves two more souls; I trust you will bring them to me tomorrow. Now, remove yourself from my presence—'

'Sir, you haven't listened to his confession.'

'Worm, what did I tell you about interrupting me?'

'You said not to do it.'

'And what did you just do?'

'I interrupted you.'

'What punishment do you think you deserve?'

244

'Anything you like, sir—thank you. Several at once, if it pleases you; or consecutively, as you wish. The more severe the better—'

'No. Your punishment is: *you* will hear his confession. If it is even moderately interesting, I expect a verbatim report in the morning. In the meantime, I have more important matters to attend to.'

I heard him crunch the insect as he walked away; then I caught a faint whiff of woodsmoke, and he was gone.

'What's your name?' I said.

'I'll tell you mine if you tell me yours.'

'I don't have one.'

'Well, that's rather pitiful... But no matter. I am Toadspit: a name feared across all nine circles of hell.'

'Are you devil or demon?'

'Devil, of course. I'm one of the higher ranking officers; the buffer between the overseer and his underlings. I ensure that they don't bother him with petty concerns.'

'And he rewards you with threats and insults.'

I heard a dry chuckle. 'I forgive your solecism, undead. Few of your kind value the twin disciplines of duty and submission. I am here to serve, not to solicit favour; and what you call an insult is merely—I seek a phrase that your tiny brain will understand—an expression of his love... But I don't expect you to see as I do. You are fragile little vessels filled with blood. Your mothers give birth over an open grave; your time in this world is spent plummeting toward death. It doesn't matter whether you are good or evil; you die, and you are forgotten. What does the mayfly know of faith, or loyalty, or service to another? What does it know of love?'

While he was talking I checked the Health app on my phone, but all it told me was that I had walked seven thousand steps and my heart rate was dangerously low. It didn't say whether I was alive or dead.

'Are you still there, zombie?'

'Yes. Do you want to hear my confession now?'

'I am compelled to do so. Therefore, I would grateful if you could make it quick.'

'My relationship with my parents was a simple one: they gave, and I received. Love, money, food, comfort—all flowed downward into my open mouth. Even when I left home and got married, the pattern continued: I looked up, they looked down. Then I followed a darker path, and I didn't see them for several years; but when I emerged into the light once more, the imbalance was restored—they rescued me from myself and provided me with a job and a flat. It never even crossed my mind that as they grew older they would need my support.'

'They sound a trifle dull. What did you do to them? Strangle them in their beds for the inheritance? Get them to fund your gambling, drinking and whoring habits?'

'I abandoned them.'

'In the sense of leaving them in peace so they wouldn't have to deal with a loser like you?'

'No. I died.'

'Death isn't a sin, it's a necessity.'

'Let me explain. At no point in my life did I consider the effect of my actions on my parents. Not as a child, nor as an adult. My death was avoidable: I could have made different choices. If I had told them what I was involved with, they would have counselled against it; but I didn't say anything... So I was murdered, and they lived on, and I wasn't around to help them as they grew older. And in the end I don't know whether they died alone and in pain, or peacefully in each other's arms—because I wasn't there. I abandoned them. That's my shame.'

'Tell me, zombie. If you were in my position, would you dare to relate such a trivial matter to your superior?'

'I'm not in your position.'

'Which is a blessing to us all... In any case, have you never considered that they might have felt relieved to be

246

rid of you? That they didn't love you half as much as you thought? That you were more of a burden than a son? Those years together without you might have been the happiest of their lives—'

'Shut up.'

He was silent for a moment. I heard him breathing softly behind the grille. Then he said: 'You, a minor vessel, presume to tell me, a high-ranking official, that I should be quiet? Thank you. You have given me something to interest my master after all. I will deliver your story, merely as the prelude to your insolence.'

'Do what you like,' I said. 'I'm leaving.'

I didn't want to sleep at the office, so I headed back to the canal. Normally, I wouldn't have returned to a place so quickly—but I didn't feel normal; I was not myself. If someone recognised me, or talked to me, so be it. I was tired of hiding.

When I reached the railway bridge, it was dry and familiar, and I settled quickly. I would have plenty of time tomorrow to decide what I wanted to be, but tonight I could rest.

Because everything was fine.

And the world was good.

PART SEVEN

Abaddon the Just

The smorgasbord of undead scents

I curled into a foetal position and wrapped my arms around my soul, and the wind and rain whispered me awake.

I stood up wearily, put on my coat and leaned against the bridge supports. The water in the canal was thick and black, but the surface came to life when the rain beat against it.

I felt no urgency to visit the workshop. I didn't even know if Malache expected me to be there. He had suggested I join him at the party, but my phone couldn't find the place he had mentioned. Two things were certain, however: the demon had told me to bring two souls tonight, and today would be my final day.

I was disturbed by a loud buzzing. It was a text from Malache. *I missed you this morning; perhaps you left early? If you do want to join us, go to the workshop and someone will fetch you.*

Nergal had sent a message, too: a link to a YouTube video posted by The Mysterious Mr X. It was titled, 'How to Lose Friends and Have No Influence On People', and claimed inside knowledge of yesterday's murder. Since I already knew the inside knowledge, I didn't bother to click on it.

I put the phone in my rucksack. The rucksack still contained my old clothes. In a moment of clarity—and developing what the demon had told me about my coat—I realised these rags were a symbol of my life to this point—which I was still carrying around with me—and if I was really serious about shedding my old self, I should throw them into the canal. Then I thought it would be useful to have a change of outfit in case of emergency, so I left them alone.

I closed my eyes and sank into daydreams.

A while later I became aware of something soft and slobbery licking my left stump. I opened my eyes and was relieved to see a golden retriever. I knelt down and embraced it, allowing it to explore my face with its tongue as I patted and stroked its back. It responded even more enthusiastically, and neither of us could think of a reason to stop, so we continued.

'Hello again.'

I looked up. It was the man who had spoken to me on the towpath three days ago.

'I see you've met Hani,' he said.

'I didn't have much choice.'

'Sorry. She's not always this friendly toward strangers.'

I stood up. The dog mirrored the movement, pinning me to the wall with its forelegs and trying to lick my face again. The man intervened, coaxing it away with soothing words, then attaching a lead to its collar.

'I'm Robert, by the way.'

He extended his hand. I offered my stump in return. He shook it firmly, but not painfully.

'Pleased to meet you.'

'Likewise... We were just on our way to the café. Perhaps you'd like to join us?'

My old self immediately refused, sensing danger, fearing exposure, knowing it would be unable to bear the contact or maintain a relationship. My new self saw his kind face and pleasant smile, and said: 'Okay.'

We followed the towpath toward town. I didn't say much. He told me about his dog and how he walked this route every morning; later, we saw a group of narrowboats tied to the bank, and he pointed to one and called it home. It was an old barge decorated with floral artwork and tubs of winter flowering jasmine. Its name was painted on the bow: The Green Man.

We continued south until we reached Jericho, where we crossed the canal to the road where the Agency used to be. The old, burnt-out shell had been demolished and rebuilt in a more modern style. I no longer felt an emotional connection to it, so I didn't mention it, and we carried on to Walton Street.

'You're my guest, so I'll let you choose,' he said. 'There are a few places to have breakfast along here.'

But for me, there was only one.

I sat beneath the awning at one of the Jericho Café's outside tables; my new friend went inside to order. The retriever stayed with me, enjoying the smorgasbord of undead scents that my body presented. My hands were a particular favourite, but she also sampled my face, neck and ankles, and spent a good few seconds exploring my rucksack.

The man returned with coffee and a flapjack for me, tea and toast for himself. We began to eat in silence, but it wasn't uncomfortable. He didn't scream; he didn't unload a shotgun into my face; he seemed content to spend time in my company. His dog liked me, so he liked me too. And when the time came for one of us to speak, I was astonished to discover it was me.

'I want to thank you for the money you gave me.'

'You're welcome.'

'I went to a café in Friars Entry. They have a shelf of books; anyone can read them. I started one but only got halfway through. I'll go back and finish it soon.'

'What was the book?'

I told him, and he nodded in recognition, and we discussed the plot, and he mentioned a few other novels the author had written.

'When you read a good story it's like being slapped awake from a dream,' he said. 'It changes the way you see the world. It can lift you out of a rut and point your life in an entirely new direction.'

'You can escape your pattern,' I said.

'Exactly.'

He smiled. I smiled too.

He returned to his tea, but glanced at me a couple of times, as though he wanted to say something but wasn't sure how he should go about it. Eventually, he found the right words.

'I'm glad I met you again,' he said. 'There's something I'd like to discuss with you... I work for a charity; we run an outreach program for the homeless. It's not about clearing the streets or forcing people into hostels—it's about talking. Befriending those who have no one else they can turn to. We're always on the lookout for new recruits—people who won't judge, who'll sit and listen and, in the longer term, help others out of that rut... Now, I don't know you very well, but it seems to me you're someone who might be good at this kind of work. Perhaps you could volunteer—'

I shook my head.

He paused, then reached down and patted the retriever on the back. 'It's not just my opinion—Hani is an excellent judge of character, too. I trust her implicitly.' The dog turned to look at him; he grinned back. 'In any case, no one can be sure about anything until they've tried it. And that's all I'm asking.'

'I don't know.'

'Fine. I've said enough.' He reached into his pocket and handed me a card. 'Here are my contact details. I'll leave it to you; you know where I live if you want to get in touch.' He finished the rest of his tea quickly. 'Come on, girl. Let's leave this gentleman in peace.'

He stood up and bade me goodbye; his retriever licked me a similarly fond farewell. When they were gone I noticed a single slice of buttered toast on his plate. It looked so attractive, I ate it without a second thought.

254

I finished my breakfast, then examined the card. It revealed the man's name, job description, mobile number and address. I put it in the zip pocket of my bag for safekeeping.

His offer had given me another choice to add to the list: continue my employment and regain my soul, walk away and give it up, return to the coffin, enter the grinder, work for a Lifer helping other Lifers—or become a personal chef to that narcissistic monster at The Chimera... It was hard to know which, if any, I should choose.

And it wasn't hard at all.

Before I left for the workshop, I went to the bathroom to see if a memento of last night's killing had been inscribed on my flesh. The last two designs had appeared on my back, so I checked that first. I saw the tattoo immediately: a golden bullet at the top of my spine, above the open end of the horseshoe.

I washed my face and left the café, wishing the barista a Happy Christmas on the way out. The rain had stopped now and the wind had slowed to a gusting breeze.

On my way to the bookbinder I passed a house with a wide gable end, which presented a trio of billboards side-by-side. All three featured the same advert, a much larger version of the poster I had seen on Resh's desk.

I wish I had a friend like Devil Joe.

The Puckered Sphincter

The workshop was locked and all the lights were off. My phone told me it was eleven-thirty. I decided to wait until noon; if no one had arrived by then, I would spend the afternoon with *Doomsday Book*.

At eleven forty-five, Malache emailed me a photograph of the note and a photograph of the two photographs that accompanied it. One photo showed the face of a woman

255

with blonde hair and blue eyes; the other was completely black. I didn't know whether the second was a technical error, or Malache had messed up, but the darkness disturbed me; I didn't know what to make of it. The note was scarcely less ambiguous. It said: *Two souls. 8861352947101+1. That gluttonous little devil. Dusk. Master of Sacrifice.*

Just before twelve, Resh pulled into the kerb on her purple Vespa. She was wearing fake antlers enhanced by red LED lights, which flashed intermittently in a rhythm I didn't understand.

'Mal thought I'd be able to persuade you. Was he right?'

'Are there many people at the party?'

'Well, they're not *all* people, but... One or two.'

'Okay, I'll come.'

'Hop onboard, then.'

'Wait. I want to give you something first.'

I reached into my bag for the yellow gacha. I held it in my hooked palm and presented it to her.

'What's inside?'

'It's a mystery. That's the point, I think.'

She cracked it open. It contained a plastic zombie wearing a checked shirt and blue jeans. He had green skin, uneven yellow teeth and black eyes, and he was holding his arms out, ready to strangle someone.

'That's very sweet of you. I'm going to put it on my workbench first thing tomorrow morning.'

'I just wanted to say thanks... For everything.'

'You're welcome, Rabbit. Shall we go?'

I put my arms around her and pressed my cheek against her back. It began to rain again as she set off, but I hardly felt it. I wasn't superstitious, but the image of a zombie escaping his capsule felt like a good omen.

The journey was short, but it took me down a road I had never been before. We headed west beyond the railway station, then north through open fields to a remote riverside inn. A crude but anatomically-accurate sign revealed its name: The Puckered Sphincter.

The outside was a haphazard arrangement of buildings, extensions and annexes, with whitewashed walls and thatched rooves; but I had no time to examine it in detail. Resh parked her scooter by a low stone wall, grabbed my hand and led me inside.

She had underestimated the number of guests. As we passed through a variety of rooms—each with its own unique style of flooring, furniture and tables—I made a nervous estimate of a hundred; and those were just the ones I could see. The sound and sight of them startled me: almost everyone was gesticulating, talking or shouting at once; and they differed wildly in form, from a tiny green devil with a high-pitched voice to a gigantic newt with a growl so deep it rattled my bones. Nevertheless, the majority of the crowd appeared human, albeit disguised by fancy dress. Some of those outfits were Christmas-themed, but a few were more eclectic: I saw an imposing Minotaur, a hulking djinn and a particularly brutish harpy. Most had gone for an unseasonal Halloween look, however—skeletons, witches, ghouls, killer clowns and, incongruously, the Four Horsemen of the Apocalypse. I narrowly avoided losing an eye to a surprisingly authentic scythe blade.

At last we reached a small room thronging with people. Here the costumes were less extravagant, and limited to headgear—boppers, bowlers, eyes on stalks, crowns, masks and leprechaun hats, rabbit ears, pig snouts and unicorn horns. It was easy to identify my remaining co-workers among them. Nergal, with a fake arrow through his head, spotted me immediately. He offered me a plate filled with chicken drumsticks. I took one and nibbled it listlessly.

'Welcome to the Bureau Christmas Party,' he said. 'In which we celebrate the death of Jesus.'

'That's Easter, you quarterwit,' said Resh.

'And he was resurrected anyway,' said Dumuzid. 'If you believe the story.'

257

'It's the same party we throw every weekend,' said Malache, who had eschewed fancy dress of any kind. 'But it's Christmas Eve, so some people have made an effort.'

'Fine,' said Nergal. 'Welcome, zombie, to our midwinter celebration. There's nothing special about it, but you can eat, drink, smoke, dance and gamble as much as you like. Our motto is: enjoy now, throw up later.'

'Words to live by,' said a hairy ape-like creature with giant fangs and multiple compound eyes, holding a foaming pint of beer in its paw.

I didn't have time to wonder what I'd got myself into: Malache grabbed my arm and took me to one side.

'I have some more feedback,' he said. 'Nothing to worry about, but Xaphan gave you the lowest score of the week on RMI. Obviously, it doesn't affect my opinion of you—which means everything is fine with the overseer, too—but in the longer term you might want to consider your options.'

I looked blankly at him.

'Anyway, enjoy yourself. Mix and mingle; see the kind of people you might be working with in future.' He patted me on the back. 'It's not a job everyone can do, but those who can, love it.'

I took my chicken drumstick and passed from room to room, watching and listening.

I saw a short devil in a sharp suit, who was outlining a marketing strategy to a taller devil in mufti. 'The core concept is The Boss vs The Seven-Eyed Lamb,' she said. 'We launch with the movie, then spin off into computer games, novelisations, TV serials, and a range of toys and action figurines. We're talking millions, right off the bat.'

'The Boss is trying to change his image,' the taller devil objected. 'I don't think he'll be onboard with violence.'

'Fine. We call it Devil Joe vs The Beast. We make him the heroic defender of mankind in the face of a grotesque, tentacled threat from space. He only becomes violent to protect the weak and vulnerable...'

Next, I saw an odd little man taking a Gila monster for a walk through the bar. The man was covered from head to toe in mucus, which he trailed in his wake like a slug. Everyone who met him backed away, but I was intrigued by his strangeness and inspired by Resh's words: *different is beautiful*. I followed him for a while, carefully avoiding his slippery secretions. At length he sidled up to a disgruntled horse, who was drinking alone.

'You,' he said. 'Do you know who I am?'

'Not really,' the horse replied, putting down her glass.

'I'm the Boss's chief speechwriter. I'm responsible for some of the most effective political slogans of the last two decades. Did you know that?'

The horse shook her head and turned away, but the man grabbed her withers with his dripping fingers.

'I'm the architect of every campaign that ever championed hope, change, trust or unity. I've written speeches both for and against immigration, the environment, big tech and big pharma... And now they're throwing me on the scrapheap. Now they're saying my ideas are old-fashioned and I have to make way for new blood. Can you believe it?'

The horse couldn't believe it.

'But that's not how this ends,' he said. 'I'm making a comeback—you'll see. This time next year, the name of Snotbush will chime in every corner of hell. They'll write poems about me, name their children after me; they'll—'

He slumped forward and burst into tears, which dripped into the horse's glass in thick, slimy drops. The horse patted him on the back, then wiped her hooves on the bar runner. The Gila monster licked its master's legs tenderly, and looked up at him with hopeful eyes.

I left them in peace and melted back into the crowd, picking up snippets of conversation as I passed.

A goat talking to a group of kids:

'He's not on camera, but the police pulled his details from the footage and traced it back to him.'

'Are they going to arrest uncle Xaphan?' bleated one of the younger kids.

'Don't worry, little one. They won't catch him in time.'

Two gruff-looking people in dog masks:

'Well, he claimed the intern woke up.'

'While he was branding her?'

'Halfway through the tattoo.'

'Didn't he use the gas?'

'He probably forgot.'

'You can't get the staff these days.'

'If you want a job done well, you have to do it yourself.'

'Amen to that, brother.'

A woman in white speaking to three horned cherubs:

'I won't get into the *finer* details of my paper, but the basic *thrust* of my thesis is that we coexist with Lifers in a kind of *symbiosis*. If we *killed* every one of them we'd be out of a job, so we let just enough of them *live* to provide full employment for the rest of us. It's a *delicate* balance, and sometimes we stray too far one way or the other—but frankly, it would be a lot easier if they weren't so bloody *uncooperative*.'

Eventually, I reached a room where three upright wild boars were laying down a rhythm with their trotters. One of them took me by the hand and pulled me into their midst, and we danced together for a few minutes through a series of chaotic moves—twirling, leaping and hopping—until clumsiness and vertigo got the better of me, and I fell over. The boars laughed good-naturedly and resumed the dance without me.

I left quickly before they changed their minds.

I retreated to the garden. There was no one else here. The storm had picked up again; it threw wind and rain against me. I looked out across the dark river to the far bank, and the green meadow beyond. The place where I had lost my hands. I still remembered the burning.

I looked back through the doorway into the pub, and saw the variant forms and faces inside. Did I really belong to this group? Perhaps not—but I was scarcely more comfortable among the living, and the dead wouldn't recognise what I had become. Why not spend my days working with devils and demons? A soul sat as easily in an evil heart as a good one.

Given time, I might even begin to love the job.

I returned to my co-workers. A devil dressed in a red spandex bodysuit held their attention. He had maroon skin, a long pair of horns and pearly white teeth. A large Komodo dragon sat at his feet.

'What's the foulest thing you can imagine?' he said.

'A fart with halitosis,' said Nergal.

'Classy,' said Resh.

'You overdosed on contempt again, my thumbscrew.'

'To answer your question, Dripcrack, my husband is the foulest thing I can imagine, except I don't need to imagine him because he's been stalking me for three thousand years.'

'Angels,' said Dumuzid. 'They're pretty foul.'

'Some of them are nice,' said Malache.

'Bunch of snooty, arrogant popinjays, if you ask me.'

Dripcrack nodded in agreement, then turned toward me. The Komodo dragon did likewise, flicking out its forked tongue and licking its thin lips.

'Being dead when you want to be alive,' I replied. 'Or being alive when you want to be dead.'

'A fine answer, but too serious for this company.' He turned back to the others. 'By the way, have I told you about the new Screaming Room?'

'What was wrong with the old one?' said Resh.

'No soundproofing—terrible oversight. But the new one is ten times as large, and even if you put your ear to the door you hear... *nothing.*'

'What's a Screaming Room?' I said.

'Therapy for the dead,' said Malache.

'The unhappy ones, anyway,' Dripcrack explained. 'Frankly, it was always rather enervating when every step you took down there was punctuated by someone wailing and gnashing their teeth—even the torturers couldn't stand people moaning twenty-four-seven—so we built a place where the miserable and the damned could go and shriek their brains out... It gives the rest of us a well-earned break.'

As this exchange was taking place, I noticed that the Komodo dragon was on a retractable leash, and it took advantage of its master's distraction by waddling over to me and licking my ankles. It was just about to take a bite when Dripcrack spotted its intentions and reeled it in like a fish. He smiled and gave me an apologetic nod.

The afternoon passed. I didn't eat or drink, but Resh gave me a couple of cigarettes, which numbed the anxiety. I tried to focus on what I wanted, but my mind was a maelstrom of conflicting desires. I felt myself being drawn inexorably into the centre, where only death awaited me.

Nergal was the first to leave. He punched me hard on the arm and handed me a bottle of Southern Comfort. 'Parting gift,' he said. 'Unless you decide to work for us, in which case I'll have it back.' He grinned as he stuffed the bottle into my rucksack. 'But who am I kidding? You have Moloch tonight. She's an absolute horror—your biggest challenge of the week. Honestly, you'll be lucky to survive.'

'Why don't you go extinct, you old quagga?' said Resh. 'Don't mind him, Rabbit. He's teasing you again.' She, too, slipped something into my bag. 'This is my gift. It's not much, but I hope it will remind you of me.'

'I got you a carriage clock,' said Dumuzid. 'It was all I could think of, and Mal says you're hardly ever on time—'

'Thanks,' I said.

He shook my hand. Nergal gave me a wave. They turned around and left.

When they were gone, I stared at Resh for a moment, wondering if this was the last time I would ever see her; and perhaps she thought the same, because she leaned toward me and kissed me full on the lips. It was a kiss unlike any I had ever tasted before: a shock of darkness, a raven's midnight cry—a kiss that, for one brief moment, filled the black hole inside me.

And it left me wanting more. My heart ached for it; my soul shivered inside its wooden prison.

Goodbye, friend

The pub disgorged its devilish clients. The day was drawing to a close. I was empty once more.

'Don't take it too seriously,' said Malache.

'I can't help it.'

'They've been married for millennia.'

'Are they happy?'

He shrugged. 'Is anyone? In the end, you get the partner you deserve. But they discovered the secret of staying together a long time ago. It's very simple: *don't separate.*'

'It felt like love when she kissed me.'

He shook his head. 'Creatures like us don't love; we take pleasure where we can. My advice is: forget it.'

He took an object from his pocket and handed it to me. It was a laminated card attached to a blue lanyard. The card was imprinted with my ID number, a grainy photograph of my face, and the words *Bureau of Infernal Affairs* at the top. There was a blank space where my name should have been.

'We can fill that in if you decide to join us. If you choose to go your own way, just pop it one of our recycling bins. But remember: whether it's the Four Horsemen, or the Bureau, or anyone else—we all share the same goal. It's just the approach that differs. The means to the end.'

'Okay.'

'Well then—'

'I have one more question.'

'Fine. Ask me anything you like.'

'What's your alternate form?'

He smiled, showing me all of his tiny white teeth. 'I don't have one.'

'But when I first saw you, your body was shimmering—'

'I don't have one,' he insisted. 'Now, if you'll meet me outside the workshop at five, I'll drive you to your final destination.'

'I'll be there.'

He looked me in the eye as if he was about to confess something; but all he said was: 'Goodbye, friend.'

He walked away. A few moments later I heard the buzz of his black scooter above the noise of the storm. I watched him leave, and thought about the answer he had given me.

I realised that I didn't believe him.

I followed the path to the river and walked south along the bank. Eventually, I arrived at a small boatyard, where I crossed the footbridge to Port Meadow; from there, I took the long, muddy track toward town. The wind buffeted me with swirling gusts, the rain fell ceaselessly; and by the time I reached Walton Street, I was soaked from hat to shoes.

I headed for Zoë's flat. There were few cars on the road and I met no one else on the way. At last, I reached a glossy red door with a brass knocker in the shape of a hand. The porch roof afforded some respite from the wind and rain, so I huddled beneath it and waited for Zoë to arrive.

264

After a few minutes, I felt a sharp pain in my torso. I unbuttoned my shirt to find a few loose stitches above the navel—my dance with the warthogs must have been more vigorous than I thought. Last time, Resh had tightened them for me; now I did it alone. But the thought of her prompted me to recall her gift.

I looked in my rucksack: between the carriage clock and the Southern Comfort, I found a pack of Marlboros and a lighter. The lighter was purple, made of brushed steel and engraved with an eight-pointed star. I drew out a cigarette with my teeth, ignited the lighter and lit the tip.

Zoë appeared almost immediately.

'Those things will kill you,' she said.

'That's not much of a threat.'

'You should throw them away.'

'They were a gift from a friend.'

'Some friend she is.'

I shrugged. 'Should we do this now?'

'Ready when you are, zombie.'

I staggered toward her front door. I didn't want to inflict on her what I had become, so I waited there, my hands black with agony, clutching a box I believed contained my soul. Then I thought: *It'll be okay, she'll understand, I can tell her everything and she'll see who I really am, and it will be fine, because love will make it fine.* I knocked on the door, but there was no answer, so I rang the bell—and this time I heard her voice through the intercom.

'Who is it?'

'It's me. Can we talk?'

'It's a bit late—'

'It won't take long.'

'Are you all right?'

'It's best if I show you.'

The lock clicked open. I crossed the threshold into the hallway: a maroon carpet, a blinding light bulb and Zoë standing before me. My hands felt like they were melting.

'What happened?'

'Can I sit down?'

She nodded. 'Come through.'

This is a mistake. There is no love.

I passed a bedroom on the left. A book lay on the bed: *Sepulchre*, by James Herbert. We went into the living room at the end of the hall—a small rectangular space with a threadbare sofa, a phone, a coffee table and a portable television. I sat down on the sofa; Zoë sat beside me. Then she saw my hands: a pair of blackened stumps that smelled of death.

'I'll call an ambulance.'

'No. Just sit with me.'

'What happened?'

'I can't tell you. You won't believe it.'

'Don't be silly.'

'I lost your pendant... I'm sorry.'

'I don't give a fuck about the pendant—'

'A demon took it from me.'

'What?'

'I'm a zombie—'

'You told me. It was funny—'

'—and a zombie doesn't have a soul. It's the thing we most crave, the missing piece of our existence. It lets us live again.'

'I don't understand. Your hands are—whatever happened to you—and you're telling me some dumb story—'

'It's the truth. The demon returned my soul in exchange for your pendant—and then he burned my hands.'

'I'm calling the ambulance. You need help.'

'No. They'll find out what I am.'

She picked up the phone. I got up and moved toward the hallway. She put the phone down.

'You're right. I don't believe you. Why can't you just say you had some horrible accident? Why do you need to lie?'

'I'm not lying.'

266

She threw her arms up in frustration. 'Look, it's late and I'm tired and I can't deal with this bullshit... We'll dress your wounds, and you can go to the hospital tomorrow, or do what you want, I don't care... But stay.'

'I can't stay.'

'And you can't leave like this. Sit down.'

I almost obeyed her; but I knew it was hopeless. Instead, with burning hands, I lifted my sweatshirt and the tee shirt beneath, and showed her the raw wounds and crude stitches on my torso.

'I'm sorry,' I said. 'But I really am a zombie.'

When you reveal your true self to another, you should not expect understanding. The best you can hope for is that they don't scream.

Zoë didn't make a sound. She just covered her mouth and looked at me in shock. Even now, I could see she didn't believe me: I couldn't possibly be undead, because no one was; it was a joke, a lie. But there was something wrong with this person standing in front of her, a strangeness to be avoided: disease, turmoil, some terrible act of self harm. All she wanted was to close the door and go to sleep and wake alone and forget. Forget whatever this gruesome, grotesque thing in front of her was.

'I didn't expect this,' she said emptily.

'Me neither,' I replied.

I turned around and walked down the hall to the front door; but I couldn't open it because my hands were broken. So I stepped to one side and pressed myself against the wall, so that she wouldn't have to touch me as she turned the catch. The door opened, and I looked at her one last time; but her head was bowed and she wouldn't meet my gaze.

'Goodbye, friend,' I said.

Two bodies, two souls

I left the shelter of the porch and gave myself to the storm.

I followed the road south toward the workshop. The rain fell on me as it fell on everything else: indifferently. I was no more important to it than a pavement, or a hedge, or a broken umbrella. My purpose was an illusion, my desires were irrelevant: I was merely an object in space, moving through time.

Malache was waiting on the threshold when I arrived. He waved, stepped outside and locked the door behind him. I thought he might put on a raincoat or a hat, but he seemed to care even less about the weather than I did.

'All good?' he said.

'All good.'

He took my thick hands in his. 'Last one. Do your best. Silence the voice in your head. This time tomorrow you'll be walking these streets as one of the living.'

'If my soul is still there.'

'It'll be there. No question.'

He disengaged the kickstand and we climbed onto the scooter. He drove slowly at first, but accelerated as soon as we reached Walton Street. The wind had eased now but the heavy rain persisted. The Vespa aquaplaned through puddles and sent sprays of water flying in its wake.

As we entered Jericho, I became aware of a flashing blue light at the edge of my vision. I lifted my head and glanced back down the street: a police bike was approaching fast. Malache saw it, too: he slowed down immediately and moved over to the kerb. The bike pulled in front of us; the uniformed officer, wearing a stab vest and helmet, dismounted slowly and strolled in a leisurely manner toward us. When he spoke, his voice seemed familiar; but I couldn't place it.

'Do you know what speed you were travelling at, sir?'

'Beyond the limit,' Malache said disinterestedly.

'I'm glad to hear you acknowledge it. And are you aware that you *and* your passenger are required by law to wear a helmet that meets British Standard six-six-five-eight-one-nine-eight-five?'

'Is that so?'

'Sir, your flippant attitude doesn't reflect the gravity of—hang on... Mal, is that you?'

Malache peered at the face inside the helmet. 'Toadspit?'

'The very same. Sorry, sir, I didn't recognise you, what with it being dark, and all this rain—'

'It's fine. Are you joining me later?'

He shook his head. 'Police Christmas Ball.'

'Well, I hope you enjoy it.'

'I'll try,' he laughed. 'Anyway, apologies again for interrupting your evening. I won't delay you any further—'

I didn't hear the rest because Malache was already speeding away.

We stopped somewhere in Jericho. I hadn't paid attention to our route; I had been thinking about Toadspit's eyes peering out of that helmet. Human eyes in a human face. I wondered what he looked like behind the grille. I had always imagined a tiny, cowering, oleaginous creature; but maybe he was as ordinary in that world as he was in this.

'The prey is over there,' said Malache. 'She's waiting for a taxi, but the taxi will never come. Keep her company until Moloch arrives.'

He indicated the woman from the photograph. She was standing on the pavement beneath a street lamp, fifty yards away. The rain had turned her hair into blonde ropes that clung to her head and face. There were three shopping bags at her feet.

'Do you have an umbrella?' I said.

'Why do you need an umbrella?'

'It's not for me. It's for her.'

He looked around, then pointed to a bin further up the road. 'Is that what you're looking for?'

I climbed off the seat and slipped into the gutter. The water immediately filled my shoes. I squelched toward the bin and retrieved a clean but crumpled black umbrella with a wooden handle. Several of the metal struts were broken. The catch no longer worked.

I returned to Malache and showed it to him, hoping we might drive away in search of another. Instead, he examined it carefully, then moved his hands rapidly over the fabric. I wasn't sure whether what he did was demonic magic or straightforward dexterity, but the struts bent back into shape, the catch suddenly caught, and the crumples were ironed out. He put up the umbrella and handed it to me.

'Thank you,' I said.

He nodded. 'I'll be back when this is over. Now, turn off your brain and do your job.'

He waved goodbye and rode away.

I didn't approach the victim immediately. Having been instructed to turn off, my brain did the opposite: it worked more furiously than ever. I stood beneath the umbrella and listened to the raindrops pattering against the fabric.

I recalled what Malache had told me this afternoon: 'We all share the same goal; it's just the approach that differs.' But that approach was precisely what made this work unbearable. In the past few days, I had wondered if there was any real difference between the Agency and the Bureau—but it was only now that I realised what the difference was. *Compassion.* Death had treated the dying with respect; the demons merely gratified themselves. The fact that the result was the same was immaterial; it was the part of the equation that could be removed. What remained was the means to the end; and I had nothing but contempt for the means.

Malache's infernal machine was the perfect example. Its banal, dispassionate processes turned people into units of production, and its insatiable demands for efficiency were worse than any torture. There was no space between its gears for any kindness, or any kind of heaven.

'Hello,' I said. 'Can I offer you my umbrella?'

She looked pale, bedraggled by rain, and I saw anxiety and exhaustion in her eyes. 'I'm expecting a taxi,' she said. 'It'll be here any moment... But—yes. Thank you.'

She picked up her bags. I held the umbrella above her head. I didn't know what to say, so I said nothing. Instead, I stood very still, and became an object whose sole purpose was to provide shelter.

After a while Zoë joined us. Her voice spoke to me in raindrops; I replied on the wind.

'I thought you were gone for good.'

'This is my encore,' she said. 'I've come to give you some friendly advice. From one ghost to another.'

'I'm not a ghost.'

'You will be soon.'

'What do you want?'

'This has to end somewhere. Now is as good a time as any. Do something before it's too late.'

'I wish you'd stop saying that. I can't do anything.'

'You don't have to lead that creature here.'

'I don't have a choice.'

'Have you seen what's in those bags?'

'What difference does it make—'

'Baby clothes.'

'But the second photograph was blank.'

'*That gluttonous little devil.*'

'She's pregnant.'

'Two bodies, two souls. One within the other.'

'What am I going to do?'

'Walk away. You've lived too long in darkness. It's time to step into the light.'

I presented my umbrella to the woman beside me. 'Please, take this—it's only a short walk home for me, and I really should be getting back.'

'Are you sure?'

'Absolutely.'

'Thank you,' she said, switching the bags to her right hand and taking the umbrella in her left. 'I'm sorry to have troubled you. The taxi should have been here ten minutes ago; I don't know where it's got to.'

I smiled, as amiably as any former corpse can, and left. For a moment, I thought I might turn around and wave goodbye, but I knew it would look odd, so I kept on walking.

Wherever I went, the demon would follow; I had to think carefully about my destination. A place without people would be best, so that no one else might suffer for my disobedience.

I was already in Jericho; it wasn't far to Port Meadow.

I walked as quickly as I could and soon reached Walton Well Road. At the end, I crossed the canal and railway bridges to the wide plain beyond. The air was dull and heavy, and there was a sense of foreboding I couldn't shake, but even in this dreary landscape there were signs of life. Nearby, I heard a man whistling for his dog; in the distance, I saw what might have been a herd of cows.

I turned quickly from the path and moved across the sodden, rutted field toward the dark river in the distance.

Black Dog

I hunkered down on the muddy riverbank and stared straight ahead. My future looked as bleak as the broad, black channel before me. I had acted on impulse, responding to a phantom voice in my mind, but I hadn't considered the consequences. I didn't know how Moloch would react to the denial of her prey, but it was likely she would vent her anger on the nearest target. This prospect didn't ease my mood.

My brain chose this moment to replay my first meeting with Malache seven days ago. I didn't know why, and I didn't fight it; I just let it run its little memory program in my head. I saw him lean forward to check my ID tag, then reach for my collar; he straightened it and patted me firmly on the back. I remembered the force of his grip, and the strangeness of that final contact...

I removed my coat and searched under the collar, beginning with the lapels. It took less than a minute to find what I was looking for: a small, sharp object pressed into the material at the neck. It made no sound, there were no flashing lights, nor even a small antenna; but I immediately knew what it was. The technology had been miniaturised since my time as an investigator, and an inexpert eye might have dismissed it as a metal stud or some idiosyncratic accessory—but I knew it was a tracker.

It hadn't been my scent that had allowed the demons to find me—although its effects at close quarters had been real enough to convince me otherwise—it had been a tracking device implanted by Malache at our first meeting. *Half of what he does is a mystery*, Dumuzid had told me. *I prefer to work in the shadows*, Malache himself had confessed. How could I have failed to see it?

The tracker was firmly attached, but after a long struggle I managed to pry it free with my teeth. My first instinct was to keep it and ask Malache for an explanation, but I suspected he would just shrug and talk his way out of it. Then I thought it would be better to put it back and not reveal what I knew; but that would change nothing. I even considered returning the favour, and planting it on Malache the next time we met—a fitting act of revenge, but one that would be quickly unmasked.

In the end, I chose the simplest option of all. I threw it in the river, which accepted it without complaint.

I felt as free as the wind, and my mind briefly unravelled. I wanted to tear off the clothes they had given me! I would never cut my nails again! I would grow my hair and beard until they were twice as long as before! I would never touch another drop of alcohol! I would never smoke another cigarette in my life!

Then I calmed down and tried to think rationally.

I stood up and put my coat back on. I found the business card my friend had given me at the café. I took out my mobile and added his details to my contacts. Then I sent him a text, telling him I wanted to discuss his offer of voluntary work. I received a reply almost instantly: *Come by the boat tomorrow morning.*

Next, I found a number for the local police. I hovered over the connect button, ready to tell them everything... But I knew it would make no difference. There seemed to be devils and demons in all walks of life, ready to hush up a scandal or silence an unfavourable story. I had neither power nor influence; my accusations would solve nothing, and would merely warn those responsible.

I felt frustrated by my weakness, and acted on impulse once more: I took the mobile phone and threw it as far as I could, deep into the eddying waters of the dark river.

I knelt down on the bank, buffeted by the storm. Was the drowned tracker still working? Could the demon follow my scent after all? I looked around and saw no sign of the creature: just grey rain in a grey field, and every shape a shadow. Between gusts of wind, I heard the man still whistling for his pet. The cows were closer now too; or perhaps they had always been standing by the river, and I had simply come to them.

I watched their slow, gentle movements for a while; it soothed my troubled mind. Eventually, one broke away from the herd and moved in my direction. It was a ghostly presence, but I wasn't afraid. I was heartened by its curiosity. It was a moment of contact with something natural and uncomplicated.

But it was no ordinary beast.

When it was only a few yards away, it stood up on two legs and began to transform before my eyes. The thick bovine torso changed into a stout superhuman frame; the angles of its limbs seemed to reverse, and became arms and legs jointed at the elbows and knees. Only the head remained the same: a broad, furry pate with a wide nose, keen brown eyes and two pointed black ears.

But the transformation didn't end there. All the subtle details of colour, texture and perspective faded and were lost, until the creature's shape became a gaping void, deeper than any silhouette, darker than any night—and it was no longer a living beast standing before me, but a rent in the fabric of space, revealing a fathomless abyss beyond.

'I have found you,' this mouthless nothing said. 'But where is my prey?'

'I don't know.'

'Then you will find them.'

I led the demon along the riverbank to the bridge, then followed the path toward town—but halfway along I cut free and headed out across open meadow. I had no particular plan; my intention was simply to keep walking until a plan revealed itself. The creature trailed me listlessly, and always at the same distance, as if it wasn't moving at all, but was some abysmal object tethered to my perception.

I continued north until I reached the wide heart of the meadow. Rain and grassland as far as the eye could see. It was a lonely, melancholy place; all that mattered on this rutted, rain-soaked earth was putting one foot in front of another. I almost forgot the darkness behind me—until I heard that hollow voice once more.

'I am hungry, undead. My mouth weeps with the thought of the little one.'

I stopped. Felt the rain on my skin.

'I have a confession,' I said.

'Yes.'

'I deceived you.'

'Yes.'

'Your prey has gone, and for the last hour we've been walking in a circle.'

I turned around. I had to confront the darkness.

The demon was still. I saw water run along its impossible edges and fall to the ground; and when I looked into that endless void an icy horror gripped my heart. Then all at once it shimmered—bending and twisting the world around it, quivering with malevolence and strength—and slowly, inevitably, it moved toward me.

'I am Moloch, from the Bureau of Infernal Affairs,' it said. 'If you wish to spare yourself a thousand agonies, stay where you are.'

In fact, I ran. I didn't even think about it; it was as if my legs had a will of their own. They careered across the grey field, splashing through puddles, vaulting over humps, scampering over open grassland, feeling so alive at this moment of death—

Until I stumbled.

I looked back in panic. The abyssal creature was gone, and I saw the beast once more, pursuing me at pace, snorting wildly. I tried to stand again, but immediately trod on something soft—a thing that yelped and nipped my ankles in retaliation. The strangeness of it unbalanced me, and I fell face down in a puddle.

But life is luck, and my luck was in.

A moment later, I felt a rough, cold tongue on my face. I looked up to see a black dog with its jaws wide open. It seemed somehow familiar.

'Hello, boy,' I said.

I sat up. The dog responded enthusiastically, nuzzling me with its snout, licking the mud from my hands, lapping at the water around me, leaping up and down, its wet tongue hanging loose from its mouth as it frolicked and skittered between grass and puddle in the rain.

Then Moloch arrived: a black beast with a hard, horned face. She didn't see the dog until it sniffed her hooves, licked her ankles, gnawed at her front legs. Her thick, bovine head looked down at her assailant, then back at me.

'Nemesis,' she said, emptily.

The dog interpreted the word as a challenge, circling her with agile springs and skips, its slim black body running forward to nip her, then leaping away again before she could trample it beneath her hooves. Moloch bellowed and lunged at her tormentor, which only seemed to excite the dog even more. It leapt at her neck with snapping jaws, tore strips from her cheeks, sent her lurching this way and that; until at last the demon conceded ground and retreated, slowly at first, then with increasing speed toward the distant river—all the while pursued by the hound, which continued to enjoy itself as if it had discovered the oldest and finest game in the world.

I watched the dance play itself out awhile; then I turned around and headed in the opposite direction.

I soon found the path toward Jericho, and followed it back to civilisation. As I reached the railway bridge, I saw a forlorn man in a blue tracksuit, looking out across the meadow and whistling for his dog.

The agreement

I made my way to The Chimera. I wanted this to end one way or the other. Even though I might leave with nothing, I had to find out.

And what was the worst that could happen? I had survived for twenty years with this box in my possession, never quite sure what it held, or even if it held anything at all. If it came to it—if my work gained no reward, or the demon broke his word—I could continue as I was.

But I would not be complicit in any more deaths.

277

A black Vespa was parked on the street outside the pub. Malache was standing by the entrance.

'Hello, friend. Where did you go? I waited for you, but you never came back.'

'I don't want to talk about it.'

'No. I don't suppose you do.'

'Is the door unlocked?'

'It is. But are you certain you want to go inside? It might benefit you to walk away instead.'

'Would your overseer leave me alone if I did?'

He smiled. 'Perhaps not. He is somewhat vengeful.'

'Then I don't have a choice. I want to know what our agreement really means. I want to know if he'll keep his word.'

'You needn't worry... Abaddon is nothing if not just.'

I walked inside and closed the door behind me, relieved that he was gone from my sight. I didn't bother to indulge my fantasies in the bar; I walked straight through to the courtyard and took the seat by the grille. Even so, it was some time before I smelled that familiar stench and heard the rustling of insect wings in the dark; and longer still until that acid voice whispered in my ears.

'Did you bring my souls, Half-life?'

'No.'

'Do you intend, then, to extend our agreement until those souls are in my possession?'

'No.'

There was a brief silence.

'Let me ask you a question. What is the most grievous of those misdemeanours you consider to be sins? Is it that your anger made someone ill, that you drowned an animal, or you betrayed a friend? Is it that you gained pleasure from violence, stole clothing from a dead man, or left your parents to die alone?'

'You said none of these were sins; I agree with you. Perhaps sin doesn't even exist. In any case, I am neither

278

good nor evil. I merely live as every human lives: as well as I am able, within the limits of what I am.'

'A pleasant response; but sin exists, it is quite real. And the only sin that matters is the one you committed this evening—that of disobedience. This is the sin from which all others spring, and it is unforgivable.'

'I don't care anymore.'

'So be it. But before we proceed, let us both reflect upon the terms of our agreement.'

An eerie quiet followed. I heard the sound of breathing—first my own, then the demon's breaths in time with mine, so that it became hard to distinguish between the two. I felt the weight of darkness pushing against me as a physical force, like innumerable claws reaching through the grille toward me. I sensed the heat of his body in the air all around: an invisible mantle ready to suffocate me.

'Tell me,' he said. 'How do you see our agreement now?'

'Until today, I did everything required of me. You should keep your word and give me my hands—and if you must, take something in return for the souls I denied you.'

'Very well. Your judgement allies with mine. And this is my first ruling: for the eight souls you gave me, I will return eight fingers.' His tone was moderate and sombre, almost reassuring. 'Now turn around. I will remove the barrier between us, so that you may offer me your hands.'

I turned and knelt down on the seat until my chest was level with the grille. It opened slowly into nothing. I clasped my stumps together as if in prayer, and pushed my arms into that thick darkness, which seemed to resist momentarily, like a velvet curtain, before it yielded and wrapped itself around my extended limbs.

'Close your eyes, friend.'

I did so, and instantly felt the weight of a clawed hand holding that darkness against me. My shrivelled stumps quickly became hot, then painful—then unbearable. I felt the skin liquefying against the bones, and the bones themselves melting into some unthinkable form, stretched and twisted by the vile manipulations of those jagged talons. I wanted to scream, but I was determined to resist, I didn't want to give him the satisfaction—but I screamed all the same.

Then it was over.

I withdrew my arms from the blackness and found my life anew. Two hands, as perfect as the day I died—but missing two fingers: the little finger on my right hand, the thumb on my left. And I couldn't contain the joy, my relief, the turmoil inside, and I bowed my head and wept for the return of what I had lost, my body shook with weeping, and I held my shaking hands toward him still, as if begging for absolution, or waiting to be manacled.

'It is time for my second ruling,' he said at last. 'You broke our agreement; it is not unreasonable to demand a penalty. I could take your limbs and leave you to crawl on your belly like a snake. I could seize that box in your possession and return it to its rightful place. But I am merciful, and this would not be justice. Your punishment is mitigated by the eight gifts you brought me; the two you did not require compensation… Now, raise your head, little Half-life. Let me darken the windows to your soul.'

I lifted my face to the open grille—and immediately the demon reached from the blackness and gripped my entire head in his scaly hands. His sharp claws dug into my flesh from the crown to the nape of my neck; but I didn't think of resisting, I didn't even move. I had invited my punishment, and I would bear it.

'Let my beauty be the last thing you ever see.'

Something else emerged from that darkness—a form so familiar, yet so hideous, that I could hardly bear the sight of it: a cruelly withered face wreathed in flames; a grotesque nose between emaciated cheeks; knife-thin lips stretched over rows of thick white teeth; and a cold, impassive, coal-black gaze.

We looked at each other for only the briefest of moments—then his taloned thumbs pressed into my eyeballs and pushed quickly inward, their path eased by an unearthly heat, which melted the jelly of my eyes and sent a scalding liquid down my cheeks, to join the tears that had barely dried.

The dark river

I felt a hand holding mine. I was lying in the alcove by the grille, but I no longer sensed the demon's presence—just this kindly figure beside me. I recognised him even before he spoke: his familiar smell, that reassuring grip, the warmth of his skin. It was as if he had been with me all along.

'I'm sorry,' he said.

I remembered shrieking in agony, and the end all of light. Then my mind had followed my eyes into darkness.

'I waited for you by the roadside. Why didn't you come? Everything would have worked out, just as it was meant to. You would have been whole again.'

'I was tired of being a slave.'

He squeezed my fingers in sympathy, but said nothing. I lay still for a while. Someone had thrust two iron rods into my skull. The excruciating bliss of righteous pain!

'I should open the box now,' I said.

'Think carefully. To choose life is to choose death.'

'I don't have to think; I know what I want... But I don't want to open it here. Would you walk me back to the meadow? I'm not sure I can find my way alone.'

'Whatever you need,' he said.

Raindrops on my eyeless face. The storm had ended, the wind was gone, but a shower of rain persisted, soothing my wounded flesh and trickling between the fingers of my new hands. Malache stayed close to me, gripping my right arm as he led me away from The Chimera, encouraging me with calming words. I sensed the strength of the pavement beneath me, heard the myriad noises of the city all around, felt the love of the man at my side. I forgave him all the wrong he had done me.

We kept walking. It was strange not to see the world I had always known; but I didn't feel afraid. I gave myself willingly to the danger.

'How far is it?'

'Not far.'

I checked that the box was still in my coat pocket; its small wooden frame was pressed against my heart. What would I feel when I opened it? I didn't know; I had forgotten what it was like to be alive. And that life would be different now anyway. A life lived in darkness.

I sensed the familiar rhythms of the city. I knew where we were without asking: here was the cinema, there the Jericho Café, now the road where the Agency used to stand, then the bridge over the canal, and the car park at the edge of the meadow.

'Take me to the river.'

The coldness of the air. The smell of mud and wet grass; the sounds of the city retreating. A field of wrinkled earth beneath my feet. Then the sluggish perfumed darkness of the river. The scent of darkness in my nostrils.

We halted on the shallow bank. I heard the water lapping softly against the mud. 'Here,' I said. Malache helped me to sit down. The ground was wet beneath me, but the rain had stopped and there was no breeze. 'What can you see?'

'Moonlight on the river.'

I reached into my coat and took the box from my pocket. I felt its lines and contours as I had never felt them before, a miniature world filled with structure and character: here was a gem, there a scratch, this was a sharp edge, that a bevelled corner. The lack of two digits was no hindrance; but I didn't pause to consider what that might mean. My fingertips caressed the veneer and felt the places where it had cracked—I peeled away a strip, then another, like picking a scab from a wound. Beneath one, I found a knot in the wood, and traced a fingertip over its lines and whorls; I pressed it, and discovered a tiny metal node at its heart; I pushed that and immediately heard a snap, followed by the sound of a complex gear working within. The box changed. Its dimensions remained the same, but on one side there was now a recessed wooden hinge—and on the other, a small metal clasp.

I undid the clasp and lifted the lid.

I didn't need to ask, because I felt it. I felt reunion, the love of being, the end of all longing, the light of the shimmering thread, the holiness and the horror and the power of life within, waiting to join me, reaching toward me, seeking its home, finding itself, wanting. I felt warm liquid rolling down my cheeks, and I didn't know if they were tears or it was blood, but it didn't matter, nothing mattered but this divine, exquisite, living essence that quivered beneath my hands, ready to fill the abyss inside me. I felt myself within it, my name, my history and future, my bliss, and I didn't need to ask, but he was my friend, so I asked all the same, because I wanted him to share this moment with me.

'What's inside the box? Tell me what you see.'

'I'm sorry,' he said. 'I don't see anything. It's empty.'

But I knew he was lying.

Printed in Great Britain
by Amazon

62478063R00168